THE
LOUDNESS
of UNSAID
THINGS

THE LOUDNESS OF UNSAID THINGS

Hilde Hinton

hachette
AUSTRALIA

hachette
AUSTRALIA

Published in Australia and New Zealand in 2020
by Hachette Australia
(an imprint of Hachette Australia Pty Limited)
Level 17, 207 Kent Street, Sydney NSW 2000
www.hachette.com.au

10 9 8 7 6 5 4 3 2 1

 A catalogue record for this
book is available from the
National Library of Australia

ISBN: 978 0 7336 4200 5 (paperback)

Cover design by Christabella Designs
Cover artwork courtesy of Nyssa Sharp
Text design by Bookhouse, Sydney
Typeset in 12/19.5 pt Sabon LT Pro and 12.5/19.5 pt TheSans SemiLight by Bookhouse, Sydney
Printed and bound in United Kingdom by Clays Ltd, Elcograf S.p.A.

 The paper this book is printed on is certified against the
Forest Stewardship Council® Standards. McPherson's Printing
Group holds FSC® chain of custody certification SA-COC-005379.
FSC® promotes environmentally responsible, socially beneficial
and economically viable management of the world's forests.

TO SAM AND THE BOYS, FOR RUNNING AROUND THE BACK PORCH WITH WINDMILL ARMS WHEN I REVEALED THIS BOOK WAS GOING TO BE AN ACTUAL BOOK.

THE INSTITUTE

The Institute. For the damaged, the dangerous, the not-quite-rights. The big mistake-makers, the ill at ease, the outliers. A hot pot. They use surnames in The Institute. Impersonal; respectful. Everyone was called Miss. The women. The workers. Miss this. Miss that. When Miss Kaye first started working at The Institute, she found 'Miss' odd. It was far from a school. Farther than Mars.

The Institute had well-manicured gardens. The women worked on them during the day between appointments. Miss Kaye never knew where she was going to work within The Institute until she arrived for the day. Or night. It's a twenty-four hour business. She looked at the running sheet and was not disappointed to see her name on 'the grounds'. Walk, make sure all was in order, chat idly to the clients, admire the odd flower. Time goes slower in the grounds. Non-eventful. The grounds, like the buildings, don't contain time. It could be 1950 or 2050. Utilitarian buildings – grey. Concrete rooms. No sign of era. No soft furnishings. Likewise, the gardens. Plants could be from 1950, and unless there's an apocalypse, a flower will be a flower in 2050. No sign of time in the clients either. Uniformed; unmanicured. Same with staff. Waiting. Wandering. No time.

Miss Kaye tried to make herself smaller in the gardens, just as she needed to be bigger in the buildings. Her presence was an intrusion as she walked past the women clipping shrubs or shovelling tanbark. There was an edging plant that turned up everywhere. The leaves didn't know if they were grey or green. The flowers pure white sousaphones.

'What are those called?' she asked a waif pulling weeds.

'Silver Moons, Miss Kaye,' the waif said in a barely-there voice.

'How do you know?' Not a lot of trust in The Institute.

'I'm learning horticulture,' she said as she stood and put her hand on her mini hip. Hard not to be defensive when it's in the air. Pea soup.

'Good for you,' Miss Kaye said as she nodded approval. In fifty steps she would reach her favourite rock. It was so flat. A stage. And as big as a car; if it was flat. It was elevated and surrounded by Silver Moons and smaller rocks. Although they weren't symmetrical, it didn't disturb her. She glanced ahead. There was a woman standing on the rock. That was against the rules. The meander became a brisk walk.

'Get down, Miss,' Miss Kaye said firmly.

'NOOooo waaaay, there's a snake, Miss Kaye. A fuckin' snaa-AAAake!' she said, dancing on the rock stage. Miss Kaye fought back her absolute desire to join her on the rock. It was not the rules. The yelling and dancing brought more women over. Tentatively getting closer. Miss Kaye put one hand on her radio. As the women drifted in, Dancing Girl told them there was a snake. An older lady with a water-stained leather face stood up straight and asked how big it was. Dancing Girl put out her pointer fingers like someone had scored a goal, but her hands weren't that far apart.

'It's a baby,' Leather Lady said, 'we need to be more concerned about the mother.' Commanding. Like Miss Kaye should be. She darted her leather face from rock to rock. Everyone else froze. Leather Lady took a step to the left, crouched down, stood up, took a step to the right, crouched down. Everyone else only breathed. But only when it was necessary.

For a moment Miss Kaye questioned her professionalism. It was time for her to take charge, to direct the women away from the baby snake. But she didn't. Baby snakes still bite. Leather Lady took a large step south-west, away from the group, and swooped down to the ground. She shot her arm out like lightning. When it emerged from a group of Silver Moons, it held a wriggling mini snake. The girls screamed and ran. Except Dancing Girl, who threw her drink bottle to Miss Kaye.

'PUT IT IN THERE,' she said loudly, crouching down into a ball.

Miss Kaye just stood there watching the running women and wishing she was one of them. Parched with fear, she opened the bottle and held it out to Leather Lady. She turned her head towards the snake just enough to look brave. Leather Lady dropped the baby snake into the bottle. Plop. Miss Kaye slammed the lid on, turned it more tightly than she'd ever turned a lid and held the bottle between two fingers at its very top.

'You can get down now,' Leather Lady said to Dancing Girl, who jumped down from the rock and stood as close to her as she could. Her protector.

'Oh. My. God. You. Are. A. Hero!' Dancing Girl said. Miss Kaye could see the Chinese whisper line that would follow this yarn. Umbilical cord thick. Hopefully the story would get so much larger than life that she would be portrayed as the opposite of how she felt. There's no visible fear when you work in The Institute. Or you don't work in The Institute.

Other staff members approached and said the Snake Catcher was on his way. Word had spread. Miss Kaye tried to hand over the bottle, but other things became more important to the others. Things in the distance. Pretend things.

'Open the lid, we don't want to suffocate it,' Leather Lady called over her shoulder.

'Yeah, we don't want it to, like, diiieee,' Dancing Girl added, her arm draped over Leather Lady. Morals get bigger with distance. Miss Kaye mimicked the motion of a partial bottle opening. The women nodded in approval and went on their way. It was normally one hundred and sixty steps down to the front gate, but it was a lot less with a snake in a bottle.

PART ONE
THE GIRL

CHAPTER 1

The girl crawled into the space between the glove box and the floor of the HR Holden and curled herself up as tight as she could – but not before she'd checked that all four door locks were firmly pressed down. The tops of the locks looked like golf tees and they had perfect swirls cut into the plastic. They felt like fingerprints looked.

'I'm just going to the chemist,' her father had said, 'I'll only be a few minutes.'

The amusement dancing around his eyes annoyed her. She had told him her fears and he explained that facing them was character building. Although she was only seven, she'd had her fill of character building.

Boland and Eastwood were criminals who had kidnapped a bunch of kids from a nearby town just a few months ago and it had frightened her to the end of her toes. Whether it had been coincidence or not, she had been given a golden

Labrador within a few days of the kidnapping. She'd been on and on about having a dog for as long as she could remember. For at least half her life anyway. Whether or not the dog was related to the kidnapping no longer concerned her. He was handsome and his tongue was big and floppy, it made her laugh. She knew she would never tire of him for as long as she liked aniseed ice cream – and that was at least forever.

Ever since the kidnapping she had been waiting for Boland and Eastwood to escape from jail and kidnap her. Life had changed. When she was alone, the threat became so imminent and inevitable that she had taken to hiding, as she was now in the car, balled up so tight she could surely fit in a matchbox. Since the kidnapping, sleeping between her Holly Hobbie sheets had become fitful and difficult and lengthy. Catching the Hepburn to Daylesford school bus was now a test of how long she could hold her breath. She could probably swim the whole pool underwater now. Not the local pool – the one they used in the Olympics. She would picture how far along the pool she would get as she waited for Boland and Eastwood to come to take her bus, hoping all the while that she wouldn't blow up like the blueberry girl in *Charlie and the Chocolate Factory*.

The taunting from the kids who went to the state school didn't bother her anymore. Nor did the fact that she had to wear a dumb tie and they could wear whatever they wanted. No one would care about that stuff once Boland and

Eastwood were on the bus. The other kids would like her once they were all on the same side against the kidnappers. She wondered if kidnappers ever kidnapped grown-ups and, if they did, what those kidnappers were called. There was no way her dad would be this scared. Or her mum.

There was no thought required when her dad asked her what name suited the dog.

'Boland, so when he kidnaps me he'll let me go because I named a whole dog after him,' she said as she tugged on his velvety ears. When it happened, she would stand tall and pretend not to be scared – she'd push her fear to the ends of her fingers. Boland would be so impressed he wouldn't notice her fingers were blue because she was so scared. Not many people had dogs named after them.

Then it happened.

Boland was at the chemist too. He had gone behind the car and he was so stealthy that she hadn't even heard him trying the door handles. But mastermind criminals aren't stupid enough to make a sound while trying the doors. He must have used his eyes and seen that the golf tees were firmly pushed down before he realised he needed a plan B to kidnap her. The only option he had left was to push the car to wherever kidnappers take kids. Panic sat at the bottom of her stomach with the cream puff she'd eaten ten minutes before. It was tight in there and she wished she hadn't eaten it, even though cream puffs were her favourite after aniseed ice cream. The car was moving. Boland and Eastwood must be pushing it.

She reminded herself to remember Boland was the boss and to make sure she gave him more attention than Eastwood. But where to? Probably a barn. That's usually where victims were taken. Even though she lived in the country, she didn't know what a barn looked like. Except that they were big, and no one would hear her scream.

Before she could process her actions, she peeked her eyes over the dash and through the bottom of the windscreen. The car was heading straight for the chemist. In Daylesford, people parked perpendicular in the middle of the street as well as alongside the shops. Perpendicular was one of her new favourite words. Maths always made the best words, like equilateral. Maths even found a new way to say pie.

'Oh my god,' she thought to herself. She'd never really believed in God, even though she did her Holy Communion. She didn't believe in God because she couldn't see him, but she could believe in Boland even though she hadn't *actually* seen him herself, because the bus full of kids he took *had* seen him. Besides, even if God was real he wouldn't like her because she hadn't respected the wafers. If only she had swallowed them instead of seeing how long she could keep them in her mouth before they disintegrated. She and her friend Claire always poked their tongues out at each other from across the church aisles with the wafers balanced on them, to see whose could last longest. One time, Sister Sylvester had seen their competition and she had her bum smacked with the metre ruler for being disrespectful to God.

Sister Sylvester had lifted her skirt to hit her in front of the whole school. She was wearing her orange undies that day and everyone saw them. It made the ruler hurt less because the orangeness of her undies was so much more painful. Fat Donna put an orange on her desk for a week after that. No; God was not going to help her now, so she put her head down as far as she could and hoped Boland would make a mistake.

BANG!

The side of her head hit the glove box so hard it hurt more than the orange undies. Through the throbbing she tried to stay calm and think of dog Boland's big floppy tongue that somehow managed to fit in his mouth, even though it was so big. She tried to focus on the humour dancing in her dad's eyes, even though it usually made her mad. Her dad's eyes were a happy place. She wanted to see his face so badly. She told herself to think of the stupid orange curl that always stuck out of Sister Sylvester's head thing. That always made her giggle; but not today.

She didn't know whether she was going to be sick in her own lap when she realised the car was no longer moving. All her bravery was summoned and she peeked her eyes up above the dash again. The front of their car was in the side door of another car parked alongside the shops. There wasn't any sign of Boland or Eastwood. Cool. Boland buggered up, like the time she got caught pouring sand in the back of Fat Donna's chair-bag so her books would be all gritty. She'd only wanted to get even because Donna left oranges on her desk and dobbed on her, even for thoughts. Boland and Eastwood must have had to run away when all the shoppers and shopkeepers came rushing out to see what was going on. She couldn't believe they had made a mistake.

'Unlock the door,' her dad kept saying really loudly as he pelted his hands on the driver-side window. His eyes weren't full of fun.

She put her fingers either side of the golf tee lock and lifted. He pulled her up through the car and past the steering wheel and gave her a huge hug. She felt like she was in heaven, even though she didn't believe in it.

'Boland came and tried to get me, Dad,' she said in between small gasps because her chest was squashed. 'But he ran away when we hit the other car,' she added, boiling with relief. She thought she heard him say a naughty word and something about the handbrake, but she was so full of happy and relief that she didn't have enough room to listen.

CHAPTER 2

She lay there between her Holly Hobbie sheets in the new concrete house thinking how slow birthdays come around, but how quick changes happen. One minute her dad was sitting her down saying that the family needed to move back to the city and SHAZAM, here she was. Her bedroom was in the front of the house and the street felt close. Back in Daylesford the street was a dirt road ages from the house. There was more noise here. She liked having a front fence. It was thick like the concrete walls of the house. It was perfect to walk along. She could be a gymnast on a balance beam – even though the fence was fatter and she never actually did backflips. But she could stand like she'd just landed and look over at the imaginary judges holding up scorecards. It was also a great place to just sit and watch people and cars go by. There were so many people here. Although she had lived in the city before moving to Daylesford, all she really remembered was a lady called Carmel who knitted her some mittens. Other than that, there was no pre-Daylesford. Strange how her dad said they were going back when she didn't remember being there in the first place.

What she did know was her mum seemed happy about it. She didn't see her mum much anymore. She floated in and out. It was hard not knowing which side of Mum she was going to get; maybe it was character building like facing her fears by being scared. Was her mum going to be a woman sitting in the corner living in her own brain, or a woman with big enthusiastic eyes wanting to dance and prance while she did normal stuff like stir the porridge? Stirring the porridge was a serious business that required the same pace all the way through to prevent lumps. It was meant to be her job anyway, not her mum's. Once, when she was stirring, she saw a ladybird on the wall near the stove and she lost her rhythm. Why a ladybird would want to crawl up a long blank wall was a mystery and before she knew it the porridge was lumpy again. When she was smaller she had a little kid's chair that she would drag over to the stove. Now she was bigger she didn't need the little chair, but it sure made a great platform to stir the porridge from back then.

After they moved to the concrete house in the city, her mum moved out to a little flat a couple of kilometres away in North Melbourne. It was made of thick bricks too. She knew the flat was in North Melbourne because that was her football team and she could almost see the players' jumper numbers when she looked out her mum's new kitchen window from the eighth storey. The Galloping Gasometer stood out a mile because he was big and square and different from the other players. She had to go and see her mum every second weekend no matter what. She had tried to talk to her dad about staying home, but he said no. 'Your mum's your mum,' he said, every time. And that was that. Even though she knew very well that her mum was her mum she still didn't want to go. But some things weren't worth mentioning. Final, like the final siren.

One day she told Helen Gallos that she didn't much like her mum. She was full of courage and chicken twist chips at the time. Helen Gallos lived down the road in McCracken Street, Kensington. It sounded good when you said it really slowly, like a prime minister. 'Mc-Crack'n Streeet, Ken-ziiinng-ton!' Before her dad would let her go for bike rides in the area she had to chant 'Sixty-four Mc-Crack'n Street Ken-zing-ton' so that if she got lost, she could help herself find her way home. She wasn't scared anymore because Boland, the person not the dog, didn't even live where there was concrete. Unless there was concrete in jail. She didn't worry about him much anymore since they'd moved. He'd never find her here. She could hardly find herself. At first she'd cried when her dad had said that the dog Boland couldn't come to the city. Now that she lived in the concrete she could see that he was better off back home. Her dad had found a nice farm for him to live on.

Helen's dad worked in a chip factory and she was fat. Probably because her dad worked in a chip factory. Whenever she went over to Helen's she got a free pack of chicken twists. There was also a Vietnamese family on the other side of the street past the school she didn't go to. They had a nice daughter called Vo, who was very good at listening and not so good at talking. It was a funny name and their dinners tasted like flowers smell, but they were lovely people. They smiled and nodded a lot, so the girl smiled and nodded a lot too. It hurt her neck.

When she wasn't visiting the people in the street, she rode her bike around the Kensington streets. As she rode she marked all the houses out of ten. She liked the ones with the curvy verandas; her dad told her they were called bullnose verandas. No matter how hard she looked, she couldn't find the bull connection. She was learning all the architecture terms that she could, and she liked the double-fronted houses the best. Double-fronted made sense because there were two sides beside the door. They were more symmetrical. The single ones looked out of balance, no matter how charming the rest was. She didn't like wire fences, she thought picket fences looked best. They were always painted the same colour as the house. She would ride by wondering if it would look odd to paint them the same colour as the window frames instead but by the time she rode home she would be wondering about something else.

The main difference between Daylesford and Melbourne was the heat in summer. In Daylesford it felt cooler and she had the swimming pool up there. There was no swimming pool near her house in Melbourne and she missed it. All the asphalt and concrete and tall buildings made it hotter. She loved going for a walk in the evening with her dad though. As the sun set and the summer evenings kicked in, the air would cool a little and they would walk for ages, looking at the houses. They marked the houses out of ten together and listed their reasons. She never gave a ten, only a nine and a half. Otherwise she wouldn't know what to do if she saw the perfect house. One time her dad gave a house twelve out of ten, but she didn't say anything. She was learning when to get upset and when not to. He was good at teaching that.

She also liked kicking the footy on the street with her dad, but she had to watch out when he kicked it too far and it went over her head. When her dad had enough of kicking the ball, he would kick it over her head and go inside when she turned around to run and get it. He would just be gone. She learned to run backwards and keep an eye on him as she retrieved the ball. This usually got a laugh out of him, so he would stay out a bit longer.

Sometimes, when she was allowed to stay up a bit late, they would sit in the kitchen together and play cards. He had taught her how to play canasta and five hundred. Her hands weren't big enough to hold all her cards, so she placed them on a kitchen chair next to her, constantly guarding them in case he cheated by looking under the table.

Even though they lived in the city, it was a quieter life. Up in Daylesford she had plenty of space and things to do. Here she was more housebound, despite her rides, and they didn't have a TV, so it was quiet. She had books, jigsaws and colouring-in but you could only tip out all your puzzles on the floor, mix up all the pieces and put them all back together so many times.

School was quieter too. Everyone already had their friends by the time she got there, so she was mainly alone. She went to St Mary's in North Melbourne, so at least she could stand at the chunky stone fence and watch Victoria Street and the trams. She did laps and laps around the church, memorising every variance in the stones. She even learned to climb the textured stone walls, though the gaps in the rows of stones were small. The ridges for fingers and toes became more and more visible the longer she stared at the walls. She planned the climbing route before she made any attempts, and hours of practice were put in during lunch and recess breaks. Once she could get about five metres up, she showed her dad when he came to pick her up. He got scared when she held position and looked down at him, courageously lifting a hand off the wall and offering a small wave. Later that year he showed her some grey hairs and said it was her fault for climbing the church.

One morning she walked out into the concrete backyard and discovered some people had broken in, lifted off the top of the clothesline and then lifted her bike and the locked chain off the pole. The big triangle bit was just sitting on the ground near the back fence. She didn't know why they would want her bike at all. It wasn't even a good one. It was from the *Trading Post*. Everything was from the *Trading Post*. It felt like even her clothes were from the *Trading Post*. They were new to her, but she knew they weren't new-new. Her dad understood how much she needed a bike. It was her peace. They didn't really have anything they didn't need. Except maybe cutlery. They had enough for more days than they did the dishes.

A couple of days after her bike was stolen, she walked out of school and saw her dad's car was parked smack bang in the middle of the schoolyard. It was odd. He always parked outside. Plus the boot was open, and he was grinning. As she got closer, so did the other kids because something different was happening. She could see some handlebars. Part of her nearly jumped up into the sky – a bike! The other part shrivelled up like an old orange that had been at the bottom of her schoolbag for the whole holidays. All the other kids were looking, and a few sniggers hit her ears. It was a new-old bike, with a big long floral seat and faded handlebar tassels. It looked like it may have had a basket with big plastic flowers on it at some stage. She was glad it didn't have a basket anymore, but her elation was brief.

Her insides knew she should say thanks, but her outsides shut the boot and made her walk to the car and sit in it. The time it took for her dad to come back, sit in the car, start the engine and completely ignore her was interminable. She felt sick sitting there as they drove away.

'Thanks for my bike, Dad,' she said, trying unsuccessfully to keep the desperation and regret out of her voice. She wished she could have the moment over again. She would run over, say thanks, hug him and she wouldn't even care about the stupid kids who weren't even her friends. They weren't worth this. Something inside her knew that a sacrifice had occurred for the new-old bike to land in the boot. And her dad had stood there looking so pleased with himself as he presented it to her. He couldn't even wait until they had gotten home because he was so excited that he wanted to show it to her straight away.

She let the stupid kids ruin her new-old bike.

They had two whole parents and snotty-nosed brothers and sisters and lives that mimicked each other. She had her dad, her crazy sometimes-there mum and a house that didn't look like the others. Not from the inside. She loved the inside and the card games and the laughs and the books that took her to faraway places. Helen the Greek girl never reacted to her bare house, neither did Vo, but these kids would have. If ever they went to her house. Which they didn't. That day she betrayed the only thing that mattered.

When the longest car ride ever finished (even the one from Daylesford to Melbourne felt shorter) her dad went inside. She ran after him, pleading to get her brand new lovely bike out of the boot. He went outside, the girl on his heels, removed the bike from the boot, dropped it on the ground, locked the car and walked back inside. She howled on the street, not caring who saw her. The concrete house was two doors from a milk bar, so there were people. There were always people at the milk bar. She knew there was no point trying to fix anything. She couldn't. Just like her mum's moods. She felt helpless.

All she had was her new-old bike. She picked it up, hopped on the dumb floral seat and rode like she'd never ridden before. Fast, careless, far away. She rode and rode, her throat losing layer after layer as she howled into the headwind, tears flying out of her eyes as she wished and wished she was someone else for just one minute.

CHAPTER 3

Sometimes Susie's fortnightly visits to her mum were only day trips to the hospital, instead of sleepovers at the flat. There were two hospitals. One was called Royal Park and one was called Parkville Private. They weren't normal hospitals with sick people lying in beds surrounded by machines. They were hospitals for the mind. She didn't like the Royal Park one, even though it had an inviting name, because the insides were shrivelled, bloated with wear and defeated; like the patients. The walls were peeling, and the lino squares curled at the edges. At Parkville Private, everything looked like a proper hospital and the nurses had crisp white uniforms. One time she asked her dad why her mum couldn't go to Parkville every time, instead of Royal Park, and he said that it cost a lot of money. She said that Pop was rich, he was her mum's dad, and her dad said that Pop only wanted to pay sometimes and that it is what it is. She didn't like Pop much, but she liked him even less then.

Rosie was at the front counter when her dad dropped her off. She liked Rosie because she always warned her of her mum's mood before she went in. Plus she gave her a biscuit every time, even though it was only an Arrowroot.

'Mum's feeling good today,' she said, handing over a biscuit. 'She's in the piano room playing away.' The girl followed the non-curly lino to the piano room. It was cosy like a nanna house. It had mixed floral patterns like a nanna house, too. It even had carpet. Once she had asked Rosie why there was carpet there but not anywhere else and Rosie said it was because of acoustics. She had nodded approvingly like she knew what it meant.

As she got closer to the piano room, she heard loud singing. It was out of tune but very enthusiastic. When she walked into the room, her mum beamed at her without skipping a note. She waited politely for the cacophony to finish and looked around the room at the other patients. Jane was there, with her wide eyes that looked at different places. So was Michael, who was really tall and skinny like a stick insect. His eyes looked so bulgy she didn't know how they stayed in his head. Old Robert was singing too, which would have been hard because he was always so slouched that he was almost folded in half. They were singing 'The Lord is My Shepherd' and she even hummed along for a bit before stopping herself. She didn't think it was appropriate to join in. A passing nurse who didn't know her might mistake her for one of *them*. When the song finished, everyone cheered and lifted their arms up. She idly thought that it would be nice to be so expressive with feelings in the real world.

At the end of the song, her mum ran over and twirled her around three times. It nearly made her sick up her Arrowroot, but she held it in her throat and kept it down with her mind.

'Look, love, I have all this lovely new sheet music,' her mum said as she showed her different pamphlets full of notes. Even though she was learning the piano herself, this conglomeration of notes looked so difficult that it hardly even looked like sheet music. It looked like a really hard dot-to-dot colouring page.

'Why is Merry Christmas written on them all?' she asked her mother as she flipped through them.

'That's my new name, but you can call me Merry for short because you're my daughter and I love you.'

Every now and then she wished her mum was the regular sort of mum, but she knew she couldn't fall into the wishing trap. She reminded herself of how hard it was when her mother sat in the corner with blank eyes, not able to listen no matter how hard she tried to be interesting. That was worse. But sometimes the boundless energy Mum was just a bit much. It made her a different sort of sick.

'Let's go to the rec room,' Merry said, marching off at full speed. She sure could walk fast. They made their way through some corridors and landed in a big room that made even the ping-pong table look tiny. She liked this room. One wall had windows all the way along and the trees outside always seemed to sway no matter how weak the wind was.

'Where are the bats and balls?' she asked her mother. Merry gave an exaggerated shrug and looked inquisitively at the others, who had followed from the piano room. Apparently Merry Christmas was also the Pied Piper.

The girl followed both of Jane's eyes and saw nothing helpful at the end of their lines.

'I'll go and ask Rosie,' she said, pleased at her own solution. She made her way back to the reception desk along the corridors, making sure she stayed in the lines of the lino squares. When she got there, she asked Rosie where the bats and balls were. Rosie said something about not having enough staff to supervise the rec room today and handed her another Arrowroot. She didn't take it.

'Don't worry, Rosie, I'll be there,' she said proudly. Rosie bunched up her lips, shook her head sympathetically and started saying that she wasn't old enough to supervise. When Rosie started saying that they could play next time, she stopped listening and headed back along the corridors to the rec room. It simply wouldn't do. It was rare to get her mother in such a good mood and she knew that the no ping-pong news would flip her mother's brain upside down. No more Merry Christmas.

As expected, her mother did not take the news well. She began ranting and raving and the piano room group started ranting and raving along with her. Jane's eyes moved further apart, Michael's limbs seemed to gain length and Old Robert stood up so much he was nearly straight. She had to think quick before things got out of hand.

'How about we all sit down and not move until they give us the bats and balls?' she said loudly. Jane clapped hard.

'What are you clapping for?' Merry Christmas asked, scrunching up her face in disapproval.

'The girl said we should sit here until they give us the bats and balls,' Old Robert said. His voice was thunderous, deep and authoritative. All at once, they simply sat on the floor. The girl sat too. A nurse came and tried to get the patients back to their rooms, but no one moved. Even when the nurse said that they wouldn't get any dinner. Susie had an Arrowroot in her tummy and a sense of pride. After all, this had been her idea.

The staff at Parkville Private became more active, more involved. But no matter who they sent, no one budged.

'Give my daughter the bats and balls so we can play ping-pong or we don't move from here forever and a day,' her mother said defiantly when the boss nurse came. The girl clapped along with the patients. She didn't even care if the staff thought she was a resident. Let them lock her up. Heck, she even decided to refer to her mother as Merry Christmas from then on.

The staff didn't bring the bats and balls, but they did bring in the big guns. Rosie walked into the rec room and sat down next to her, but not too close. Jane and Old Robert clapped at having a new member for the protest. Merry Christmas and Michael weren't so convinced.

'It's time to stop,' Rosie said, looking mostly at Susie.

'We'll stop after we get the bats and balls,' she said. Her face went red as she thought of all the times Rosie had been nice to her when her mother had been difficult. All the times that she'd sat with Rosie behind the reception desk instead of watching her mum in a trance. All the times her father had picked her up and Rosie had told him that she had a nice visit, even when it wasn't nice. Because it made it easier for her. It meant she didn't have to talk about how hard it could be in there. How character building. She felt so terrible at her betrayal of Rosie that she got pins and needles in her arms and legs and neck and brain, but she couldn't back down. She looked at Rosie and hoped that she somehow understood her thoughts.

'If I can get the bats and balls, and I'm not saying I can, it is one game and one game only,' Rosie said. She was stern. The group nodded excitedly. Michael made a noise like a foghorn and nodded so hard it looked like his head would fall right off.

Rosie left the room. The atmosphere deflated like a two-day old balloon. The girl crawled over to her mother and gave her a hug, hoping it would help keep a bit of Merry Christmas in her. But she was also the Pied Piper and the Pied Piper wasn't playing the pipe anymore.

Old Robert was the first to stand up. He returned to his ninety-degree angle as he shuffled out of the rec room. Jane's eyelids drooped as she stood, and Michael briefly stretched his long limbs before rising to the roof and following Old Robert. No one wanted to make life awkward for Rosie because she helped make all their lives less complicated, more justifiable. The girl stood next, allowing her mother to lean on her as she rose. Neither knew what was next, but her mother put in a real effort.

'Want to play a duet, Susie Shoes?' Merry Christmas said to her daughter.

'Yes, please,' she said back, looking up at her mother who wasn't quite Merry Christmas anymore. Neither of them touched the lines in the lino squares as they headed back to the piano room.

CHAPTER 4

*H*er mother drifted in and out of the mind hospitals. When she saw her mother at the flat, she had to pack a bag and stay overnight. She felt miserable as her dad dropped her off, but she decided she didn't have to go to her mum's straight away so she meandered over to the milk bar nearby. She bought twenty cents of mixed lollies and was quite happy with the proportion of jelly-based versus cream-based ones she'd chosen. The cream ones – like teeth and milk bottles – probably didn't have any cream in them at all, but she called them creamy. There were a couple of Mates in there as well, and although chocolate wasn't her favourite she didn't mind sucking it off the square of toffee, which would last ages.

After crossing two roads, she wandered over to sit on a swing in the park. She pushed herself so high that the chains bunched up and clunked back together in the middle. Up and down, up and down she went as she made her way through her bag of lollies. But she couldn't stay there forever. She had to face the inevitable. It was like arriving at the top of the Faraway Tree – she never knew whether a good or a bad land awaited. And like the Land of Topsy Turvey, Mum Land was fun until she realised that being upside down was only fun for so long.

As she got near the flat door, she could hear laughter and people. There was a little glass panel that ran down the side of the door and she peered through. There were a couple of people she knew from the mind hospitals: Michael the stick insect and Jane with the different direction eyes. There was a fat lady in a spotted dress who was slapping her knees while her head was really far back, laughing hard. The girl smiled. It didn't look so bad today. At least with guests there she wouldn't be the centre of her mum's world.

She knocked and her mother rushed to the door, threw it open with gusto and spread out her arms, flinging them around her daughter. She felt skin. When she was released, she could see that her mother was wearing an apron on her front. And when Merry Christmas turned around, saying something about a pancake party, she saw her mother was wearing nothing else. She could see her mum's bare bum. Her insides shrivelled up as her face reddened. She looked around the room at the guests, but no one else seemed to care. As she debated saying something, the fat lady in the spotted dress signalled her over with helicopter hands. She walked over. The lady spun her around, picked her up and sat her on her knee. It happened before she could say she was too old to sit on people's laps, but as soon as she landed, she liked the cuddle and comfort. The fat lady said her name was Sally Bellally. The girl laughed and said her name was Susie Manoozie.

'Who isn't a floozy,' said skinny Michael in a sing-song voice, deep like an opera singer.

'But she's a real doozy,' said Jane, looking at Susie and the kitchen door at the same time. The group clapped. A small birdlike woman with a pointy nose and tiny lips emerged from the kitchen and handed Susie a green enamel plate.

'My name is Frances, and on the menu today we have lemon and sugar, jam and cream, or maple syrup,' she said expectantly as she took a small notebook from her apron pocket. She had one of those mini half pencils.

'Hmm,' Susie said, taking her time. The room became more and more curious the longer she thought about her choice. She crossed her legs, uncrossed her legs, rubbed her chin thoughtfully as she repeated the options out loud, overacting her thought process the whole time. Michael leaned further and further over the longer she took. If she waited much longer he might topple over.

'What did you have, Jane?' Susie asked.

'JAM and CREAM,' Jane said as she clapped loudly once. Susie hadn't heard such a staccato clap before. It was sharper than her metronome.

'I'll have jam and sugar, thanks,' Susie said decisively.

'NOOOO YOOUU WON'T, young lady,' Frances said in a decrescendo, flipping her notebook shut. 'THAT is not on the menu. Wait here, please, while I consult with the manager.' Frances turned on her heels and burst into the kitchen just as Susie's mother was coming out, frypan in one hand and a laden plate in the other.

BAM.

Frances ended up on her bottom with a lemon and sugar pancake sliding ceremoniously off her head. Her mother stood on it when it hit the floor and she went down with a crash. The pan circled round and round on its base making a dreadful racket before stopping at Michael's feet. He picked it up with one hand and swooped down his long arm and picked up the bird lady with the other. She was instantly upright, patting herself down to make sure all her bits and pieces were in place. Tight bun of hair on her head – check; notebook in pinny pocket – check; eyes, nose and mouth still on face – check.

Susie's mother laughed uproariously. Unlike the bird lady, she enjoyed the chaos. Michael scooped up the pancakes and began shovelling them into his mouth, mumbling something about not liking things going to waste. Jane stood behind Merry Christmas and tried three times to help her up, but her mother was having none of it. Her apron was askew and one of her boobs was laughing along with her. Susie was momentarily mortified and then she stood up and gave everyone a job. Jane was to get a cloth; Michael was given her enamel plate and told to pick up the remaining fallen pancake pieces. Sally Bellaly provided a strong base from which to pull Merry Christmas up and Susie got on her knees to use the cloth Jane had rinsed for her. As each section was wiped down, Jane attentively took the soiled cloth and brought it back fresh as a daisy and smelling like lemon. It made Susie want a lemon pancake.

'Can I have a lemon and sugar pancake please, Frances?' she asked, as she wiped the last dirty bit of floor. Frances had a burst of purpose, ushered herself and Merry Christmas back to the kitchen and the party guests resumed position. Susie returned to Sally Bellaly's lap.

Frances poked her head out of the kitchen and looked left then right before risking the move to the lounge room. She gave Susie the pancake, and Susie said thank you. Frances patted her on the head ever so lightly and said 'The girl has good manners' to the room at large. Everyone nodded approvingly. Susie had spent enough time with people from the mind hospitals to know that they liked good manners very much. Nearly as much as they liked God. What they didn't like was the news. It ended up with lots of head shaking and walking around in circles and noises instead of words coming out of their mouths. It got louder and louder the more news they heard. After her experience with Boland, Susie understood this reaction. Merry Christmas emerged from the kitchen, enamel plate in one hand, spatula in the other and her boobs back in place.

'Will you marry me?' skinny Michael said, getting down on one knee. It was a long way down.

'Marry Merry, marry Merry,' Jane said, clapping with vigour.

Her mother froze in the doorway for a moment before elegantly placing the spatula under the fresh pancake, walking towards her daughter and placing it on Sally Bellaly's empty plate. She then stepped back to the doorway to give Michael her full attention. She swung her now empty enamel plate and hit him fair and square on the side of his head. BOING.

'You're lucky I didn't use the frypan,' her mother said, matter-of-factly. 'If you ask me again, I will,' she added grimly.

'Yes, Merry, I'm very lucky,' Michael said as he erected himself.

'I'll marry you, Michael,' Sally Bellaly said. Susie fell to the floor as Sally Bellaly stood up, put one hand in the air and gracefully walked over to her new husband like she was about to dance the waltz at the Queen's ball. Susie thought of Maid Marian and Robin Hood. Michael took Sally Bellaly's hand and guided her to the chair next to him. It was gentlemanly. The group burst into a round of 'Happy birthday, to Michael and Saaaaa-llllly,' before a boisterous standing ovation. The bride and groom sat down in the chairs like they were thrones. Jane ran to the kitchen and emerged with two serviette rings.

'I now pronounce you man and wife,' she said, looking each of them in the eye simultaneously. Frances got out her notebook and wrote down the exact time and date according to her watch.

'For posterity,' she said tightly. 'On this fourteenth of July at five o'eight and sixteen seconds,' Frances pronounced. Michael and Sally each placed a few fingers in their respective serviette rings to prevent them from falling off and bouncing across the floor. Susie clapped along with the group and smiled at her mother, who had managed to find a red vest to put over her in and out boobs when Susie hadn't been looking.

CHAPTER 5

Things had changed for Susie. It was near the end of her last year of primary school and she felt, for the first time, that she had power. Not on the outside, on the inside. There were actual changes too. She had a job and she had got it all by herself. There was a newsagent close to her mum's. She rode her bike down there, told the man that she loved riding and that she would be an excellent delivery girl. When she found out the start time was five am she didn't even care.

'Well, sir, I can ride just as fast in the morning,' she said, nodding at the man.

'One chance. See you at five tomorrow. Do your parents know? Normally the parents come in too,' he said, leaning over the counter seriously.

'They're working so they couldn't come. And now I'm working, too. See you tomorrow,' she said, leaving before he could ask her any more awkward questions. Her dad wouldn't mind, even though the shop was a fair ride away. Kensington didn't have a newsagent, even though it had loads of shops, otherwise she would have tried to get a job closer to home.

She rode home in a westerly direction to tell her dad about her new job. She was learning to tell north, south, east and west. The middle of Melbourne was on a compass grid, and she could now see, for example, the south-west corner of an intersection.

A new girl had come to St Mary's Primary, and she lived in Carlton in a two-storey terrace house. It was as close to a ten as Susie had seen in a house that wasn't double-fronted with a bullnose veranda. The front door was painted bright yellow and it had a sparkling silver decorated knocker smack bang in the middle above the equally silver letter slot.

The best gelati shop ever was on the corner of her new friend's street and Lygon Street, on the north-west corner. When she told her dad about the wonderful gelati and the precise directions to the shop, he immediately suggested that they go for a night drive after dinner to give it a try. Susie was thrilled. They sat out on the streets watching the passers-by as they ate their pear gelati. Pear! It was almost better then aniseed ice-cream; but not quite. It was hard to get aniseed ice-cream in Melbourne.

As they ate their gelati, Susie told her dad about her new job. He nodded approval at her initiative and so, from then on, she got up early every weekday morning and turned up to the newsagent's ten minutes before she was due to start.

George, that was the newsagent's name, would stop work and sit down on a stack of papers for a chat as she loaded her side bags. He seemed to be interested in her descriptions of the houses she flung newspapers at. Together they made up lives for the imaginary people who lived inside them. There was an old single-fronted rundown worker's cottage near the Lost Dog's Home, and they often talked of old Betty who lived there, though no one had seen her for many years. As the story grew, it was decided that old Betty was a widow whose heart had never recovered from losing her husband in the war. She only left her house once a day to pick up the paper, and she had a room devoted solely to the growing stacks of newspapers going back for years – even before George had the newsagents. George didn't feel the need to tell Susie that there was a young couple living there, who came in to pay the bill monthly. Susie liked sitting with George, but she liked riding more. She especially liked the sounds of the birds, which seemed to grow louder as the dull dawn light brightened and the sun came up.

Months went by. Whether she was living with her dad or visiting her mum, she made sure to be at work ten minutes before her start time. Before she knew it, it was almost the end of the year, and the time came to pick a high school. All the kids in her year were going to some Catholic high school near St Mary's, but Susie explained to her dad that she didn't much care about following them there. The kids weren't her friends. He suggested she try out for a high school in Parkville that required her to sit a test, so she did. She sat in a room for a couple of hours answering questions about what the odd one out was – like lion, ringmaster, trapeze artist and circus tent. In the last section, she had to write a made-up story with the theme 'loyalty'. Instead of writing a made-up story, she wrote about the time she went to visit her mum and there was another crazy lady there who had a son who was older than her. He was called Wexley because his mum liked the name Wesley, but also liked to have a Bex and a lie-down. Bex was a gross powdered drink; nearly as gross as Wexley. And that was how the sinewy, pimply boy Wexley got his name. The two crazy mothers decided that their offspring were a match made in heaven and decided to marry off their children.

When Susie wrote the story, she used expressions like 'arranged marriage' because she read in a book that they do that in India. She enjoyed writing the story very much, especially the bit where the two crazy mothers left the girl and Wexley in the flat to get to know each other before their impending nuptials. Wexley was stinky and tried to kiss Susie, but the girl in the story was having none of it. She kicked him right hard in the shins and told him to 'fuck off' with thunder on her face – just like the kids who lived in her mother's flats who sometimes kicked her in the shins, called her a snob and told her to fuck off back to where she came from.

She didn't put that part in the story but it had become more and more perilous entering her mum's flats. She was never attacked out the front, because the flat kids knew her dad sat out the front until she hit the staircase. She didn't even know half these kids, and the ones she did know were because every Saturday and Sunday, when her mother was Merry Christmas rather than a zombie, she would open up her flat to as many kids as would fit. She called it Saturday and Sunday School. They would be greeted with snacks, followed by games, stories and songs. Only a few loved her for it, the rest used her. Her mum invited them all in, even Kathy who was as big as an adult and as mean as the desert. They were all nice to Susie at her mum's, but they sure were mean in the hallways or the stairwells. So, when Wexley put his arms around her and went to kiss her, she did to him what they did to her. The girl in the story should be grateful the kids had been mean, because it gave her the tools to save herself from being married off to ugly spotty Wexley whose mum was way crazier than hers.

'You reckon we can pretend that we're happy and going to get married when our mums come back?' he asked. It was more like a whine than a voice, and it crackled between a girl and a boy voice the whole sentence.

'Yeah, as long as you sit there, and I sit here and you don't say one more word to me,' Susie said, sliding her bum down to the floor with her back to the lounge wall under the window. It gave her a clear view to the front door. He slid down his wall and they waited for their crazy mothers.

That's where she ended the made-up story part of her entrance exam to University High School. It wasn't a university, even though it was in the name, and her dad seemed pleased with her when he picked her up and she told him she enjoyed the test. She told him it was easy to pick the patterns and the wrong one out and that she wrote an interesting story about mixed-up loyalties. It had to be the best story in the room because no dragon, witches or magic potion story was ever going to be more interesting than the two crazy mothers, the kid named after a headache powder, the girl and an arranged marriage. It was then she decided that real life was much more interesting than the lands above the Faraway Tree.

She had almost forgotten the story she wrote until there was a bit of a kerfuffle a few weeks later. Susie and her dad were called to the school for an interview and she was asked whether she would like to talk to someone; that perhaps some things were happening at her mother's that should be discussed. Susie explained that there were certainly some colourful characters in her mum's building and she'd used them for inspiration but she had made the story up after reading about arranged marriages in the *Encyclopaedia Britannica*. She got the feeling that this was better than telling the whole truth. She told Mr Negas that she decided to write a story about anti-loyalty and asked him what he thought about it. He took a moment, looked down at her through glasses that seemed way too small for his long, pointy nose and told her that it was quite well written. Susie beamed as she sat outside the office while Mr Negas and her dad 'had a little talk'. She decided that she didn't fancy growing all the way up, if for no other reason than there must be nothing worse than 'having little chats' with each other.

When her father emerged from the office, he handed her the Year 7 booklist and suggested they drive to the bookshop to pick up her required reading – so she'd have the chance to get a jump-start for her new school. She couldn't think of anything else she'd rather do.

CHAPTER 6

*A*s Susie and her friend neared the tram stop at her new school on Royal Parade, she cringed. Her mother was there, adorned with numerous chunky Catholic necklaces and six canvas shoulder bags. Susie still resented her fortnightly visits to her mother but she tried to smile. A grimace was the best she could manage. Susie quickly introduced her friend Sasha to her mother and looked neither of them in the face. A tram screeched to a halt in front of them, but her mum held her arm and suggested they catch the next one so they could 'have a chat'. Susie waved miserably at Sasha through the window and let her shoulders slump.

'I would never have introduced my mother to my friends when I was your age,' her mum said, as the tram rattled past, piercing her with sincere appreciation. Her mother was a beautiful woman with the palest blue eyes imaginable. Their colour was more like mountain haze than the sky.

High cheekbones, a slender nose and perfect rosebud lips surrounded them. Susie didn't look like her at all.

'I wouldn't have either, Mum,' she said as she looked away, trying to cover her embarrassment with a bit of humour.

'Been practising the piano?' Mary asked. She was more Mary than Merry Christmas that day. 'The only thing that will separate you from everyone else are looong, haaard, sloooow scales,' she said, tapping Susie firmly on the chest.

Susie scowled and dropped her bag as loudly and emphatically as she could. Her mum still bore her bags on her shoulders and Susie wondered what they contained.

They got on the next tram and, after a few stops, Mary decided that it would be more exciting to walk.

'Where are we going, Mum? Can't we just go back to your place?'

'I've got a few things to do first and I want you to say hello to Don Sing, he's known you since . . .'

'I was this high,' Susie said, trying to sound enthusiastic. There was always good food at Don Sing's Chinese restaurant, and she liked the sound of clicking mahjong tiles. There were definitely worse places to go. Mary stopped to have a drink at a water fountain, but no water came out. Susie watched her mother's face transform and wished she could disappear.

'The goddamn fruit-tingling council are in on the conspiracy too,' Mary said, getting louder and louder. 'What do I do if I'm thirsty?' she asked sardonically, tapping her foot on the asphalt and putting her hands on her hips. 'I have no choice but to go and *buy* a drink. It's a Coca-Cola conspiracy and even the council are in on it.'

Susie tried to explain that the tap was just broken and that the council would get around to fixing it, but to no avail. Mary ignored her and stomped into the nearest takeaway food shop. After flinging open the doors to the drink fridge, she picked up a can of Fanta.

'Product of Coca-Cola,' Mary said, pointing at the can and winking at Susie triumphantly. Both the pudgy man behind the counter and Susie shifted uneasily. Then Mary picked out a bottle of milk and began telling the man about the dirty business practices of the Coca-Cola company. Some other customers came in. After Mary began to insist it was time to boycott Coca-Cola products en masse, much to the amusement of the other customers, the man pushed the milk towards her, refused the money in her hand and pointed to the door. Mary stormed off; Susie followed in a slow jog.

'Where are we going, Mum?'

'We are going to see your father.' She kept walking towards the train station. Susie was secretly pleased and began to concoct excuses to remain at home once they got there, rather than go with her mother back to those flats.

After getting off the train, Mary resumed her brisk pace. They walked in silence. When they arrived at Susie's newish old house, her dad was in the yard painting the picket fence with his old clothes on. Susie felt a flush of anger. They were meant to do that together.

'Well, well, well!' her mum said, leaning dramatically against their car.

'What, what, what?' her dad said, grinning at Susie who was too fed up to respond. Mary swung the milk bottle, still half full, and hurled it at the windscreen of their Holden. It missed, hit the bonnet and left a dent; the bottle didn't even break. Her dad emerged from behind the fence, flicked the bottle into the gutter and ushered them all into the car. As they pulled up outside Mary's place, he searched for Susie in the rear-vision mirror. She ignored his eyes and he laughed and told her to smile, while her mum sat silently sulking. He seemed to enjoy telling her to smile at the most inconvenient times, like after beating her in a board game. More character building. Susie looked out and counted eight floors up the housing commission building and wished, yet again, that she could disappear.

'See you in the morning,' her father said with finality.

Before entering the building, Susie looked up to make sure that no one was dropping anything from the top floors, then raced inside as fast as she could. Her mother watched her in amusement and loitered in the danger area looking pleased with herself. Mary began to tap dance and hold her arms over her head protectively, laughing hysterically to herself. A lump developed in Susie's throat. Too proud to let her mother see her cry, she took to the stairwell and ran up to the eighth floor in record time. Her frustration had dissipated by the time she got there, and she waited for her mum to catch up.

As they entered, Susie noticed some initials scratched into the side of her mum's new piano. 'What happened?' she asked.

'Someone broke in, scratched the piano and poured honey through the cupboard. I'm just glad they didn't pour honey on the piano keys,' her mum said genuinely. Susie looked at the cupboard. She felt sad for her mum because it used to be full of paper, pens and other stationery items. The paper came in all shades and the pale lilac was Susie's favourite. It had taken ages for the stock to build up. She went to the cupboard and threw open the doors. There were a couple of sad-looking piles left but the best colours had been ruined. Susie had always enjoyed sorting through the things inside and rearranging them – it was one of her favourite things to do. She went to take her bag to the spare room, but her mother stopped her.

'You're sleeping in bed with me tonight,' her mum said as she put her arm around her. 'A girls' night.' Susie didn't argue, dropped her bag in her mum's room and then ventured to the spare room to see the real reason why. The floor was covered with 'Save the Children' money tins, the type roadside collectors rattle.

'What are they for, Mum?' she asked as a dread ball grew in her stomach.

'I know at least eighty people in this building and I'm going to give them a tin each. Imagine how much money we can raise?' She was so enthusiastic she was almost Merry Christmas, but Susie immediately felt sorry for her. She knew the kids around here would fill the tins, but not for the charity; they would open them and keep the money.

Susie went over to the blue trunk with gold hinges that sat under the long lounge room window so she could put the tins out of her mind.

'How's the lolly collection going, Mum?' she said, smiling to herself. When she opened the trunk she saw Mars Bars, Coconut Ice, Cherry Ripes and even Liquorice Chews amongst the growing collection. Her mum was going to ship it to the Queen when it was full, so Her Majesty would know what confectionary delights were available in Australia. Mary sent a book to Her Majesty once; it was returned with a letter saying that she couldn't accept unpublished material. Susie was happier than her mother about receiving a letter from the Queen herself. As she dug through the lollies, she picked up a Turkish Delight and turned it over and over in her hands. Eureka! It was made in England.

'Mum, there's one here that's been made in England, so I can eat it, can't I?' Her mum emerged from the kitchen, her face red, stormed over to the trunk, slammed the lid down and locked it. Susie wished she had never asked.

'Go to bed,' she said. Susie obeyed even though it was too early. She knew that her mother would get over it by the morning and having some time to herself appealed to her. As she lay there, she indulged in misery and self-pity for a while. She thought about her friends and wondered why she was the unlucky one in the parent department. Once, just once, she wanted to come home from school, be greeted by both parents and a fridge full of ice-cream and drinks of all flavours. 'What would you like, dear?' the mother would ask. A family dinner would follow and then they would watch the news together. She got bored with hoping so she gave up sulking and turned to the book her real mum had left on the pillow for her. She always left a story for her and it was often the highlight of her visit. She opened *The Happy Prince* with high expectations and she wasn't disappointed. Afterwards she lay there with a tear-stained face, thinking of the loyal swallow and the broken-hearted worn-out statue. Even though it had been sad, Susie was full of good will; even for her mother. She fell asleep.

She woke up early, even though it was a weekend, and she didn't remember her mum getting into bed. Mary was fast asleep, so she crept into the lounge room. The sun was streaming through the window and she sat in the warm square of light it created on the floor wrapped in her orange fluffy blanket. Her mum had cleaned up, which was a good sign. As she looked out the window, a little sparrow landed on the window sill and Susie marvelled at its many shades of brown. She decided that brown was the most underrated colour in the whole world.

As her eyes wandered, she noticed that the blue trunk with the gold hinges was gone. She hadn't heard any noises in the night and she wondered who had helped her mum move it and where it had gone. She opened the front door and there it was in the outside hallway, open for anyone to help themselves. She helped herself to a Turkish Delight and as she ate it, she looked down the never-ending balcony and noticed a figure approaching. It waved as it got a little closer. The blonde hair became evident. It was Kathy; her mum's favourite (and Susie's least favourite) flat kid. Susie didn't like her at all, and she was scared of getting a kick to the shins. Kathy said 'hello' as she folded her arms and stood there all up herself.

'What are *they* doing here?' Kathy asked after a long pause.

'Dunno,' Susie said, trying to look like she didn't care.

'They're those chocolates ya mum's been saving for the Queen, aren't they?' she asked as patronisingly as she could. 'Your mum's a fuckin' loony.' She was so close to Susie's face that she could see the flecks in her eyes. Susie kept her fear in her stomach. She was getting better at controlling her face. Character building helped that, at least.

'Yeah, well, your mum wouldn't eat if my mum didn't give money to your mum,' Susie said, pleased that she had stuck up for herself. Then she realised she had actually stuck up for her mum.

'Yeah, well she only gets money from the government because she's a loony.' Kathy spat on the floor in triumph, grabbed an armful of chocolates and walked away with a toss of her head. Susie knew it wouldn't be too long before others came for their share, so she went back inside.

As she shut the door she felt strange. She was so resentful towards her mother, yet she had stuck up for her. Usually she didn't. She was hurt by what that horrid girl had said. A lot of noise started outside the door and her mother emerged from the bedroom, sleepy-eyed and yawning. She smiled and Susie smiled back – a real smile.

'Enjoy the story?'

Susie nodded vigorously and followed her mum to the kitchen. Mary put the porridge on the stove and handed Susie the wooden spoon. She stirred while her mum set the table. Silently, they ate their breakfast and sat for a while afterwards. Susie decided that she could have done a lot worse in the parent department. There was no friction in the air, they were just happy in each other's company. She wouldn't have swapped mothers at that moment for anything in the world; even if she was a loony.

Later, Susie and her mum walked downstairs together. As her dad pulled up, her mum shook Susie's shoulders, looked at her firmly in the eyes and said: 'Remember. Looong, haaard slooow scales.' With a conspiratorial wink, she turned and walked up the path. She didn't look back.

CHAPTER 7

Susie ran through the danger zone and headed up the stairs. Her dad had a new rule. Once she got to the eighth floor, she had to wave with one arm after her mum had answered the door. If something was wrong, she was to wave with both and then go back down to the car. On a recent visit, her mum hadn't been home. Susie had to wait and wait until eventually it crossed her mind to go down to the fifth floor and knock on Bill's door. He was a human blueberry. Round and ripe and even his nose was purple. He looked at her like Wexley did before he tried to kiss her, but she ignored his creepiness so she could use his phone to call her dad. When he came to pick her up, he was furious and worried at the same time. He kept asking what would have happened if he hadn't been home, but it was a one-way question that didn't need an answer. It was like the time she got lost at Moomba. When he finally found her, he hugged her tightly but was angry at the same time. Which was strange because he was normally patient and nice; even if his sense of humour was mostly annoying.

When she passed the fifth floor, Bill was out on the balcony. He lived in the end apartment near the stairs. She noted that his nose was more purple than usual. Probably because it was cold. Her dad said that's what happens when you drink too much and get gout. She called out a quick hello and kept moving. The least amount of manners required. But manners nevertheless. After all, he had saved her bacon that time. She got to her mum's door and knocked. And knocked. She started to feel sick because when she looked through the glass panel at the side of the door, she could see that the inner foyer door to the lounge room was open. It was only ever open when her mum was home. Fact. And she wasn't answering the door. She felt sick and her eyes went dry like the desert as she pounded and pounded. No answer. It was blind panic, and it shocked her. Normally she would be grateful that she didn't have to stay, but the absoluteness of something being wrong brought out her love.

A figure walked down the hallway towards her – her dad.

'You didn't wave, love,' he said. His sentence went from frustration to kindness as he got closer. She had no control over her face this time.

'Mum's there, the inner door is open, she's there, and she's not answering,' she said. Her words got quicker and quicker. She vaguely heard her dad saying that she wasn't home, that it had happened before, that it was time to go. Susie planted her feet on the ground.

'Something's wrong, Dad, you *have* to believe me,' Susie said, trying to keep the worry out of her voice. Her dad always responded more positively when she was calm; measured. Again, she explained that the inner door was *always* open when her mum was home, and *always* shut when she wasn't. His face changed as he started to believe her. For an instant she was relieved, but then panic set back in.

'Bill has a key,' he said, heading to the stairs.

'He's on the balcony,' Susie replied, hot on his heels.

They got to the fifth floor and the human blueberry was still there.

'Give me the key, Bill,' Susie's dad said. She hadn't heard him so authoritative before. Bill just stared at him. He was almost smirking. Her dad rushed at him, spun him around and put his forearm across his neck. Bill went even more purple. Susie just stood there, frozen by the violence. She struggled with her feelings. Although she felt proud of him, she also felt sorry for Bill. She wasn't sure what her job was or how she was supposed to feel.

'Give me the fucking key,' her dad said menacingly. Bill nodded, her dad let him go and he went inside. As he entered, Susie stood right in the doorway so he couldn't shut the door on them – *and* he tried to. Her father's arm stuck out and helped her hold the door open.

'You don't want me to come inside, Bill.' The words sat in the air. Bill disappeared for a few moments and her dad winked at Susie. Not a joking wink; a team wink. Bill emerged with his arm extended out the front, a key in his outstretched hand.

Susie grabbed it and headed back up to the eighth floor, her dad behind her. They'd slowed a little by this stage. It was a combination of using so much energy in gaining the key and trepidation about what awaited them.

When Susie got to her mum's door, her dad held out his hand for the key. She shook her head. It was her mother and she would open the door. After opening it, she rushed through the mini foyer, took a right and went straight into her mum's room. There she was sitting at her desk under the window. Relief flooded through her. Her mum looked like she was concentrating hard, leaning right over her words. Probably writing a poem, Susie thought to herself. But something was wrong with her position. She looked a little too slumped; maybe she had fallen asleep from all her concentration. Her dad pushed past her and began shaking her mother.

'Mary, Mary,' he said loudly; desperately. It had all happened in seconds. Susie was instantly full of dread. She just stood there, watching. Tears burned the back of her eyes, but she tried to wish them away. It was time to be brave, time to hope. Her dad rushed back to the foyer and picked up the bright red phone. It was the same red as her mum's vest. Susie noticed her mum was wearing her nice shirt under it. A crisp, white, long sleeved, button up shirt for special occasions, like the concert at Parkville Private that she'd organised a while back. 'Merry Christmas and Her Singing Elves' she had called it. And it was a great concert, even if Susie and Rosie from the reception desk were the only guests. They had lime cordial to drink while the show was on, and Rosie had given her a cream biscuit instead of an Arrowroot. 'An occasion biscuit,' her mum had said.

As she stood there she could hear her dad calling for an ambulance, but she couldn't make out the words. She took a step back, so she could keep an eye on her mum and also see her dad on the phone. Bill appeared at the front door. Her dad covered the mouthpiece of the phone and told him to fuck off. Susie had never heard her dad swear before, and that was the second time in one day. Bill slunk away. Susie decided that her dad could look after himself and went back to her mum's room. This time she walked right over and stood by her side. She was asleep sitting down, her head resting on the desk covering her pages. The part of her face that Susie could see looked grey; wrong. Susie picked up her mum's hand that was flopping down at her side. She stroked her hand, but she couldn't find any words. Everything was flashing before her eyes like a Japanese bullet train. All the visits to the hospitals, all the visits to the flat, all the bush walks back when they lived in Daylesford, all the one cents she had earned by picking dead daisies from the daisy bushes.

Her mum had a particular aversion to dead daisies and Susie got more pocket money than anyone because of it, even though they weren't rich. One dead daisy equalled one cent. When she had a half bucket load, she would take it to her mum and say, 'There are one hundred and one daisies here, Mum.' When she held out the bucket, her mum would step back from it like it was full of spiders or snakes. Her mum would watch her take them straight to the outside bin and then pay her for doing it. Susie liked even numbers and preferred to have exact numbers of dead daisies in her bucket, but her mum always looked at her with doubt when she presented even numbers. Susie learnt to say odd numbers so her Mum would believe her. Even though it was a lie to say one hundred and one when there were actually one hundred and two, it made them both feel so much better. And she always rounded down because rounding up would have been immoral.

Susie stood there holding her mum's hand, wishing she hadn't worried about other kids thinking that her mum was crazy. She wished she had been more proud of her mum, instead of trying to hide her. All those times she wished she had a different mum rushed into her brain and she felt just horrible. Like the girl with the curl in the middle of her forehead who was horrid. Still she couldn't speak.

Her dad came back in the room and told her the ambulance was on its way and that perhaps she should wait in the lounge room. At first she acquiesced. She went and sat under the window where the blue trunk used to be. Then she paced and found herself in the kitchen. She climbed up onto the bench and looked out the kitchen window across to the Arden Street Oval, just past the park where she liked to swing – even though she was too old for swings. She watched and waited until there was the sound of people. Then she slid down off the bench and headed back to the lounge room.

The lounge was full of bags and ambulance men. There was even a lady. They bustled, talked, came in and out to get their bags. There were almost as many bags as her mum walked around with. She went to the bedroom doorway and saw her mum lying on the ground. One man was trying to get a needle in her arm. They had cut her good shirt practically right off, but she knew her mum wouldn't mind. She walked around the house with no shirt all the time, so she wouldn't be embarrassed. All of a sudden blood spurted out of her arm. Heaps of blood like a thin fountain and the ambulance men and lady bustled even harder. They were walking fast and they looked disorganised; like they didn't know what to do. That was fine though, because Susie didn't know what to do either. Someone muttered something about getting the kid out of there. Susie put on her 'I'm not moving' face, but she was forgotten straight away. Bustle, prod, chest presses, poke, feel. Round and round in circles. Eventually they wheeled a trolley past her, counted three, two, one, put her mum on it and they were gone.

'We'll meet them at the hospital,' her dad said quietly, putting his arm around her shoulders. She pushed him away and headed to the stairs. The trolley was up near the lift when she looked over. They walked even though they were in a hurry. Words that weren't being said hung between her and her dad as they made their way to the car. Her dad sat behind the steering wheel with his forehead on it for a few moments and then started the car. Susie noticed that his eyes were wet too.

CHAPTER 8

It didn't take ages to get to the hospital, but it took ages to get to the hospital. Most of it was spent in silence, but at one stage Susie asked whether her mum was going to die.

'I don't know,' her dad said, 'but whatever happens it's not your fault.'

Until then Susie hadn't thought it was her fault, so she gave it some thought.

'It's not anyone's fault that she's sick, Dad. What's wrong with her?' she asked after a while.

'I don't know.'

Susie could tell when to stop talking.

When they got to the hospital, her dad asked the desk nurse where her mum was. The lady wasn't as nice as Rosie. She had a hard face and her bright red lipstick looked silly on her barely there lips. Susie felt like everything was going to annoy her at that moment, so she told herself to be careful and not to say her thoughts out loud. The lady probably thought she looked nice in her stupid lipstick. They walked down a corridor and a jolly nurse approached them.

'Let's get you a biscuit and a drink while you wait, young lady,' she said, crouching down to Susie's height. 'I'm Judy,' she said in a voice aimed for children younger than Susie, but she didn't mind. She liked her face.

'Nice nurses always have biscuits,' Susie said, smiling. Judy smiled right back, put her arm around her and took her to a small room that had a table and chairs in it. Nothing else. Susie sat down, and Judy said she was going to steal her father for a while so he could chat with the doctors. She added that she'd be right back with a biscuit and a drink. Susie appreciated that she said 'steal' him. It was accurate.

'Do you have Fanta?' Susie asked. She figured she might as well get a soft drink while everyone was being so helpful.

'I'm sure we can manage that,' Judy said decisively and left the room.

Susie just sat there swinging her legs. She pretended the table was a piano and practised long, hard, slow scales. When her mum woke up, she'd tell her that she didn't waste her waiting time and that she sure was getting better at her scales. A list of things she would say to her mum began forming in her mind; things that would make her happy. Things that would bring out the Merry Christmas in Mary. Like how they used to have stone pillows in ancient Mesopotamia. That would show she'd been doing her homework and make her laugh. The best thing about her mum was how involved she got when she was feeling up. Susie bet herself that her mum would take her for a walk after hearing about stone pillows so they could find pillow rocks and try stone pillows in real life. Susie secretly liked this about her mum and when she woke up she would tell her mum just how much fun she could be.

'Here we go, love,' Judy said as she came into the room. She knocked on the door before coming in, which Susie also liked. It made her feel respected.

'Thank you,' Susie said as she cracked the Fanta can and inspected the plate of biscuits. There were two cream options, but she chose the Scotch Finger, even though they went better with milk. Judy put some note paper, a colouring book and some textas down on the table.

'I thought I'd bring you some things to keep you occupied, you might be here for a while,' Judy said as she pulled out a chair and sat next to her. She crossed her chubby legs, put her hands in her lap and looked at Susie expectantly. Susie was feeling suddenly petulant, so she didn't take the unsaid invitation to ask any questions.

'I'll leave you be and check on you soon then,' Judy said after ages and went to leave the room. Susie pulled herself together.

'What's wrong with her?' she asked.

Judy sat back down. 'She's very unwell but the doctors are doing everything they can to help,' Judy said, touching Susie on the shoulder. Susie pulled away.

'Where's my dad?'

'He's talking to the doctors and he'll be here as soon as he can.'

'Is she going to die?' Susie asked. It was really the only question she had.

'Maybe.'

'I'd like to be alone now,' Susie said, picking up a texta. 'I'm also too old for colouring books and I want my dad.' Judy said that she coloured in sometimes, even though she was a grown-up, and added that she would send Susie's dad in as soon as she could.

When she left the room, Susie wished she'd stayed. But it was too late, and she didn't know what she'd talk about with Judy anyway. There were tears inside her, so she let some out while she wished for her mum to be okay. There wasn't even a clock, so she couldn't see if time was going as slowly as she thought it was. She opened the door, poked her head out and decided to go for a wander. As she headed up the hall, she almost played hopscotch on the lino squares. Mostly, she felt like running – and Susie did not like to run. Running seemed pointless, but she could have run to China and back right then. After a few lengths of the hallway she returned to her little room and ate another biscuit. It tasted like cardboard and the Fanta made her feel sick. It left a gross film on her teeth.

She began scribbling, harder and harder as she went. The paper began to tear. She remembered the time she had a bobby pin when she was lying in bed. It was dark, and she drew invisible pictures and wrote invisible words on the wooden bedhead above her head. She couldn't sleep. It was when she was living in Daylesford and her mum had been in Melbourne for a few days. Susie wondered if her trips to Melbourne back then were really mind hospital trips in disguise. She made a note to ask her dad. When she had been drawing imaginary pictures with the bobby pin, headlights had appeared in the driveway. Her mum had come into her room and turned on the light, even though it was late, to give her a present. It was the *Chess for Children* book, Volume 2, and Susie was thrilled until she saw the look on her mum's face when she looked behind Susie's head. She had seen many faces on her mum, but never had she seen her so . . . heartbroken. Susie looked behind her and saw that all the imaginary bobby pin thoughts and pictures had actually scratched into the wood. They weren't invisible after all. And right in the middle were the words 'I hate Mum'. Susie felt like her chest was going to explode; that her face was going to blow up.

'I'm sooo sorry, Mum, I didn't mean it,' she had shrieked as she sat in front of the words. Her mum had simply stood up and left the room. When Susie looked up, her dad was standing in the doorway. He followed her mum. Susie had cried and wished every magic force in the universe to turn back time. Shame seeped into every nook and cranny of her body and mind and she wished she was dead. It was the worst night of her life so far and she couldn't ever imagine having a worse one. Until now.

She scrunched up the scribbled on paper and threw it into the corner. Even though she didn't think of it very often, the shame of that night managed to come back at its every memory. It didn't even shrink with time.

When Judy came back, she had her dad with her. He had red eyes. Susie's stomach shrivelled into a sultana. She knew. Her dad and Judy took it in turns talking about the doctors doing their best, there was nothing anyone could do, that her mum had died. Susie was already cried out and genuinely surprised that her mother would never be herselves again. Judy edged her chair closer and closer to Susie as they spoke and she pulled her into a big hug. Susie just sat in that hug. She wondered why she wasn't crying. Why she wasn't as sad as she should be. She was angry that her mum had died; angry that her mum was crazy. All the things her mother could have been, but wasn't, filled her with rage. She sniffed and Judy made the hug even bigger. It had to end at some stage, so Susie reluctantly pulled herself away. Her dad sat there with his face in his slender hands. Susie felt just awful for him. So awful that she started crying. She didn't know what to do. Judy pulled her in again and Susie soaked it up, hoping that Judy didn't know she was really crying for her dad; not her mum. It was definitely the next worst night of her life now.

CHAPTER 9

Susie was angry. She knew her mum wouldn't want to be cremated because she was Catholic. But her pop was paying for the funeral, and he was Church of Christ. And they like cremations. No matter how hard she tried, she couldn't quite calm down. It didn't help that she was wearing a skirt. She hated skirts. It was made of itchy felt and her button up shirt was tight around her neck. She was in the wars.

They pulled up to a pretty church atop a mini hill in a faraway suburb. She thought she saw a sign saying Balwyn at some point. When they pulled up, there were loads of people, but she didn't recognise most of them. Susie rolled her eyes on the inside as she hopped out of the car.

'Here we go,' her dad said as he squeezed her shoulder. They both took a breath in and went to face the throngs.

The first group she saw was Kathy and a few of the flat kids. Kathy was wearing a skirt too.

'You look as ridiculous as me,' Susie said as she walked over. She wanted to get any meanness out of the way. Her tank was nearly empty.

'Yeah. It itches,' Kathy said, giving her thighs a quick rub. Susie smiled and explained that she was going through the very same thing.

'I'm really sorry about your mum. She was always real nice to us kids, you know,' Kathy said to the air near Susie. This was a turnaround. Susie decided she had two options. To make Kathy pay for all her horridness by listing all the awful things she had said and done – or to let it all go. She was tempted to let it all out, but she knew her anger was powerful. There was no need to let it destroy Kathy as well as her insides. It was bigger than Kathy. Besides, Kathy had even bothered to wear a skirt. Susie simply thanked her for coming. She might have seen her breathe a sigh of relief, but it was so quick she might not have.

Susie looked over at her pop and was filled with hate. He smiled at her as they approached each other. There was no avoiding him, and she wanted to get him out of the way too. He hugged her to let all the people see that he was a good person. She let him. His suit felt as itchy as her skirt.

Once she extricated herself from Pop without even saying one word, Susie looked around and saw some mind hospital people. She raced over to feel their kindness; their loss.

'Hey Snoozie Susie,' Michael said, enveloping her in his long arms.

'Hello. Where's Sally?' she asked. Sally was definitely the best hugger.

'She's in hospital,' tight little Frances said. 'This is very, very sad.'

'Yes it is,' said Susie.

'Will we still see you?' Michael asked with quick words.

'I don't see how,' Susie said. There was no point in lying. 'I'm not old enough to come on my own. But if I was, I would,' she added. She couldn't imagine her dad driving her to the mind hospitals without her mum being at the other end. The others nodded and muttered agreement.

'We'll miss you, Susie Shoes,' Michael said as Susie went to walk away. She was more emotional than she thought she'd be at never seeing the pancake crew again. Her throat got tight as she waved over her shoulder, Susie didn't want them to see her feelings, so she kept her tears in. There was more than one funeral that day.

There were so many people that they couldn't all fit in the little church. There were people standing around the edges and even some people outside. Susie sat in the sixth row and when she looked up at the front, she could see her pop sobbing. His shoulders were shaking and he was whimpering. Susie wanted to stand up and tell the whole crowd that he had no right to cry. That he let her mum stay in Royal Park when he had the money to put her in Parkville Private. That her mum only needed a piano because it was what made her happy. He could have bought her one instead of her having to save from her pension for years. He could have made sure that she was buried, like she wanted to be, not burnt to a crisp. She wanted to stand and shout it all out, but her feet just wouldn't. Nor would her throat. It was practically closed over and she struggled to breathe. As always, Susie's anger never lasted long enough for her to use it. It just spiked like a heart machine when someone comes back to life and then it evened out. Part of her wished it would stay in her stomach a bit longer so she *could* use it. Part of her didn't.

Father Peter and Father Frank were in the crowd, and she wondered if they were allowed in another church or whether they were disobeying God. They had their uniforms on, so Susie decided it must be all right. When her mum was full of misery and Mary, not Merry Christmas, the Fathers often came to visit. They made her cups of tea and poured all Mum's black beer down the sink. Susie helped. It was called stout and it stunk like rotten socks. She made a mental note to talk to them at the end of the service. To inquire about their moral dilemma and about their thoughts on cremation for Catholics.

Her dad came and sat next to her and he was too sad to cry. His sadness spread to her and she wallowed in it. She was tired from being angry, so it was a relief to only feel sad. The day before, Susie had walked past her dad's room and he was just sitting on his bed looking at a small piece of paper. She walked in, sat next to him and put her arm around his shoulders. He was holding a black and white photo of her mum that looked like it was taken before Susie was born. Her dad told her it was the photo her mum used on her taxi licence when she was younger. Susie never knew her mum was a taxi driver. She wondered how she managed to drive people around with her up and down moods. The people would have had interesting trips either way, she figured. Her dad was genuinely fraught and she could see that he loved her mum. She hadn't been able to see that when her mum was alive. It was comforting. He probably had on-again off-again love for her just like Susie, but she didn't ask him about it.

The service went for too long, and when it was over everyone stood around on the grass out the front talking in low voices and shaking their heads. Kathy came up with the other flat kids and said goodbye. Apparently it was a bus and two trains to get home. Susie was glad she hadn't given Kathy a hard time beforehand. She was relieved that she never had to see her again, but she wished that she had seen Kathy's nice side earlier – everything could have been so different.

When she saw Father Peter and Father Frank, she asked why they were allowed in another sort of church; and were they as mad as she was about her mum being cremated when she wanted to be buried; and while she was at it, did they ever go anywhere without each other. Father Peter smiled. Father Frank said sometimes it's about the people left behind, not the person who died. Susie said that wasn't true because she was a person left behind and no one bothered to think about her. Father Peter smiled a different sort of smile when she said that. They had been there for her mum and she would miss seeing them around. Her dad wasn't Catholic, so she couldn't imagine him driving her to church to see them. She gave them each a goodbye hug. The Fathers had obviously never had hug lessons and both stood there like robots.

As she walked over to a fat old tree to have a sit and wait for her dad, she realised how much she was going to miss her mum. No more dim sims at Don Sing's, no more Father Frank and Peter chats. No more visits to the mind hospital, or piano recitals, or pancake parties. No more Merry Christmas.

POLE DANCING

There was a large, somewhat vulnerable woman who came in and out of The Institute, depending on the level of her mental health. Prone to bouts of violence. Birthed in frustration rather than cruelty. Although Miss Kaye was wary when she approached her, the fact that she was hugging a pole allayed her concerns. She decided that if someone was hugging a pole, they weren't a current threat. Risk assessment.

'Hello, Miss D,' Miss Kaye said when she finally arrived at the pole. When they first became acquainted with each other, Miss Kaye had asked if it was okay to call her Miss D — given that Damaskinos was a bit of a mouthful. Miss D had looked at Miss Kaye's name badge and said that would be fine, as long as she could call her Miss K for short. Both had smiled and nodded briefly in agreeance. The Institute wasn't without little in-jokes. Little things pumped its heart line.

'Hello, Miss K,' she said, her big floppy lips almost wrapping themselves around her words. Even though her teeth were XL, her lips were XXXL.

'We're going to have to go in for lunch in a minute,' Miss Kaye said. Laidback. No pressure. The lure of food.

'I'm not going anywhere,' Miss D said so resolutely that her words were clear. And a little loud.

'Well, you can't stand there hugging the pole forever.' Just as resolute. Let the battle begin. Miss Kaye imagined game show music. Fast with lots of dah-dahs.

'I think I can actually,' Miss D said. Softer. Miss Kaye could see her calculating how long she could actually stand there. Thoughts rolling through her eyes. Toy cash register. Ka-ching, ka-ching as each thought passed through.

'Why are you here?' Miss Kaye asked, carefully keeping the question out of her question.

'The other girls were teasing me,' Miss D said. The eyes stopped ka-chinging and filled with sadness. The best poker player in the world couldn't win with those eyes. They belied her every thought. Even if they were covered in sunglasses her thoughts would pierce their way through. Laser beam feelings.

'Hmm. It's not nice being teased.' Keep it simple. True.

'They said I look like Mrs Shrek,' Miss D said. Outraged. Miss Kaye tried not to smile. Reminded herself that teasing is not about degree – it's about the effect. She did look like Mrs Shrek. 'Do you think I look like Mrs Shrek?' Cripes. Dishonesty didn't work inside The Institute.

'Well, one of the girls said I looked like Chucky the other day. Do you think I look like Chucky?' Miss Kaye asked. Miss D's faced transformed into a big Mrs Shrek smile.

'Yeah kinda. But only because of your hair.'

'Well you look kinda like Mrs Shrek, but only because of your smile.'

They both stood there in contemplation for a moment. Miss Kaye knew Miss D would let go of the pole at some point soon. Miss D knew she'd let go of the pole sometime soon too. But that's not how the game worked. It had to be harder. Just how it was. It's okay to cave, but not too soon. Miss Kaye had an idea to move things along. Risky though.

'I tell you what, Miss D. How about I hold the pole for you while you walk back to your room?' Bam. The game show music came to a climax in Miss Kaye's head.

'Promise?' Miss D asked as the side of her head left its resting spot. A slow pole peel.

'Well, promises are dangerous. I can promise, but what if a bolt of lightning hits the pole and throws me up into the air? Then I've broken a promise and it's not even my fault,' Miss Kaye said, increasing the speed and the mystery of her words. Drama.

'Well, promise except if it's not your fault,' Miss D replied, putting one arm by her side.

'Deal. Bluetooth handshake.' Miss Kaye and Miss D stuck out their hands and shook from two feet away without touching. There's no touching in The Institute. 'Now, look over to your building.' She did. 'I think it's about eighty steps to the front door,' Miss Kaye said.

'I think it's less,' Miss D said. Distracted. Shiny new thing.

'Well, you go and count. Next time you see me, you can tell me how many it was.' Finality. Being ten metres out straight in front does not, however, mean it will result in a goal. Good odds though.

Mrs Shrek took off. She took the longest possible steps her unco-ordinated body could manage. She didn't quite topple six times and she kept looking over her shoulder to see that Miss Kaye was still holding the pole for her. Smiling her Mrs Shrek smile on each occasion. Each time she looked back, Miss Kaye would nod in vigorous support; her Chucky hair bouncing along.

Everyone had different strategies in The Institute. Some would make strict headmaster instructions. Some negotiated tirelessly. Miss Kaye found that simply being herself was mostly effective. As Miss D entered her building, she waved. As Miss Kaye let go of the pole, she waved back.

•

Prone on the fence. Jesus on the cross. Wind had picked up a while back. Wind was as bad as a full moon inside these walls. Or what a full moon mythologised anyway. Miss Kaye didn't have an opinion on the effects of a full moon. But she did on the wind. It was only a few hours after the pole, and here was Miss D stuck steadfastly to a cyclone fence. Patterns of behaviour form quickly in The Institute.

'How many steps was it from the pole to the unit?' Miss Kaye asked on approach. Flippant.

Nothing.

Too much too soon. Soldier on.

'I'd like to know who won the step bet.' Statement.

Nothing.

Interminable.

'I did, it was sixty-six,' Miss D said. No victory in her tone. Lispy messy esses.

'Righto. You win then.' No defeat in Miss Kaye's tone.

Nothing.

'It's a little chilly,' Miss Kaye said, pulling up her collar. Legitimate.

Nothing.

'I watched you walk back and I thought you took longer steps than normal. That would make it less steps than normal,' Miss Kaye said. Trying to open the unopenable.

'I'M NOT A CHEATER,' Miss D said. Oops. Not quite the top of her voice so Miss Kaye was still in the game. Bases were loaded.

'I never said you were.' Even.

'You impicated.' Fair call.

Nothing.

Two can play that game.

'Leave me alone,' Miss D said.

'You know I can't do that.' True. Another staff member passed by, pretending not to see what was happening. It could be hard in The Institute. Sometimes it was just your turn. Sometimes it wasn't.

'We've known each other for a while now,' Miss Kaye said. Sometimes history is all you have. 'I reckon a couple of years now.' Not true.

Nothing.

'You're wrong,' Miss D's big lips managed. Her head straightened ever so slightly. 'I reckon it's at least four.' Ka-ching, ka-ching.

'That means I'm getting old.' True.

'You're all right for an old person,' Miss D said. Also true.

'Thanks. We've been through a bit,' Miss Kaye said. Return to history. The only play left in the book. She was tired. Too. Miss D half smiled. If you didn't know her, it would be leering. 'Remember when you needed new pants?' Miss Kaye asked.

Regardless of the memory, shared ones are shared ones. The smile got bigger. Spit lines between her lips.

'No one would give me any, even though I needed them.' True. Sometimes you had to be loud to get things done in The Institute.

'Well I wouldn't say wouldn't.'

'You have to say that.'

'True,' Miss Kaye said. She could half smile too. She wondered how she looked to Miss D. Through her big Mrs Shrek eyes. 'Well you sure know how to get a pair of pants, Miss D.'

On Miss D needed pants day, she simply walked around without any pants on — until she was presented with a pair. No pants; no undies. Just Miss D. Miss Kaye had asked her to go and put a pair of pants on. Said that she simply could not walk around with no clothes on. Miss D said she could take her top off too. Miss Kaye had tried not to smile. But her eyes did. By the time Miss D sat on the couch in a communal area, a staff member had found a pair to give her. Miraculous. Miss D put them on and the rest is history.

'It works in the real-life shops too,' Miss D said. Delighted with herself.

'Well, we need to get you and your pants back inside.' Back to business. No outward support for her pants superpower.

'I hate the wind,' Miss D said. Her face matched her words.

When she wandered her mind back, Miss Kaye could see the wind history. She'd missed it then, but she picked it up and put it in her armoury now. So many clients. So many armouries.

'I can see a way. Can you trust me?'

'No, but my ears are open.' Trust. Open ears. Close enough.

'I will walk alongside you.' Simple. True.

Miss D's face peeled off the cyclone fence, diamonds imprinted on her cheek.

Waiting. Patience. Miss Kaye didn't recall having patience before working in The Institute. Now she was so patient it had cost her a friendship or two.

'I don't know how to make my hands let go,' Miss D said, looking at them like they were strangers.

'Sometimes you have to wait for your body,' Miss Kaye said.

'That's true,' Miss D said with her words and her brightening eyes. Revelation.

'We have time.' Home run. Miss Kaye could almost hear the crowd.

For the second time that day, Miss D pulled away from the metal. No big almost fall-over steps this time. Ginger little cartoon creep steps. Eighty steps can take sixty-six and eighty steps can take a hundred and nine.

PART TWO

A GROWING PILE OF UNSAID THINGS

CHAPTER 10

Life for Susie became more predictable after her mum died. On one of her now frequent walks among the skyscrapers, she approached a kid selling newspapers on a corner and asked him how he got the job. It looked more appealing than the five am deliveries. It turned out he went to her new high school, but he was in a different house, so they weren't in the same classes. He told her his name was Geoffrey and that he had seen her around. It was easy to get a paper stand, he added, and told her to go to a banana alley on Flinders Street not far past the station. After she said thanks, she wandered down Flinders Street, keeping an eye out for a banana alley. When he had spoken of it, she pretended she knew what it was, so he didn't think she was dumb. She liked his face. Those big kind eyes made her hope she had made a friend.

It was a dead zone past the station. There were rats climbing the matted weeds on the hill on the south side of the road. Just when she thought he had lied, she saw a strip of short, stumpy, joined together shops. Banana Alley. They were new-old. They looked a hundred and they looked new. She wondered whether they were copied from old buildings or fixed up old buildings. Either way their score was only a four.

Mid-City Newsagency sat plainly in the middle. When she went in, there was a short bald man with a shiny head and blue overalls fussing over some paperwork. She told him that she delivered papers in the mornings but that she was looking to change jobs now that she went to a high school in the city. She was trying to appear older than she looked. He explained that there was a pecking order. New people get a paper stand at the quietest corners and as people leave, you move up to stands that sell more papers. Two cents per paper sold, and twenty percent of the face value of magazines. If she played her cards right, she could even sell flags at the Moomba parade. Ten cents each. Susie reckoned a whole lot of flags got sold at Moomba. Just when she thought she had a new job, he said it wasn't really a job for girls. Her face coloured and she said that she was just as entitled to get a stand as a boy and that she was more reliable than any boy in the world anyway. A trial of two weeks was offered, and she took it. It was after school every day and she would be on the train home by half past six each night.

Her dad didn't need much convincing. They lived opposite the rifle range in the back blocks of Williamstown these days, and he said he'd pick her up at the station of a night. But he added that it was all over the first time she missed a train. He'd do his bit if she did hers – she agreed that was fair.

Susie settled into being an inner-city kid. She loved the hustle and bustle of all the people going home after work and most people bought the paper for twelve cents, paid with fifteen cents and said keep the change. Especially when they said 'thanks, mate' and she said 'you're welcome'. They would feel bad for calling her 'mate' after hearing her girl voice and they always let her keep the change. It happened a lot. She didn't think she looked like a boy but her hair was short, so it made sense. Besides, these people were in such a rush they probably wouldn't notice if half her face was missing. Every night after work the paper kids went back to Banana Alley to count out their coins. Susie always stood next to Geoffrey. The other paperboys would laugh and say 'wash your hands, Geoffrey', in a teasy voice at him. Apparently it was an ad. Susie didn't have a TV so she didn't know what this ad was, but she told them to shut up. One kid was Turkish and his name was Teddy. Susie let off a barrage of teddy bear jokes at him one night until he had tears in his eyes. She then said that she'd leave him alone if he left Geoffrey alone and it all died down. Teddy's dirty looks got worse, but Susie didn't care. Geoffrey was her friend now.

They started sitting together at school lunchtimes and going to each other's houses as well. Mostly they played jacks in the corner of the library and talked quietly about not too much. He was gentle, and he lived on a houseboat on the Yarra. Susie loved visiting the houseboat – it even had red velvet seats. And the dining table was round and there was the tiniest little room up the back near Geoffrey's bedroom for her to stay in. Cosy, safe, cocooned. She had to let him come to her place sometimes because he loved going to an actual house. Even if it was old and crap. Susie wished they could swap. Geoffrey saved all his paper money and said he wanted to buy a house before he grew up so he didn't have to live on the boat anymore. Susie didn't save at all and became a member of the Pancake Parlour Breakfast Club. She would go twice a week before school and sit there enjoying her three-stacker. Sometimes she thought about her mum when she ate pancakes, but they still tasted good anyway.

One day an old man called Cliff Young ran a really long way, and he was old. Crinkly crepe paper old. His face was on the front page of one of the papers. A man who lived in the building near where Susie sold papers always came and stood with her for a while. At first she thought it was creepy, but as she got to know him, he became more interesting. After seeing Cliff Young, he designed a jumper with running cartoon gumboots on it and he asked whether she wanted to come and pick one up for free. She did, but her instincts said not to go to a stranger's house. His name was Mack and one day he said that he liked bowling and asked whether she wanted to go with him. She figured that it was safe to go to a public place, so she met him in the city on a Saturday. He paid for the bowling and the food, even though she had her own money. Near the end of a game, he sat really close and put his arm around her. She didn't really know what to do. He stroked her chest and she just sat there frozen to the bench seat. Eventually she stood up and said she was going to the toilet, but she ran out the front door instead. Sometimes running was good.

When her dad asked her how her day went with her friend, she said it was just terrific and that she wanted to be a ten-pin bowling champion. She pretend bowled down the hallway as she spoke. As she lined up for a strike, she scrunched up her feelings into a ball and threw them down the hallway. She raised her arms in celebration of her strike. Even her dad had a pretend roll and they laughed like they hadn't in ages.

The next Monday, she asked her boss, Ross, for a different stand because she had been reliable and deserved a better one. She was given the one in the foyer at the bottom of the tax building on King Street because that kid never showed up anyway. Ross said she could go straight there and not to worry about who would do her old stand. She didn't worry at all because she never had to see Mack again.

CHAPTER 11

Susie loved the new stand. There was a man with a red beard called Max who worked at the front counter just inside her building and he was actual nice, not creepy nice. He always wore light blue shorts, a white button up shirt and long white socks. Like it was a uniform that he invented for himself. He had a girlfriend called Fiona who worked upstairs. She had bright blue glasses and she wore flower print skirts. Susie thought flower skirts were gross, but not on Fiona. Max and Fiona always brought her little snacks and made sure she was okay.

Every time Susie and her dad played cards, she would talk about Max and Fiona and how they were going to get married. In her mind they were going to make a perfect couple; a perfect family. They'd have the ten out of ten house she had always imagined. Max was so understanding about feelings. She just spat them at him like her brain was a high-pressure fire truck hose. She wished she could help herself, but she couldn't. When she set up her stand every afternoon, she would lay out the magazines with all the desirable headlines displayed. Then she would sit on one milk crate, put her papers on another (she was convinced that she sold a few more if the papers were on the green one) and she would put another crate in the corner of the windows nearby – in case Max had the time to come over and have a sit. He never complained that the crate was uncomfortable or anything.

Spending time with Max made her feel so much better that it was hard not to tell her dad how great he was. She didn't mean to make him sound so good, because it was important that her dad felt good too. But she had never been able to ask her dad if he was *sure* it wasn't her fault that her mum died. That if she had arrived a little earlier maybe she wouldn't have died. That kids at school thought she was a weirdo. And they said so. She had a couple of friends, but mostly Geoffrey, and she told Max all about him. And Fiona, when she had time to come downstairs. Sometimes they even brought her Twisties. She wished she was their daughter, but not really, because she wouldn't have swapped her dad for anything. It just felt nice to be able to speak her brain without judgement. The kids at school would rabbit on about how crap their lives were because they weren't allowed to buy the new Duran Duran record. She felt like smacking them in the face and saying 'imagine if your mum was so sad she killed herself'.

The paper kids had been getting more and more mean to Geoffrey. Susie told him that he needed to stick up for himself. Geoffrey didn't think so. He said he didn't care, that they meant nothing to him. It sounded plausible, but Susie couldn't ever imagine not caring – so she didn't believe him.

One night Susie had packed up the tiniest bit early. It was fish and chip night, and if she caught the earlier train there would still be a sliver of light when she and her dad got to the beach. Dusk was her favourite time of the day; except for dawn. It didn't matter whether the light was coming or going, as long as it was coming or going.

As she was leaving Banana Alley, Teddy was walking in behind Geoffrey. He was calling him a girl and a sissy and a poof in his nasty voice with his curled up mean lips. Susie rushed towards him, shoved him in the chest and sat on him after he fell. She started slapping him and pulling his hair and screaming at him in a voice she hadn't heard before. She sounded crazy in her own head.

All the paper kids had rings with little metal hooks on them, so they could open the tape on the paper bundles with ease. Teddy began thrashing his ring around. Susie waved her arms, trying to stop the ring from connecting with her face. She received two large skin tears on the back of her hand, and even though there was blood dripping all over the place, she kept trying to hurt him. Two arms reached around her and pulled her up. They held her tightly around her waist and she still kicked and screamed. Other kids had arrived and were holding Teddy back. He had a sore ego. All the kids were saying that Susie had won the fight. The bald-blue-overalled man carried her back inside, Geoffrey by his side. The other kids were told to stay outside. Ross let go of her after she promised not to go anywhere, and he got out a wet flannel and some Band-aids. After the blood had been wiped off, the cuts weren't that big.

'Hands bleed a lot, so do heads,' Ross said as he placed criss-cross Band-aids on her cuts.

'It's just going to get worse now, Susie,' Geoffrey said. He was normally so calm, but she could hear a little hysteria creep out from the hidey-hole in his brain.

'I'm sorry,' Susie said, using all her strength to will her tears back inside and to stop her bottom lip from quivering. She ran. And ran. Past the other paper kids, past the old dump of the rat covered hill and all the way to her train platform. She caught the train she would have normally and rued her stupid personality all the way to Williamstown. Self-loathing, self-pity and self-righteousness made a thick soup in her stomach. She decided that Geoffrey could get stuffed – she didn't need his stupid friendship anyway. She wasn't as misguided as everyone thought. By the time she got off the train, she was tired and nearly defeated. She walked down the ramp to the phone box to ring her dad, but there. He. Was. He was holding a paper parcel of fish and chips and he grinned at her. She grinned right back. He tousled her hair and they drove to the beach. She almost felt better.

'We missed the light, Dad,' she said when they got there.

'Yes, but the moon is big tonight.'

She looked around at the waves and saw tinsels of light dancing on them. She found a good spot and they sat down to eat, huddling into themselves. Even though it was cold, the wind whipping on her face felt refreshing. Her dad started explaining about genetics and eye colours. He spoke of the percentages of getting your eye colour depending on dominant or recessive genes.

'Mum's eyes were blue,' Susie said. He explained that because his were brown, and brown was dominant, that her eyes were always more likely to be brown. Her dad had gone back to university this year, and he had so many interesting things to talk about. He was doing biology and drama this term.

'What happened to your hand?' he asked her, looking at her criss-cross Band-aids. She started explaining that she had cut herself with the sharp rings by accident, but they both knew there was more to the story. He didn't ask for the truth. He just sat there looking at the waves and waited. Susie found herself blurting out everything that had happened. How for months these kids were mean to her friend and that even though Geoffrey thought he didn't need help, she helped him anyway because that's what friends are supposed to do. And that she hated Geoffrey now because he wasn't even grateful and that he said she had made it worse. Her dad just listened.

'So anyway, my boss fixed up my cuts and I ran and ran and now we're here,' Susie said in conclusion. She was a bit breathless by then. Her dad took in a few deep breaths and let them out slowly. Susie wondered if she was in trouble. It appeared she wasn't. He just asked her a series of questions. Did she really hate Geoffrey? Did she think that fighting was the only option? What was she going to do tomorrow when she saw Teddy again? Her boss again? Although the questions were annoying and a bit unfair, he asked them nicely. He wasn't asking for explanations; he just wanted her to look at herself. That wasn't anywhere near as bad as having to answer for herself, so she engaged. By the end of it she decided that she still liked Geoffrey, that she would say sorry to her boss and that she would only say sorry to Teddy if it was absolutely one hundred percent necessary. Because it may not be. She decided that she might ignore him instead and that was acceptable. Unless it truly wasn't.

Susie licked her finger and rubbed it across the paper to pick up any salt remnants. As she did that, her dad told her about how the drama class had to demonstrate obsessive behaviours in class that day. He told her that one lady sat there and pretended to wash her hands over and over non-stop. And that a man continually walked around the room having pretend meltdowns every time he accidentally touched the lino lines with his feet; which happened a lot because he was tall and had massive feet. Susie laughed and asked what her dad did. He said that he stood near a wall banging his head against it. He said that he tried to do it gently but sometimes his head hit the wall too hard and that he had a headache. Susie said you didn't have to hit your head against a wall to get a headache. Her dad said they should take their headaches home to bed. They did.

CHAPTER 12

*W*eeks later, after apologising to her boss and ignoring Teddy, things were back to almost normal. She was walking down to Geoffrey's houseboat one evening after her paper stand, when she saw some people sitting in a line on the street. They were young and sounded happy. It was on the west side of Russell Street near Bourke and the line started at a ticket outlet. She crossed the road and ambled past as slowly as she could. One girl looked at her and asked her name.

'Susie Shoes,' Susie said. 'Well, that's what my mum called me.' She didn't know why she said so much.

'That's a great name. I'm only Lisa,' the girl said. She was older than Susie. Probably at least sixteen. She had lipstick on and had big boobs that popped over the top of her tight shirt. 'Are you here to camp out for tickets too?'

'Well, it's a last-minute decision,' Susie said, plonking herself down next to the older girl. The girl snorted.

'Clearly, or you'd have a sleeping bag. Here you can share mine,' the girl said as she unzipped her cocoon and turned it into a big square. Susie shuffled onto the warmth. Only Lisa launched into a soliloquy about Spandau Ballet and how much she loved them, how they spoke to her, how they sung her feelings, how they understood her. She got out some magazines and they looked through them together with differing degrees of admiration. Susie felt like she was in a documentary about the inner workings of a teenage mind. She wondered if she would ever be like Only Lisa. She didn't think so. At the very least she hoped she wouldn't get big boobs. As they flicked through the pages, Susie adapted to her environment. The magazines were really just a montage of pretty boys – like Geoffrey. She placed her friend's face on the boys Only Lisa liked, which enabled her to contribute to her maybe new friend's imaginings. She almost felt like she fitted in.

After a while, Only Lisa got a silver bag out of her backpack. It had a round plug in it.

'Oh, a mini waterbed,' Susie said. It's what it looked like, so she said it.

'Oh, a big one of these would be the best bed ever on the whole planet,' Only Lisa said, looking at the wine bladder like she'd never really appreciated its true value. She put the plug to her mouth and took a swig. Susie wondered what was inside it as she put her schoolbag behind her back so she could lean against the wall almost comfortably. More and more people joined the line. An Only Lisa lookalike sat on her other side. It was an uncomfortable sandwich. Susie couldn't imagine lasting very long between them. They would figure out she wasn't like them sooner or later. The girls passed the bag between them and, on one of the trips, Susie took it and had a swig herself. Her eyes instantly watered as she swallowed the acid. She nearly puked on the inside, but she didn't show it on the outside. Her throat and stomach heated up immediately. It was the first time she had been able to track anything going down her throat and she revelled in the experience. It was like a slow-motion heat x-ray of the digestive track.

'You okay?' Only Lisa asked, smiling warmly. She put her arm around Susie protectively. 'You're a different sort of cat. I like you.' Susie was glad she was sitting down. People didn't like her very often and she was pleased that it was too dark to see the surprise on her face. The glee. Susie did her best miaow and turned her hands into paws. This got a few giggles. Susie felt like a bag of live snakes on the inside and had another swig.

'How old are you, anyway?' Only Lisa asked.

'Fourteen.'

'You look younger,' Only Lisa said, knowingly.

'Well, clouds look like you can touch them, but it doesn't mean you can,' Susie said confidently, but her pink cheeks betrayed the lie. Susie had another acid swig. It wasn't half as bad as the first time. The crowd kept growing. She knew she was out of her depth, but she just wanted to feel a part of something for a little longer. After a few more sips she felt like her neck wasn't strong enough to hold her head up. And her eyes were blurry. Maybe that's how crazy Jane had seen the world through her different facing eyes.

Claustrophobia set in. She needed to be in air, not wedged in a line of people. Susie managed to reach behind herself and grab her bag. In one movement, she stood up with it and walked away from the line. She stumbled over to the gutter, fell to her knees and vomited her guts up. She felt like all her organs were coming up through her throat and she retched until nothing was left. Perched there on all fours, she started to feel very sorry for herself even though she knew self-pity was bad. Her dad had told her that you need to be able to laugh at yourself and that feeling sorry for yourself was a one-way ticket to misery. She sat there thinking that drinking wine was a one-way ticket to misery. A warm hand started rubbing her back and she glanced over her shoulder. It was Only Lisa. She was making soothing noises as well as rubbing her back. Susie just wanted to be enveloped in her arms, but she knew it would be somehow inappropriate.

'You need to go home while it's early. This isn't for you,' Only Lisa said to Susie who nodded weakly. 'I like you, though. Are you okay to get home?' Susie nodded again, picked up her bag, tried to spit out the acrid taste in her mouth and headed towards the station. She decided against going to the houseboat – she needed her own bed.

When she eventually made it to Williamstown, she was better at walking and she called her dad from the phone box. He didn't ask any questions. Perhaps he knew how weak she was from her voice. He picked her up and she didn't say anything on the way home. When they pulled into the drive she wanted to tell him that she met some people in the city and she had some wine and frankly felt quite ill. That she regretted it, that she was sorry. But she couldn't. He felt too far away. Even though she didn't want to be alone, she went to her room. He let her.

CHAPTER 13

Susie waded through the motions at school the next day and trudged to her paper stand. Her head was thick and foggy and her mouth was parched, even though she drank a lake of water. That made her almost smile. She liked the word parched and didn't get to think it much. Her words were few but her thoughts were through the roof. Most of them were miserable. She just didn't have much hope left and nothing was exciting. When she sat playing jacks in the library with Geoffrey, the gibberish they usually shared was almost non-existent. They normally went to places that didn't exist and made up lands and lives they would live in when they grew up. And the ones they wouldn't. But not that day. Susie wanted to tell Geoffrey about the night before, but she didn't know how. He had been disappointed that she didn't show up to the houseboat and his mum had even made sauerkraut. He said it was embarrassing – and that he was worried. She tried to be sorrier. As sorry as she was for herself. She wanted to say that he didn't even know what embarrassing was, sitting there with his sauerkraut. Embarrassing was chucking your guts up in the gutter and going home full of stress and wine and shame.

But she didn't want him to think she was dumb. Instead of telling the truth, she said that she just needed to walk last night. To think about her mum. As soon as the words left her mouth she felt infinitely worse. Now she was more than dumb. She was horrible, and a liar, and the worst person she could ever imagine. Her face glowed fire engine red at her mortification. Geoffrey thought it was red because she was speaking her true feelings about her mum. He even gave her a hug. The hug felt like jail. It wasn't earnt, it was stolen. This just made her even more quiet and they were both relieved when the bell rang.

Usually they rushed up to Royal Parade to get the first possible tram. Every second at their paper stand mattered. All sales counted. But Susie hung back a little when the final bell went. She saw Geoffrey running for the tram. He kept looking back and around for her. She was usually the quickest. Even if a tram came before he got there, she always waited for him. They'd sit on their bags on the floor, so the old people could sit down on the seats. The mini stairwell on the non-get off side was their favourite spot. Today, she stayed close to him, but not too close. She ducked and weaved behind other kids as he looked back. She could see that he wished she was with him, but her legs wouldn't go to him; her body just kept hiding itself. By the time the next tram came, she was fighting back tears. Regret seemed to be more and more frequent. She hoped that growing up didn't mean feeling more and more regret.

Susie was good at mustering herself. Pulling herself together. Putting on a face. Her feelings were usually deep stabs that didn't last too long. Except today. She promised herself never to drink wine again. How she wished she had run with Geoffrey. She'd just about had a gutful of hurting herself.

When she got to the tax office, she set up her stand. She didn't bother putting a crate out for Max. Or worry about the way the magazine headlines were placed. She made a fan with them instead. After a while, she wished she wasn't there. She folded her cloth money bag over and left it on top of the papers. She put her coins in it and wondered whether people would pay for their own papers if no one was looking. Or whether they would walk past to the next paper kid. Or whether anyone would wonder where she was.

Susie stood outside the building behind a pillar to see what would happen. Most people looked around for her. Some took a paper and left the money in the bag. Others, who normally bought a paper, looked around in confusion. They wanted a paper, but it felt wrong to take one – even if they were leaving the money. Max came over. He rocked back and forth a few times on his heels, but he didn't look around closely enough to see her peeking from behind the pillar. If he did, of course he'd see her. He decided to sit on her crate. He moved the grubby cloth money bag and as customers came, he folded the papers for them and took the money for her. Each one was sold with a flourish and Susie promised herself to put more performance into her selling from then on. Most of the people laughed. She couldn't hear what they were saying, but she imagined it was stuff like 'got a new job, Max' or 'found a new purpose, Max'. A couple of them winked at him. Her heart came back and she felt like her life mattered again. She went back inside to say hello.

She cheerfully set up Max's normal crate when she walked back in and plonked herself down in his spot. He laughed. She thanked him for sitting at her stand and told him how much it pepped her up, and then the fire hose of feelings spouted again. The wine, the spewing, letting Geoffrey and herself down (not necessarily in that order) and feeling so far away from her dad. From herself.

'I chucked up like I chuck up my words and feelings when I'm with you,' she said in conclusion with a wry smile. It's always good to finish with a joke, even if it was an almost joke. He looked like he had a bit of hayfever and she asked if he was all right.

'Always,' he said, standing up and blinking away his hayfever. 'Better get back to it. I'll bring you a bickie later.' He went back to the counter and she went back to reading the paper upside down between customers. She was getting really good at it. Nearly as fast as reading it the right way around. When that got boring she brought out her Rubik's cube. She was getting really fast and the customers often watched her moves. FUDLUDR was her favourite. It got the middle pieces in the middle layer into place and it sounded good. Fud-luh-dar. When she said it in her mind she added a dahhhr at the end. Like a pirate.

After a while, she felt a presence at the entrance. She focused on the exit because the people leaving the building bought papers. The people coming in did not. Usually they looked worried about tax stuff. Max did a great job calming them down. They left happier than they entered. Mostly. And Susie figured Max had the hardest job in the building. The stressed people never seemed to go upstairs. Max would have made a wonderful drawbridge guard in the really olden days. The upstairs people must have it easy. Susie reminded herself to ask Fiona what the upstairs people even did.

She looked over to the presence and there was her dad, leaning against the same pillar she had hidden behind earlier. He was grinning. He liked turning up in strange spots. Once at the museum, he just disappeared in the dinosaur exhibition. She panicked for a while but then remembered who he was. He'd be hiding somewhere looking at her. Grinning. And he was. From the next level up behind the brontosaurus head. Although it was largely funny, it was always a bit scary too. She wondered if that's why she didn't like surprises – even good ones. She smiled at him and waved him in. He looked down at her arrangements and nodded.

'You might sell more magazines if you place the headlines out,' he said. She knew he wasn't being critical, but near everything he said sounded critical recently. She hoped that finding things critical didn't happen more as you got older. It felt like it wasn't going to be much fun with all this rising regret and criticism and these little chats.

'I normally do, Dad, but I wasn't feeling great today. A bit disinterested actually,' she said, hoping he'd be impressed that she knew it wasn't uninterested. Or maybe it was. There was only a little bit of defensiveness in her tone and only slightly more on her insides.

'Those days happen,' he said, leaving space in the air for her to talk if she wanted. She used to love that he gave her options, but sometimes she just wanted to be guided. It was tiring guiding yourself. Now there was a stack of unpleasant growths forming a pile of sick in her stomach. Regret, criticism, self-guiding. Instead of talking, all her words volcanoed up her throat and stopped just before her mouth. She searched her brain for mind draino but she came up empty.

'Well I thought it was about time I came and saw what you do,' he said after waiting a while. When she sold the next paper she presented it like she was a butler. Her performance earned her a big smile. And she got to keep the change. She told her dad that this was a much better stand than the last one, five blocks down and half a block left.

'The stands on the little streets – Little Collins, Little Bourke etc – are all crap,' she explained, 'unless they're at the subway entrance.' She spoke of the ideal stands and showed him how to hold coins so you could access change really fast, so you could sell the next paper within milliseconds. She'd been practising for when she got a really busy stand. He said that this one was very well sheltered and casually asked if Max was there. Although he sounded really casual, his body language showed interest.

'Who might this be, sitting in my spot?' Max asked as he emerged from the foyer. Even though he said it playfully, he was on alert, which Susie had never seen.

'Good timing, Max. This is my dad,' Susie said, presentation style. They shook hands and they both relaxed significantly upon meeting each other. Susie wondered why there'd been any tension in the first place. The three of them froze for a few moments and then her dad and Max started talking at the same time. Nice to meet/would you like/I'd love/coffee. They both said coffee at the same time. A suspected conspiracy flew through her feelings so quickly that she couldn't grasp it. She let it go and smiled at their awkwardness.

'I'll take your dad in for a coffee,' Max said, gesturing him inside before Susie could say anything. Then they were gone. Before too long Fiona came and sat down. Although she'd visited before, she had never sat her floral skirt down on the crate. She tried to look comfortable as she handed Susie a packet of Twisties. Susie wolfed them down and it completely distracted her from her dad and Max. She asked about what the upstairs people actually did. It was interesting for a bit, but after a while she just nodded and said 'Oh' and 'Hmm' without hearing the words. When Fiona had a speaking break, Susie said she had to pack up soon and go and count out her coins. Fiona said she'd get her dad.

Her dad came back and told her that he had driven in to the city and offered to wait while she counted her coins so they could drive home together. Maybe even get some fish and chips, even though it wasn't fish and chip night. Or Chinese if she felt like it. Susie chose Chinese, thinking solely of the banana fritter at the end. There was a pep in her step as she trotted down to Banana Alley while her dad went and got the car. She felt three worlds better than she had before.

CHAPTER 14

'Shall we go to the Chinese place in Kensington, Dad? It's on the way,' Susie said when they were in the car. Because they moved a lot, she loved going back to where they'd been before. 'I'm feeling sentimental.' Her dad grinned and nodded. He had his striped scarf wrapped tightly around his neck. It was always so tight it looked like it was holding his head on.

As they drove, Susie pointed out architectural highlights. She told him that even factories can be interesting. Even though she was too old for hide and seek, she pointed out that it sure would be fun to play it in these buildings.

'For posterity,' she said in case he thought she was being childish. Back when they had lived in Daylesford, a boy had managed to climb up to the top shelf of the linen closet in one of their games. It took so ages for them to find him that her mum and dad nearly called his parents to report him missing.

As they passed through North Melbourne, Susie didn't point out the flats her mum had lived in. But she looked. She counted up eight floors and saw the kitchen window she used to sit at. Her mum's orange fridge used to stand out in all the beige. There was no orange fridge now. She supposed not many people had one. The inside of the car was especially quiet once they'd passed the flats. Luckily Kensington shops were not too far up the road, so it didn't last long.

Susie pressed her reset button as she got out of the car. She didn't want Mum memories to seep into her fritter. Her dad held the restaurant door open for her, doubling over in a big flouncy bow as she passed through. She walked with her head held high and pretended she was the fanciest person in the world.

'Where would madame like to sit tonight?' her dad asked in a posh accent. She examined her options, looking down her nose the whole time.

'Madame would like to sit there,' she said, pointing at a table with a spinning platform at its centre. A Lazy Susan. It wasn't busy, so her dad asked the waiter if they could take the larger table.

'With a Lazy Susan for my Susie,' he said, tousling her hair. When they sat down, she asked him why it was called a Lazy Susan.

'Because a lady called Susan invented it,' he said, before telling a tale of a lonely lady who went to live in China after she suffered a terrible heartache. She was so heartbroken that she could barely move her arms and she asked the restaurant she frequented daily to find a spinning mini table in the middle – so she didn't have to reach too far when selecting her dishes. It was simply too hard to lift your arms when your heart was so broken.

'So how did Lonely Susan's Lazy Susan get to Kensington from China, Dad?' she asked, letting the prawn cracker sit and tingle on her tongue as it disintegrated. It reminded her of the communion wafers and she wondered how the Daylesford kids were going. Except for fat Donna – she didn't much care how she was.

'Funny you should ask,' he said as their dishes were placed on the Lazy Susan. Susie spun it around each time her dad went to pick something up with his chopsticks. She knew it would only be funny once or twice, so she sat on her hands to stop herself from doing it endlessly. Now that she was growing up, she tried harder to stop. Stopping things once she'd started had been a problem her whole life. Like holding up the bucket of dead daisies to her mum, even though her mum reeled at them. Like aiming spit-balls at the girls who had long hair. They got sick of telling her how hard it was to get dried spit-balls out of their hair and to please, please stop it. She couldn't. She always went too far and everyone she had ever met had told her the same thing. It was getting easier now she was older, but not by much. At least she was trying, she thought, as she sat on her hands and watched her dad fill his bowl, wanting to spin the food away over and over. And over again.

As they ate, her dad told her how Lonely Susan had terrible trouble learning Chinese, even though she felt she had a Chinese soul. Although she wanted to live in China with her kindred people, she just couldn't go another year of not being able to speak to a single soul. She ordered her food in restaurants by pointing at other people's meals, which was most annoying because she liked to eat early and whenever she went out she had to stare at an un-understandable menu until others arrived and ordered their food.

'Surely she learned to say chicken or rice, Dad,' Susie said. It sounded fantastical that you could live in a foreign country and not learn a single word for many years.

'Heartbreak stops the brain from learning,' her dad said. Susie could believe it.

'Why was she heartbroken?' Susie asked. She wished Geoffrey was here. He loved it when he stayed at their actual house and her dad told stories. She bet he would love Chinese food too and made a mental note to ask him. There was a big difference between sauerkraut and Chinese. While she was at it, she could ask him why they ate German food when they were Dutch. Maybe the Dutch didn't have their own food.

'You tell me,' her dad said as he poured himself a glass of wine. It was a rich dark red, unlike the watery pale yellow acid she had tried the previous night. For a minute she remembered the smell of it, so she put her chopsticks down for a food rest.

'I don't think anything happened specifically,' Susie said, frowning in thought. 'I think she was just born to be in the world alone.'

'Yes, she was born lonely,' her dad said, not skipping a beat. 'That's why she thought she'd be less lonely in China. How can you be lonely when there are millions of people around you?' he asked before he explained that Lonely Susan had trekked to the most populated country in the world to chase friendship. But there she was after many, many years – still so lonely that she could barely lift her arms.

'Maybe she just stood right up, Dad. Maybe she didn't even wait for the people to come and eat. Maybe she just picked up the round spinning mini table and caught a plane straight back home to Melbourne,' Susie said, picturing this spritely, but old, lady called Lonely Susan simply walking out of the restaurant and coming back home. 'To face her loneliness.'

'That's exactly what happened,' he said. 'How did you know?' They laughed. It was time for sweets. Her dad asked if she was sure she could fit a banana fritter in. 'Your eyes have always been too big for your stomach.' This was true. She thought back to the times they went to Myer in the city. It had a large cafeteria with winding metal bars going around glass cabinets filled with many foods all laid out ready for selection. They went there once a year on her birthday, except once when she chose McDonald's.

That hadn't gone well.

She had heard all the kids at school raving about it, but when she went, her dad said he didn't want anything from that American conglomerate and sat there waiting for it to be over. She had ordered a hamburger and chips and it tasted like cardboard. She went back once with her own money to see if it had really been that bad. It tasted better when she went by herself, but it still wasn't terrific or anything. So, every year, except for the McDonald's disaster, she had chosen Myer for birthday lunch. He always said she could have whatever she liked, and she piled her tray, that slid so smoothly around the metal curves, with anything that looked delicious. Like meatballs and jelly slices. By the time she got to sweets, she could never fit much jelly slice in and every year her dad said her eyes were too big for her stomach.

'How about we share one?' Susie said hopefully. Her dad agreed, and a banana fritter was ordered. Her dad resumed the Lonely Susan story. He told Susie that Lonely Susan literally picked up her lazy table and came home, even though she had a bit of trouble at the airport. The Chinese airport staff were suspicious of her carrying a round wooden mini table, so she missed the first plane. The mess was all cleared up when she was taken to an interview room and she placed her table on their table and spun it around a few times. The Chinese airport people all nodded and clapped at her lazy table invention and she boarded the following plane home with many airport staff waving her off.

'She had to get the bus home from the airport because she was so lonely there was no one to pick her up,' Susie said. 'And she got more and more sad as she watched the people from her plane hug their friends and family when they arrived.' Susie's dad nodded in agreement. 'If I came home from a plane trip, you'd pick me up, wouldn't you, Dad?' Susie said and asked at the same time.

'As you would me,' he said matter-of-factly.

And so Lonely Susan had caught the bus home from the airport, walked straight to her local Chinese restaurant and placed it on their biggest table. The staff looked at her like she was a strange old lady, which she was, until the food arrived. The waiters put the food on the tablecloth and Lonely Susan picked up the dishes and placed them on her mini round table that she had carried all the way back from China. She spun the food around and gestured for the staff to sit and eat with her. They turned the door sign from open to closed at the front of the restaurant and Lonely Susan and the ten staff all sat down while the cook brought out dish after dish. They spun the Lazy Susan around to reach what they needed with great ease and all of a sudden, Lonely Susan wasn't lonely. Every night she went to a different Chinese restaurant all around the country, becoming less and less lonely as she travelled.

'Behind her as she went,' Susie's dad said, 'Lazy Susans were built at each restaurant. And that,' he said as the fritter was placed between them with two spoons, 'is how the Lazy

Susan was invented.' By the time her father had reached the end of the story, he was standing up and gesturing. Susie clapped. It had been quite the show.

'Those drama classes are really paying off, Dad,' she said. He sat back down and they polished off the banana fritter even though they were both full.

CHAPTER 15

Susie didn't go to Myer for her fourteenth birthday. Geoffrey and Susie had a new person join them in the library at lunchtimes, and she played jacks better than both of them. Her name was Lotte and she was Dutch, like Geoffrey. She was pretty and had long luscious hair that Susie envied. She was mighty sick of her short, stick up all over the place hair, but she had accepted that there was nothing she would ever be able to do about it. Lotte wore her hair in plaits and wore dowdy clothing. Susie asked her whether she was trying not to look beautiful. Lotte went pink in the cheeks, all the way up to her eyes and changed the subject.

Geoffrey and Susie were most curious about Lotte because she was one of ten children. Ten! They were both only children and marvelled at how exciting it must be to have all those people around all the time. Lotte said it was actually quite annoying because she shared a bedroom with three other sisters and they had to sleep in bunk beds. Susie said it must be wonderful sleeping in bunk beds and that she would swap any day. Or maybe merge Geoffrey and Lotte and have nine brothers and sisters and bunk beds and a houseboat. Lotte was a serious girl and got A pluses in everything.

'What do you want to be when you grow up?' Susie asked. When Lotte replied 'a child care worker', Susie told her that it would be a waste. With all her brains and looks she could be a surgeon and an actress and why would anyone want to be a child care worker anyway. They often imagined their future lives. Geoffrey was going to join the Labor Party and be a politician, or maybe even a journalist who told the truth. Like Mike Willesee. Susie said he should start by writing about living on a houseboat, but Geoffrey said he'd much rather write about being in an actual house. Susie was going to be an architect, or a lawyer who fights bullies. The three of them copped their fair share of teasing, when the other kids bothered to notice them.

Susie spent one evening making birthday invitations for Geoffrey and Lotte. Each word was written in a different colour and she cordially invited them to spend the day with her in the city, where they could 'roam to their heart's content, anywhere they wanted'. She added that the State Library had a lovely dome to stare at from creaky old wooden swivel chairs. Her invitations were accepted.

Between sitting out for Spandau Ballet tickets and her birthday, music had suddenly become interesting to her.

Each song took her away to a new imagined place with new imagined people and she was a new imagined version of herself living a new imagined life. Even though songs only went for a few minutes, the transportation to these other worlds felt longer, and each song provided her a new world where she was the hero, the vision of sorrow, the brave, the centre of the universe. She mattered in songs. Her dad said he understood that she wanted to spend the day with her friends and accepted her invitation to play cards at the end of the day. Susie was pretty sure he was being honest.

On the night before the big day, he presented her with a portable tape player. An actual portable tape player. She hugged it and then hugged him. They didn't have much money, so she made sure he understood just how grateful she was. She could play whatever she wanted, without having to wait for a good song on the radio or listen to those interminable ads where they screamed bargains at you. He even gave her some blank tapes and she headed to her room to tape some songs off the radio.

The next day came and Susie headed into the city to meet her friends under the Flinders Street clocks. She was way early. Since her mother died, she found herself early for everything; even school. She would just sit out the front and watch the people trickle in until the big rush when the entry was busier than Bourke Street. Mr Pauly was always early for school as well. She wondered if he was late for his mum's suicide too. She couldn't think of any other reason to be so early. They never spoke or anything, but they would nod at each other when the other one got there. She wondered if they were having a who gets there first race, but she didn't think so. And if they were, she mostly won. He'd nod, go inside and come out with a steaming mug of coffee. He always stood over the way. They waited together every morning without being together. It was nice.

One day he wasn't there, and Susie got more and more worried as the minutes ticked by. As the kids started coming in, there were whispers and mumblings. Something was different. Something had happened. Susie asked a kid called Darius what was happening. He was sort of approachable, compared to the others. He sat with his friends in the library at lunchtime too, but his friends played Dungeons and Dragons. Susie desperately wanted to learn this game, but she didn't know how to ask. Darius said that Mr Pauly had fallen off the tram and that he was taken away in an ambulance. Susie became desperately sad, but she managed not to show it. She didn't want to look like a dork. Mr Pauly was away for two whole weeks and then, one day, he just showed up at school early again. Susie wanted to say how glad she was that he was okay. That he hadn't died. She wanted to ask if he had a family, and whether there were people to look after him at home, but all she did was nod and hold the main door open for him, so he could get in the door with his crutches.

Susie sat on the steps under the Flinders Street clocks just looking at all the people coming and going. She generally saw people at the end of a work day, when she sold them papers to entertain them on the way home to their lives. They looked a little different on the weekend. There were more smiles, a slower pace, anticipation for the day ahead. Most days were like a lifetime to her, and each one took a little something from her. But, she supposed, each day replaced what it took with something else. That's why people look a little fresher at the start of the day. Nothing had been taken yet.

'HAPPY BIRTHDAY, SUSIE,' Geoffrey and Lotte said in unison from behind her. She beamed and added the hip hip hoorays at the end with her whole body. They chatted and walked aimlessly, taking up more space than required. They sung at the top of their voices, they skipped and sometimes they sat. Susie felt impregnable as she danced her way through the people down Swanston Street, her friends in tow. Top of the world, in which she now had a place. The world needed to get used to her, because she was untouchable – a part of it now.

They set about their missions and fulfilled them one by one. They didn't quite get thrown out of the State Library when they swirled around the raised centre console on the top floor. They almost ate too much at the Pancake Parlour and Susie laughed as she said that all their eyes were too big for their stomachs. Susie blew raspberries at the people who looked down their noses at them and told Geoffrey that other people were jealous because they were so happy. They caught a tram up to Lygon Street and managed to avoid the inspector, so it was free. They went to the Poppy Shop and looked at all the Puggles and miniature wooden toys, pointing out what they would buy for each other if they were rich.

The day passed in three minutes and they sat down under the clocks at five o'clock for a debrief. They chatted idly about their day and they all wished they didn't have to go home. Geoffrey peeled off first because his mum was quite strict about curfews. Susie tried to talk Lotte into waiting for just one more train, but she had to go and help her mum with her little siblings. She was the oldest. Susie pointed out that she was already a child care worker and they laughed. Susie waited one more train, just watching the people looking not quite the same as they had in the morning. Susie felt different than she had that morning. She had belonging now. When the time came, she wandered down to the train and looked forward to playing canasta with her dad. Perhaps, because it was her birthday, they could go out for ice-cream beforehand. Or afterhand.

The closer she got to home, the bigger the ball of trepidation in her stomach got. A few months ago, they had a lovely dinner out. Chinese. When they got home, her dad had invited her into the lounge for a chat. He explained that he came to see her paper stand because he was concerned about this Max person she kept talking about. He did a speech on how careful she needed to be of strangers. That their intentions were not always clear. Susie said she was old enough to take care of herself and that he had no right to decide who she spoke to and who she didn't. The tension grew throughout their 'chat'. The fact that she had identified Mack as one of these people and taken care of it herself sprung to her mind, but she kept her mouth shut. Her dad wouldn't listen anyway. Or congratulate her on how she'd handled the whole Mack thing. Then he started on about not wearing her bathers while she walked to the pool now that she was getting older. She said she bought them with her own money and she would wear what she pleased when she pleased.

The conversation had provided no winners. Only losers. They both sat there befuddled at how they had landed in this place where they couldn't speak without it becoming a major event. An unpleasant one at that. The growing pile of unsaid things sat between them. Susie wondered if she kicked it, whether it would crumble and scatter like autumn leaves. But it would probably be made of concrete and she didn't want to stub her soul.

She'd had such a good day, and she had been looking forward to playing canasta with her dad – not so much by the time she got off the train.

But he was waiting for her, smiling. He was trying to set the tone. She appreciated that at least, and the perfect day she had flooded back through her. She chatted away as they drove home, leaving out the bit where they nearly got thrown out of the library. They both enjoyed the card games and sat up late together. The pile of unsaid things was there between them, but if no one disturbed it, it didn't cause any harm. Susie idly wondered whether this is what people meant when they talked about an elephant in the room. Probably.

'Late night birthday gelati?' her dad asked. It was nearly eleven o'clock, but Susie knew the shop would be open. It seemed to never close.

'I might even try a new flavour, Dad,' Susie said. She tried and tried to try new things, but old favourites always won the day. Her dad always tried new things. He said there was nothing wrong with old favourites to make her feel better. She was going to say, 'Like you, Dad.' But she didn't.

CHAPTER 16

*A*s time went on, Susie's new-found confidence and certainty of having a place in the world, wherever that may be, led her to start making her own life choices. She knew what was best. Wagging school began in small doses. An afternoon walking the streets of Melbourne here, a morning sitting in the State Library there. When she walked down the street, she eyed strangers with knowledge, with challenge. She pretended she was an Atari car, speeding down the street, carefully dodging the other people. The image of the game, which she only got to play once a year at her cousin's house, was super-imposed on the people she passed. Her hips were the back wheels. She ducked here and zipped there, and she knew Melbourne better than anyone. One day she found a door. Just a door. It was rusty and dusty and slightly ajar. She saved the door for when she and Geoffrey had a day in the city. They weren't as often as she would have liked because Geoffrey's mum was big on homework and achieving straight As. So was her dad, but he allowed plenty of down time. Besides, As were easier to come by for her.

On their next Saturday, Susie packed a torch in her backpack before hopping on the train. And it was a proper torch too. A square Dolphin one that had an enormous battery, not a tube one that needed two Cs or Ds. It was bright yellow. When they met under the clocks, she told Geoffrey about the door. It was on the north side of Little Bourke between Spencer and King Streets. She said it was in nearly the same spot as her new paper stand on Little Collins Street, above the subway station exit, except on Little Bourke. He nodded and said he could picture the location.

'We just have to explore it. No one explores anything anymore because it's already discovered, and no one has been through that door for many years,' she said, trying to instil some mystery and intrigue into her proposition. Sometimes Geoffrey was reluctant to do new things. He was as reticent to adventure as Susie was to new foods. She found this annoying because how would they ever do anything if the requirement was having already done it. 'I mean, if you're too scared,' she said, drawing out her last word.

'I'm not scared,' he said, his tone clipped. 'It's just that you lead us into trouble sometimes.' Susie pooh-poohed his statement and said that they wouldn't ever have any fun unless they took a few risks. Like the time they took the blocked door at the zoo and ended up being in the emu feeding room.

'We would never have seen those emus if we hadn't taken a chance,' she said.

'One of them nearly ate my head off,' Geoffrey said. Susie wondered why he always saw the bad things. 'Yes, the emus were cool but one of them was vicious and anything could have happened,' he said with his hands as well. Susie threw her head back and laughed at the memory of his cartoon fear face. Geoffrey had to join in. It's how it was. Her laugh was catchier than a cold. He subconsciously checked his head for his beanie. It was still there. She liked when he did this. God knows where he thought it was always going.

Susie finished laughing and stood up. She motioned him to follow, and he did. As they wandered across town, Susie shouted him a doughnut. They went halvies. She got the bigger half on his insistence and they ate in silence. When they got to the door, Susie did a presentation bow. Although it was ajar, it looked stuck. They both took turns in pulling the door open. Susie said how funny it was that you always think you can do it better than the person doing it. Like watching someone struggle with a jam jar lid. All you want to do is take it off the other person and do it for them, even though it usually ends up being just as difficult. Geoffrey said he thought he knew what she meant, but his face didn't. A screech sound rang out as the door finally gave way. Susie and Geoffrey both popped their heads out of the alcove to make sure no one saw what they were doing. Clear. From there the door gave way easily. It dropped from its upper hinges and sat there at an awkward angle – as if it was unsure which way to go. To fall or not to fall.

Susie took the torch out of her backpack, and Geoffrey congratulated her on being prepared. She said she must have learned something from being in the Brownies. He laughed and said he would like to see her in a dress and a beret. She nearly punched him in the shoulder, but she managed to control herself. They walked down a staircase made of only concrete, with no slip strips or banisters down the side. He commented on the lack of safety and she said it was probably like the stairs the servants had to take in the olden days, except they would be carrying arms full of plates and still manage to get down without falling. Geoffrey laughed at the image of her in a maid's dress; Susie said she didn't like where he was going with all these dress comments but laughed along too.

Even though they had the torch, they couldn't see very far in front of them at all. Susie was in the lead and she started running her hand along the wall in front of her, so she'd be alerted to any upcoming perils. Geoffrey screamed. A short, sharp one. Susie stopped, and her heart raced faster than any Atari car ever could.

'What happened?' she whispered hoarsely. Geoffrey said nothing before he admitted he just wanted to give her a fright. She swallowed most of her anger in two goes and she was grateful for the darkness. The only thing she hated more than surprises were frights. Or maybe it was the other way around.

It seemed like the tunnel went forever. And it stayed almost dead straight. Twice Geoffrey suggested they go back the way they came and once Susie thought it was probably a good idea too. But she held firm.

One night she and Geoffrey had walked to the Williamstown cemetery in the middle of the night. She reminded him how scared they felt and how they talked themselves out of fear and played a great game of hide and seek. He reminded her that he had become hysterical when he couldn't find her after ages and that it hadn't been as much fun as she remembered. Like the emus. He said she only ever remembered the good bits.

'What, like when we sat under a tree and ate cherries in the moonlight next to the grave of John Wilkinson born 1883 and died 1921?' Susie said. Geoffrey said he had forgotten that bit. Susie had posed that Mr Wilkinson was a victim of bad luck – he had managed to live through the war only to die a few of years later. Geoffrey had said that at least he didn't have to live through the Great Depression. Susie said Geoffrey was way too obsessed with money.

As they walked, they felt light changes in the gradation of their tunnel. Susie felt it when the path turned upwards and Geoffrey felt it when it made its way down. Susie said the tunnel was probably shorter than it felt, with it being so dark and a little scary. Geoffrey said he didn't think she got scared. Susie said she never got as scared as he did, but that she felt a bit like vomiting because it was so dark. Darker than Daylesford at night. They were quiet for a while and Geoffrey said the quiet made him more scared, so Susie told a story about an old lady who wore tin foil on her head, so she didn't get brain cancer. Which was fine until she had to take her granddaughter to a parent teacher interview because the girl's parents couldn't make it. Having an old lady turn up to your parent teacher day in a conical tin foil hat was a frightening thought. Way worse than a dark tunnel. Susie stopped walking as the path took a sharp right. They couldn't see up ahead.

'What if we get lost,' Geoffrey said, hissing his words and pulling on her arm. Susie suggested that it was only one turn, which was one left turn on the way back, and that they could surely remember that. Besides, it wasn't a T-intersection. There was still only one way back. Geoffrey only agreed to go further if there were no more turns. None. Zip. She had to agree, because she only had two other options. Go back where they came from or leave him where he was. Although option two was tempting for a moment, she agreed to his no more turn condition and they set off.

After only twenty-two or so steps, there was another spartan staircase, made of the same rough concrete. Susie expected there to be more light at the top. Daylight meant a street. When they got to the top, the door had a push bar on it. Susie creaked it down and shoved her weight against the door. It budged, but only slightly. Geoffrey thought he could do a better job and gave it a firm shove himself. It gave a bit more. They both agreed, without discussion, to hold the push bar down together and shove the door as one. The door flew open and Susie and Geoffrey tumbled out into a carpark.

They picked themselves up and shrugged at each other. Neither had any idea where they were. They followed the road up, because that's where the ground level had to be, and they saw sunlight at the next level. They exited the carpark and found themselves at the bottom of the Bourke Street mall. They just stood there in disbelief on the south-west corner of Elizabeth and Bourke Streets, looking around for potential reasons for such a tunnel.

'If that was Parliament House and not the Post Office, I could see that the politicians in the olden days might need an escape tunnel. Like in the war,' Susie said, breaking the silence.

'The stairs are too new,' Geoffrey said, shaking his head.

'Well, it's definitely time for lunch,' Susie said. Someone had to put the tunnel to bed for a while. It was too incredible to think about. Geoffrey nodded, and their legs took them to the Pancake Parlour. The one down the laneway off Bourke just past Russell Street. They both agreed that this one had the most character, even though it was like the others. It was more maze-like and had more wood.

They sat at the table with the big chess pieces and had a game. After Geoffrey's second move, he casually mentioned that she had missed a bit of school recently. She maintained eye contact with her pawns and said that her dad didn't mind if she went to the State Library and read books. Geoffrey shrugged. It sounded true. Susie shook off the lie and told herself that her dad would absolutely let her skip school if she was at the library.

'Next time I'm there, I'll try to find out about our tunnel,' Susie said as she let her bishop out. Geoffrey thought that was a great idea. He said the school library was lame and wouldn't be able to tell them anything anyway. He said that home schooling herself must take a lot of discipline. She nodded gravely with a mouthful of short stack. The lie settled.

CHAPTER 17

*O*nce the lies started, they didn't stop. They kept spewing out of her mouth, much like the wine on the Only Lisa evening. There were lies she told others and lies she told herself. Projectile lying. All over the place. She told the school she was having counselling about her mum when she handed in forged notes three afternoons a week. She told her dad that everything was going swimmingly at school. Although she was having more and more time off, she was spending most of it in the State Library. She learned the catalogue system and dutifully filled out the book order cards. She would then sit in the upper reading room and stare at the dome, occasionally checking the number board. Her number would light up when her books arrived. She read voraciously on a variety of subjects and was completely convinced that she was learning more this way than she ever would at school.

She read about foot binding in China and marvelled at the few available pictures of folded over feet. The toes were folded underneath the foot and damn near touched the heel. Western culture slimmed women's waists with tight corsets, so she thought it was a bit hypocritical to diss the Chinese. This led to her ordering a book on corsets. Apparently having a tincy-wincy waist meant the women were visibly unfit for work and therefore they were part of the leisure class. Susie laughed and thought that she was part of the leisure class, sitting in the library all day reading. When the First World War started, women were asked to not wear corsets and twenty thousand tons of metal was saved and used for the war. Then she ordered a book on the importance of metal in the war and on and on it went.

Sometimes she went and sat in St Paul's Cathedral. She'd genuflect and sit on the pews, thinking back to her mother's religious days. Although she didn't feel religious, the routine of it all appealed to her. Occasionally she went back to St Mary's church, which wasn't far from the Vic Market – which sold the best freshly cooked warm, round, sugar covered doughnuts in town. They made them in a bus, and Susie thought that driving around the country in a doughnut bus was an attractive career option.

Sometimes she went for a swim at the City Baths. She enjoyed swimming, especially now she wasn't doing lessons, like up in Daylesford. Up and down, up and down. Apparently, she was an excellent swimmer, but she just had no interest in it. One day she had told her dad that there was no point continuing her swimming and that she only really did it because he bought her a cream puff at the end of each lesson. It was never spoken of again. Susie really missed those cream puffs.

The one thing she did religiously was go to work. She never missed her paper stand. She would always wait for the tram she knew Geoffrey would be on and they'd head off to their stands together. One day he said he was worried about her and she said not to be silly. She reminded him that nothing had changed, that they still stayed over at each other's houses and that she still loved his mum's sauerkraut.

Geoffrey didn't mention her absences from school when he sat around with Susie and her dad and played canasta. He never won, but he loved playing and chatting as much as she did. Susie had never asked him to lie and, in fact, had told him on three separate occasions that her dad was most supportive of her sojourns to the library. He couldn't work out whether it was true or not. It would certainly seem in character for her dad to support Susie's endeavours, so he left it alone. Susie's dad often spoke about his university studies when they played cards and postulated about the benefits of university and the importance of being an autodidact.

On one of her day trips into the city with Geoffrey and Lotte, they wandered around tapping their left feet to Split Enz. Every fourth beat, they all slapped their left feet on the ground twice in quick succession. Every time an adult looked at them disapprovingly, they looked at each other knowingly. Jealous. They just wished they were having as much fun. Six months in a leaky boat – tap tap . . . tap tap. Susie carted her portable tape player everywhere now and milkshakes became the new doughnuts. Susie loved blue heaven, but only when you couldn't get lime.

They tapped their way into the Myer store and sprayed perfume on each other. When they got to the sunglasses section, Lotte picked up a pair and looked at herself. Susie could see that she was in love with them. She wanted her to have them. When Lotte reluctantly put them back, Susie eased them off the shelf and put them in her milkshake. She turned off the music and told the others it was an outdoor thing. She didn't want any unwanted attention. The milkshake was feeling twice its weight. Guilt can be heavy. She didn't really know what to do, so she tried to laugh along with her friends as they weaved their way through the watches section at the back near Little Bourke Street. Susie expressed a sudden and insatiable desire to leave the store. She said the lights and all the perfume were making her sick. She needed some air. They walked out into Little Bourke street and a man in a suit with a name tag appeared out of nowhere and stood in front of them.

'What have you got there?' he asked pointing at Susie's milkshake.

'A milkshake – der,' Susie said with as much bravado as she could muster.

'I'm going to have to ask you to drink it,' he said.

'RUN!' Susie said to the others, 'I'll meet you at the dome.' They ran. Susie wanted to run too, but her body cemented itself to the floor. The others were gone, along with her courage. The man suggested she come with him, to have a little chat. It was more of an order disguised as a suggestion. Susie went where she was led, which was to an elevator that wasn't advertised in behind the watches. They went up two floors and down a little corridor to a little room. The man said the police were going to be called and that she was to drink the milkshake please. Susie said she wasn't thirsty. He waited; Susie drank. It felt like liquid mercury, barely making its way down her throat until the top of Lotte's sunglasses revealed themselves. He asked her why she had taken them.

'My friend fell in love with them and I just did it,' she said with her arm up like she was in class. Her father had always said that if she got into trouble to stick her hand up and tell the truth. That things go better for you if you're honest. She still managed to put a sullen disinterest on her face when the man babbled on about consequences. After forever, the police came, and she was put in the back of a police car and taken to a police station. She wondered why she wasn't handcuffed. There was a metal grille between her and the front seat and she wondered if that's what jail felt like. It was stifling, and she struggled to keep her milkshake down.

When they got to the police station, there was a whole lot of desks all crammed into one massive room. Susie wondered how the police on the phone could hear anything with all the chatterbuzz. She was taken to a small room off the big room and given a piece of paper to write down who she was and what her parents' phone number was. She wrote everything down.

'Is your mum likely to be home?' the tall skinny policeman asked.

'She's dead. But Dad should be. He's painting the laundry today.' The tall skinny man looked a little awkward for a second and then said he would be back. She sat there looking out the window at the big room. She didn't realise that police did office work and she wondered if this was what the upstairs at the tax office looked like. She missed her stand there, but her new one was much more lucrative. She sold three bundles early and then the late edition got thrown out of a van at her feet. She was usually able to sell at least six bundles for the late rush. She dropped in to see Max once and explained that she had no weekday time to see him regularly. They'd exchanged an awkward hug.

The policeman who was shaped like a tree trunk came in and told her that they'd spoken to her dad. He said that she had to wait until he came in to pick her up. Susie said she was fine to catch the train thanks, but she was told that shoplifting was a serious matter and that they were going to work out what to do with her while her father made his way into town. Now she really felt sick. She didn't think she'd ever be able to stomach another milkshake in her life. For a moment, she let tears stream down her face, but she stopped them as soon as she could. She wasn't a baby anymore and crying was embarrassing. So was being in the police station. It was the longest hour she had experienced for some time. Since being late for her mum's death, which was how she described it to herself, she had become obsessed with time. She could guess the time within a few minutes of whatever time it was. She often checked this skill. Right then she was thinking it was 2:06 in the afternoon. She desperately wanted to check it, so she popped herself out of the little room to scan the walls for a clock. There was one, and it was five seconds to two. Time was going even slower than she thought. She watched the big red second-hand tick towards two o'clock when the skinny policeman came up behind her and asked what she thought she was doing.

'I need to go to the toilet,' she said, thinking this would sound more reasonable than 'I needed to check the time to see if I was right'. She didn't want him to think she was loopy. He escorted her to a toilet and he even waited outside for her. It was intimidating, and she slouched her way back to her little room. After ages, she could see her dad enter the big room and look around. Tree Trunk Policeman fetched him and the two of them stood outside the little room having a chat. Susie never wanted to see or be part of any more 'little chats' in her life. She could hear little grabs, like 'warning' and 'too much' something that could have been 'freedom'. Her dad looked in at her occasionally and Susie felt dreadful when she saw his sad and disappointed eyes. Her dad's eyes got watery, but he never cried, even though he looked like he was going to.

Tree Trunk Policeman and her dad came into the room and sat at the other side of the table. The room felt like it shrank to the size of a lift. Susie felt like running. Just getting up and running as fast as the wind. But she listened instead. The nice policeman, as her dad called him, was going to let her off with a warning and she promised she would never steal again. She tried to explain that it was an impulse decision and that she didn't even mean it in the first place, but she remembered her task was to be quiet and listen. So she did. She nodded contritely when she thought she ought and eventually it was time to go.

They walked silently to the car. Susie wanted to ask her dad whether they could stop by the State Library, so Geoffrey and Lotte knew what happened to her – so they didn't worry. But she knew this would not be received well. It was a mostly silent car trip as well. Susie kept trying to think of things to say. She tried saying how sorry she was, but her dad just looked out the windscreen and didn't even turn his head towards her. Not even once. So she stopped trying. She leaned on her seatbelt and let her head rest against it. Her head was surprisingly heavy. She just looked out the window all the way home. When they got there, her dad got out of the car and went inside without waiting for her. It reminded her of the time he brought her home after the new-old bike fiasco. She'd forgotten about it, but the memory came back along with all the feelings of guilt and regret. All piled on to the shoplifting guilt and regret. A big fat double dose. It was too much. She went to her room, knowing that anything she did to try to fix things would just make it all worse. She took her tape player out of her bag and didn't even turn it on. There were no songs to take her away from this mess. She just went to bed, with pounding ears, even though it was only nearly the evening.

CHAPTER 18

On one of the days she actually went to school, she was half listening to the Geography teacher talking about topographic this and geomorphological that. Her attendance had improved since the shoplifting incident. She had her pen in her hand, but she wasn't taking notes. Mostly she was looking round the classroom at how grown up all the other girls looked. They had boobs and all-knowing expressions when they looked at each other. Susie had some movement on her chest, but she just wore bigger shirts so no one, especially herself, could see. She didn't wear makeup like the other girls and she couldn't fathom why they paired off with the boys who looked like half men. She smiled across the room at Geoffrey, who still looked boyish. She didn't know if she could be friends with him if he had fluff on his chin or was big like an ape.

Lotte sat in the front, as usual, and seemed so interested in everything. Susie wished she could be more like Lotte. But she wasn't. Lotte was different from the others too, but in a better way than Susie. She wasn't quite so out of place, and she chatted easily to everyone. Even though she could sit with whoever she wanted, she still sat with Susie and Geoffrey at lunchtimes. Rather than sitting in the library, they chose to sit under a tree in the far corner of the oval these days. Even in winter, except if it was really pouring. They'd all read *The Lord of the Rings* recently, and Susie used to pretend they were sitting in the Shire when they sat in their spot. It was a safe and removed part of the world. They no longer played jacks.

There was a rap on the classroom door and in walked Susie's dad. Susie's insides did backflips and she automatically stood up. He signalled her over, and when she headed towards him he told her to bring her bag. She didn't have any idea what had happened, what had gone wrong. There must have been some terrible disaster, one so big that he turned up in her classroom. At least he wasn't dead, was all she could think. The walk to the door took forever and when they got out into the hallway, he pulled the classroom door closed behind him. On closer inspection he looked furious. She hadn't seen him look like this. Ever. Not even when she got caught shoplifting.

He marched along at such a quick pace that Susie had to half jog to keep up. They went down the stairs and up the stairs of the front building to her form coordinator's office. He rapped on the door, opened it, entered, sat and pointed to the chair next to him. Susie sat. Mr Higgins looked a little sorrowful, but Susie didn't know why. He began explaining that they had compiled all the notes she had forged to excuse herself from school. A brick formed in her throat and she couldn't talk, even when she was spoken to. She could explain everything – that she was an autodidact, that foot binding and communism were more interesting than geographical formations and that she hadn't been doing nothing. She'd been productive. At one point they were both looking at her, searching for explanations but the words couldn't get past her throat brick. She tried not to look sullen, but she was downright miserable. Even her face was ignoring her instructions. Her dad started saying that if that was the sort of attitude that she was going to have, then there was nothing more he or Mr Higgins could do for her. He stood up and then sat back down.

'Susie won't be returning to this school, Mr Higgins.'

Just like that.

Mr Higgins looked even more sorrowful and Susie wanted to smack some sense into him. To make him stick up for her because she couldn't stick up for herself. Teachers were supposed to help. Her world was caving in around her and she felt like she was drowning. All her body did was cry and wail like a baby. She pleaded with her dad to give her a chance, to listen to her. He gave her a few seconds to do so, but the brick was back and presto, her moment was carried away by the wind. She tried to chase it, but it was gone. So was her dad. He had left the room and was marching downstairs to the main entry. She followed, taking the steps she normally sat on early in the morning two at a time. She would never see the day start around her again. Or Mr Pauly across the way greeting her with a nod.

She kept following her father, trying to hold back her tears but they were plentiful and in complete control of her. He got to the car and hopped in. She hopped in beside him and slumped in her seat. Maybe he would change his mind. Hope began to sprout. She pictured them having a game of cards and talking about it, resolving it. It had all been blown out of proportion and they would laugh at the whole thing. They would even laugh at the pile of unsaid stuff that sat between them most times. Tomorrow was a different day and she would be back at school; her dad would say what a terrible mix-up it had been, and Mr Higgins would smile and welcome her back to school. Her sliver of hope was slippery and difficult to grasp, but she held onto it harder than when she played tug of war in PE class.

Instead of going the usual way, her dad was driving into the city. She wanted to ask where they were going but the brick was firmly cemented now. She wondered if she'd ever be able to speak again. He drove down towards Flinders Street and turned right. When the car pulled up outside Banana Alley, her stomach sank into her thighs. She felt like she was made of plasticine and she was about to melt. Anything but my job, she thought to herself. He couldn't. He wouldn't.

'You go in there and tell them you won't be working tonight,' he said. His voice sounded far away. It sounded like it wasn't his. Susie began to open the door. 'Tell them you won't be back and that they'll need to find someone to take over your stand.'

Susie couldn't move. She just sat there. Her dad listed a litany of her sins. Her wagging, her lying, the stealing. He told her that her life was out of control and everything that was happening was a consequence of her actions. Her choices. When he finished, he was like a deflated balloon. There were a few moments of nothingness.

'I can't,' she said meekly.

'If you don't, I will.'

That would definitely be worse. Even though she'd thought it couldn't get worse, it had. Susie steeled herself and her feet walked her over to the newsagency. Ross was there in his blue overalls comparing the various piles of magazines to the various pieces of paper in his hands. He looked surprised to see her and smiled until the look on her face registered. He asked her what was wrong. Kindly. Susie knew he had a soft spot for her. Even if she did fight with the other kids from time to time. He was like a second dad. A work dad. Susie stood up straight and found some words. She said that she could no longer work for him and that she was grateful for having the job in the first place. She said that her life circumstances had changed rather suddenly and that coming to the city would no longer be practical.

The lie came easily to her. She'd read about the Chinese notion of saving face one day in the library. Susie struggled with the concept at first, because it sounded like everyone was being a bit sensitive about feelings and that perhaps being honest was more beneficial. Right then, as she stood there talking to Ross, the concept became clear. It's okay to lie if it serves to protect the face. To avoid shame. She wanted Ross to remember her positively. It had nothing to do with her bruised ego. It was about honour. Not that she had any honour left. Or any face.

She held herself straight as she walked back to the car. She slumped as soon as she sat back down and she lowered her head to below window level as they drove past. Just in case Ross looked out and saw the real her. On the way home, her dad took a detour just before the rifle range. Susie wondered where he was going now, but decided that nothing could be as bad as what had already happened. He'd already taken her life away from her. Tears came again, even though she thought she had none left. What was she going to tell Geoffrey? Maybe she'd be better off just disappearing and never speaking to him again. That would save having to explain what had happened. Anything would be easier than that, even losing her best friend. The car stopped in front of the local high school. Not just any local high school, a girls' high school. She couldn't believe things were about to get even worse.

'I'm not going in there,' Susie said. She was only defiant for an instant.

'Yes, you are.' Her dad got out of the car. Susie followed. Her life as she'd known it was behind her.

CHAPTER 19

The house was quiet for months. Susie hadn't found a way to forgive her father and her father hadn't found a way to break through her walls. They had spasmodic conversations and one night they almost had a proper conversation about what had happened over a game of canasta. But Susie developed a headache and went to her room.

One Saturday, Geoffrey had come over to her house. He told her that her dad had told him what happened and that he was really sorry. Susie acted like she didn't even care.

'Come on, let's go to the city,' he said. Susie could see he was trying. 'Your dad said it was okay.' Susie shrugged. 'We can go to the library and get pancakes,' he said, trying to seal the deal. His voice broke up when he said pancakes and she laughed and said that it looked like he might become a man after all. It felt good to laugh.

As much as she wanted to go to the city and tell Geoffrey all about how awful the new school was and how the girls just talked about The Angels, wore lipstick and gossiped about boys – she couldn't raise her spirits. She would love to tell him how much less she fitted in there and how much she missed him and Lotte. But she was proud, and she didn't want him to know how sad she was. How much she missed her paper stand and how much she craved having her own money to do what she wanted. She said that he really shouldn't come over without telling her because she hated surprises. Even more than she hated her crap life. She got tears in her eyes, so she faced the other way. He hugged her from behind and she allowed herself to cry. Geoffrey let her; and held her. He said that maybe next weekend would be better for her and that they could go to the city then. She said that would be much better than today because she was busy, even though they both knew she wasn't.

Her dad dropped Geoffrey down at the station and Susie hopped on her bike. She had bought it before her life fell over. It was a silver racer with ten gears, and she could go ages without holding the handlebars. She could even take most corners hands free. It was all she had these days and every time she took off, she planned never to return. She rode and rode and rode. That day she rode to Werribee and couldn't find a house even resembling an eight out of ten. They were all brick boxes with no features. She wondered whether she loved houses at all. Maybe it was just looking at the idea of different lives. What she did know was that marking houses out of ten had become a compulsion. Like knowing the time. Down near the water at Williamstown, she would sit on the sand and face the water, but inevitably she'd find herself turning around and looking at the houses.

The following Saturday she did go and meet Geoffrey under the clocks. Her dad had given her ten dollars for pancakes and whatever. She wanted to tell him to jam his money up his bum, but she took it – even though she knew the pancakes would probably taste like memories; like acid. It was different when she bought her own. Even though her dad would say no, she asked the local newsagent for a job. Just in case. But there were no jobs anyway. The man delivered the papers himself. In his car. That seemed ridiculous to Susie, but he was free to do as he pleased. Unlike herself. The tape player didn't accompany her to the city, so there was no foot tapping or stamping. Or singing. They wandered the streets, but it wasn't the same. She expected Geoffrey to put some sort of effort into injecting some fun into the day, given how miserable she was, but he didn't. Maybe he didn't know how. She was so full of self-pity it took her ages to realise that something was wrong with him.

They walked and walked. Up past the Vic Markets and down Errol Street in North Melbourne. It was one of her favourite streets, full of old double-storey shops with iron lacework. She would love to have a shop here and live above it, sitting out on the upstairs veranda watching life happen.

It almost cheered her up. But not quite. By the time they got to the park, they were both tired. Susie suggested they sit on the swings.

'What's wrong?' she asked him as they swung. She felt bad for not seeing his misery beforehand.

'We're moving to Sydney. Dad got a job there,' Geoffrey said. He was melancholic. Susie felt terrible for him. She knew exactly what it was like to have your life flipped upside down. Geoffrey said that they were leaving in a month and the only good thing was that they were moving to a three-bedroom apartment. He said most people in Sydney lived in apartments. Susie said that high density living was the future. She'd read a lot about population back when she was learning things.

'Well that's as good as an actual house, Geoffrey,' Susie said with enthusiasm. 'It's all you've ever wanted.' She was trying to switch his focus onto the good things – to cheer him up. 'You'll even have a spare room. I can come and visit,' she said excitedly. They sat there imagining all the plane trips and all the visits. He said they were moving to Manly and Susie said that was handy now that he was becoming manly. They laughed properly for the first time that day. Susie told him there were lovely beaches there and Geoffrey said he had no idea how she knew so much about random stuff. Susie said she paid attention to things and that he should be right chuffed about living there.

'Why don't you come with us?' Geoffrey asked. And just like that, life became exciting again. They plotted and planned how to talk their parents into it. After all they were practically brother and sister anyway. Susie said she would be no bother at all, that she was an expert in staying out of the way (Geoffrey raised his eyebrows and told her not to go too far) and that she'd never wag school or anything again. That she would get a job and give all her money to Geoffrey's mum, so she didn't cost anything. Geoffrey said they'd get paper stands together and that it would be just like how it used to be.

By the time they left the park to walk back to Flinders Street, they might as well have had the tape player. They tapped and stomped and skipped past the people down Elizabeth Street and, at one point, Susie grabbed on to the back of a tram. When the tram started moving, she shouted that she was moving to Sydney to all who would listen as she hurtled along. Geoffrey ran as fast as he could to keep up with the tram and when she jumped down at the next stop, he made her promise not to do that again. He said she could have died and then he would have died of heartbreak. Besides, if she got caught behaving that way, their Sydney dreams would go up in smoke.

Before they hopped on their trains, they sat on the steps and rehearsed what they'd say to their parents. Susie decided that stating the facts would be best with her dad. That she would simply inform him that she was moving to Sydney with Geoffrey's family. That it was the best option for everyone. Geoffrey was going to try a gentler approach. Drop hints. Leave ideas hanging in the air in the hope one of his parents would pick one up. After all, they both agreed that Geoffrey's dad liked her. Perhaps even more than he liked Geoffrey. He always laughed when they played Monopoly. Susie was always pretending to be different types of landlords in a variety of accents. Geoffrey had never made his dad laugh – not like that anyway. They left each other, full of jubilation. It was the best idea ever and now all they had to do was make it happen.

When Susie got home, she saw her dad reading a book on the big brown velvet chair. It was both of their favourites. His cheeks were pink from the wine. She could see the bottle was more than halfway down and his glass was near empty. Perfect. She sat opposite him in the floral chair that used to be his mum's before she died. He looked so far away. The distance was winning. The battle between wanting to fix things and knowing that it was all too far gone. He didn't understand her. Either that or she didn't want him to. She wondered which it was for a moment and then dismissed it. It didn't matter. The result was plain to see. The months had gone on and he went out to avoid her and she went to her room to avoid him.

'Geoffrey's family is moving to Sydney and I'm going with them,' Susie said as a matter of fact. He looked at her. No surprise, no nothing on his face. She stood up and went to her room. She put on her headphones and listened to some music, but she wasn't in the mood to be removed to other worlds. She wanted to live in the new dream. The real dream – Sydney with Geoffrey. A whole new life. She lay in bed and watched the light squares from the window move slowly across the ceiling. The sun had faded and the moonlight was bright. After she heard her dad go to bed, she snuck out the back to look at it. It was one of those really low, really big almost orange moons. Her favourite. She lay on the grass until the night moisture seeped through her pyjamas and she went to bed shivering. It didn't feel cold though, her mind was too sunny.

CHAPTER 20

The next few days passed, and nothing was said of the Sydney mission between father and daughter. Geoffrey rang her every night. There was a phone box near the houseboat, and even though she knew he'd be uncomfortable out there in the night air, he obviously didn't mind too much. He said he'd rather be there on the phone than anywhere else anyway. On the twelfth night, he said that all the hints he'd been dropping were working. His mum had rung her dad and they were going to have dinner. Dinner! Susie said that could only mean one thing; Geoffrey said he knew, it meant she was coming to Sydney with them. It must. It couldn't mean anything else.

Geoffrey said that he'd been quite clever and told them that if they were living together, it was probably best if they went to different schools. Susie didn't like this idea at all. Geoffrey said she must trust him. So she did. Mostly. He said it showed maturity; that they were looking at ways to make it work long term. He even told her there were two high schools near Manly, in a suburb called Harbord, and that they were next door to each other. Literally. She asked him how he could possibly know this, and he said he had asked Mr Higgins for some information on schools up there and that Mr Higgins said there was Manly High and Freshwater High. Right next door to each other.

'I'll go to Freshwater High, it sounds so . . . exotic,' Susie said dreamily.

'I'll go to Manly High because I'm so manly,' Geoffrey said. They both laughed their heads off at that one. And so they spoke every night until her dad and his mum had dinner. Susie asked where they were going. She said that her dad would be in a better frame of mind if he ate Chinese. Geoffrey said his mum hated Chinese food and that it would go much better if they went for Bratwurst. Susie said her dad liked Bratwurst because when he was young he went to Berlin and he had told her that there were men on every street corner with a sausage stand that they wore over their shoulders. Like a backpack, except it was a front pack, with a semi-circle on the front with a heated base and bratwursts galore. Geoffrey thought that was a bit far-fetched. Susie said German street corners wasn't a subject he excelled in. Geoffrey agreed.

On the night his mum and her dad went for dinner, Susie and Geoffrey talked for ages. Because her dad wasn't home, there was no whispering or having to go silent if he entered the room. She was set up perfectly on an old-fashioned tapestry chair near the back door. It had buttons all around the upholstery, except they looked more like flattened stars that raised to a point in the middle. She supposed they were called buttons, even though they weren't warm. Buttons had a warmth. The flattened stars were cold to look at, and to touch, but she fiddled with them endlessly anyway.

When they hung up, Susie was so beside herself that she paced around the house. She paced through the yard. And then she paced through the house again. Then she heard her dad's car; it was a big noisy green Ford these days. It didn't have the character of the old HR, but the sound was distinctive. She didn't want to appear desperate, so she jumped under her blankets and pretended she was asleep when he pulled into the drive. She heard him pottering about and summoned all her brain strength to stay put. To not move in case he popped his head in. It was terribly difficult just lying there, but she managed until eventually she fell asleep somewhere in the thoughts of this new school, these new people, a place where she would fit right in from the start. Where there were beaches and her face had no pimples. Where she was funny. And popular. And where she needed her diary for things other than due dates for assignments. Where she had a new mum and a dad and an actual brother. Geoffrey had fallen asleep earlier, but with similar visions of their new life. Where he didn't have curly hair and his ears didn't stick out so much.

The next day took three forevers. She rode her bike to school early, continuing her tradition of allowing the day to develop around her. She carried a new disposition, and it sparked the interest of a few girls in her class. They kept looking at her, whereas before they'd sneer at her then look away. Each day seemed to require each girl in the school to let her know she didn't belong. She didn't much care because she would rather eat brussels sprouts than hang with them anyway. The other girls thought they were having an effect on her, but Susie was stainless steel. Nothing took her shine. Well not them anyway.

Susie wondered why she didn't feel lonely when she was so alone. It felt strange that she had spent so many months with so few interactions. She even thought she would miss her dad more. But she didn't need any of them. She had her worlds. Like the Helen Reddy song she loved so much. This lady called Angie-baby lived her life in the songs she heard and had no inclination to live in the actual world around her. Nor did Susie. She read, she listened to music, she rode her bike, she looked at houses. During lunch breaks, she had taken to looking through books full of paintings in the library. Bruegel was her new favourite. The pictures were full of almost cartoons – but not really. Such busy scenes. Her favourite was a big banquet, but the guests at the table hardly drew her attention. It was the servants and the wait staff walking around with huge platters, so big there was a man on each end of them. They wore chef's hats and aprons and their eyes smiled. She lived their lives as she pored through the pages. She didn't need the real life in front of her, except when Geoffrey was around. When she read Asterix books, even though her dad said she was too old for that shit, she was whatever character she wanted to be. Sometimes she even walked around her room with a ramrod straight back being Caesar. Her nose even felt bigger from the inside. She could see it grow when she crossed her eyes.

There must have been thirty times that day where she checked her time power. It was going so slowly that even when she minused ten minutes from her instinct, it was way earlier than the real clock. It perturbed her. Her world was so dependent on knowing the time. On feeling it.

When she rode home after school, she was pleased to see the car in the yard. It was crunch time. To Sydney or not to Sydney. She knew her dad didn't have uni on Fridays. Apparently there were very few classes on Fridays. Lecturers liked a three-day weekend. But he went to the library on Fridays more often these days, and he wouldn't get home until after dinner. She was grateful today wasn't a library day.

They used to sit down for dinner together but these days he often left a note with two dollars saying something like 'Get yourself a pie'. Which she didn't mind. Pies never got old. Not like doughnuts or milkshakes. She hadn't been able to get through a whole milkshake since the shoplifting incident. It was like her brain associated the taste with trauma. Acid shakes. Sometimes she put two pie moneys together and rode down to get fish and chips on the beach. She didn't do it with her dad anymore, but it was still a favourite. Especially when she ripped open the paper and the steam rose and warmed her face. The first chip would be so hot that she had to pass it around her teeth with her mouth open. Up and down teeth chatters to stop it from burning the hell out of her mouth. The steam was almost visible under her nose. She usually ate way past the point of being full. Her dad used to say 'Just stop, Susie,' when she said how full she was. But she always kept stuffing her face anyway. She couldn't stop even if she tried. Besides, all the times she didn't eat, for whatever reason, meant that it was okay to overstuff herself at other times. It all evened out in the end.

When she walked inside, her dad was sitting on the big brown comfortable velvet chair that was both their favourites. He wasn't drinking wine. Nor was he reading a book. He was just sitting there. Like he'd been waiting for her.

'Be ready at six. We're going for Chinese and a chat,' he said, looking away as the last words came out.

'Okay.' She suspected he could see her heart booming with anticipation, but she remained unattainable. It was time.

Susie asked which restaurant they were going to when they hopped in the car at exactly six o'clock. Regardless of everything else, she appreciated that he wasn't late to the car – even if it wasn't for her. He always said that it was arrogant to be late. There was a local Chinese restaurant that wasn't as good as some of the others they'd been to, and he said it would do for tonight. When they got there, there was no flouncing around pretending to be fancy people. It was just Susie and her faraway dad going in for some Chinese.

'So, Sydney?' her dad said, opening the menu. The contents seemed fascinating.

'Yeah,' Susie said back, pretending that her menu was fascinating too.

He closed the menu and looked at her. He said that he had gone out with Geoffrey's mum and that they had come to an agreement if, hypothetically, she was to move with them. He would pay board for her, which included food, and that it was a tenant relationship. They were not her family and did Susie understand the difference? Susie said she did and asked if Geoffrey's family were having money troubles. He said that their life would be a little easier if they rented out the third room. Susie hadn't expected things to be so formal. She was pretty much grown up now and she could take care of herself. Except for the board, she supposed. After they ordered, they resumed their conversation. Her dad said he would pay board for her as long as she stayed at school. The minute she left, or wagged, his support ended. Susie nodded vigorously and said that not only did she understand, but that she was very grateful. She was so excited and yet her chest shrank, and tears lined up in single file behind her eyes. She excused herself and went to the toilet for a cry. It was everything that she wanted, but she was sad, scared and felt like her insides had smashed into tiny pellets. She pulled herself together enough and returned to the table.

The meals had arrived. Susie thought she'd puke if she ate, but she forced her mouth to accept the food. She didn't really know what to say. She wanted to ask whether they'd ever be friends again. Whether a part of him didn't want her to go. He said that he would keep his distance, but that she could phone if she wanted to. He said that he would keep in touch with the school to monitor whether she was breaching their agreement. If things went sour in Geoffrey's household, she would have to find alternative accommodation. Coming back to Melbourne was not the preferred option. For either of them. It was time for her to make it on her own.

Susie's sweet and sour pork got stuck in her throat and she thought she was going to choke. She coughed it back up and her dad asked if she was all right. She said she was fine, thank you very much, and drank some water. It gave her a moment to take it all in. Maybe she wasn't leaving for Sydney, maybe he was throwing her out. Regardless, she was going to maintain face and not reveal her wounds.

'Well that's that, then,' Susie said. Her dad shrugged.

He explained that he had to convince Geoffrey's parents to take her with them and that she was not to let him down. Susie was still convinced that she and Geoffrey masterminded the whole thing and that her dad was saving face. He said that he would provide an extra twenty dollars a week to Geoffrey's parents to give to her and that was all she was going to get. This sounded like a lot to Susie, and she thanked him again. She said she wouldn't waste this opportunity to start fresh. To start her new life. He said that it was a shame it had come to this, but that she was going nowhere at the moment. That her life was stagnant, and she was too full of resentment to see it. He said that maybe she stood half a chance if she went to Sydney. Susie swallowed her shock at his analysis of her life and told herself that he was right – her life with him was destroying her slowly.

He didn't bother suggesting a dessert and she was not inclined to ask for one. They automatically sat at the table when they got home, and her dad brought out the cards. He laid out a timeline and said she must continue going to school until the day before she left. She thought that would be best, given that she didn't want to spend one more minute with him than she had to. They only played one hand. Her dad went to the lounge to read and Susie went to her room; less jubilant that she had expected.

INTAKE

The girls were at their most vulnerable on entry. Life had ballooned and they found themselves at The Institute. There are some that come and go. Revolving door. Leave better than they came; arrive back worse than they left. The new-new ones did it the hardest. Learning the system. Frightened. Deer in the headlights. The Institute is here to help, but it's hard to see.

Miss Kaye walked in on a Thursday. No different to any other day except that it was the last day of her week and she was going away for a few days. One day to go. There was quite the kerfuffle when she walked in. A young girl was yelling at staff, yelling at the other women, yelling at the world. Top of her lungs. Stream of consciousness. She was really yelling at herself. At her life. But she hadn't figured that out yet. Miss Kaye didn't intervene. The others were handling it. The girl had dirty blonde curly hair with a big matted knot on the back of her head. Grubby. Spotty. Big tear-filled dark brown eyes.

Miss Kaye walked through the office to drop her bag off and make a coffee. Every day started with coffee. She sat at the desk facing the service window. During intake the girls get a phone call, but Miss Kaye had to ring the numbers first. To make sure the people at the other end wanted to talk to their sisters, mothers, friends, aunties, daughters. Families are complicated. Miss Kaye knew this personally. She had the smallest family going around, but that didn't make it easy. Less people didn't mean less issues. She looked up the intake sheets to see what the new girl's name was. Samantha Broom. Unusual. Miss Kaye's name was so dull she revelled in those with more pizzazz. Broom. She found the sheet with the name and phone number. It was the girl's grandfather. She rang the number.

'Good morning, is that Mr Broom?' she asked.

'Speaking.' His voice creaked and crackled like old floorboards.

'I'm calling from The Institute, your granddaughter —'

'Oh dear,' he said with great sadness. Miss Kaye found the desolation in his voice contagious and her heart dropped an inch. 'I can't talk to her. Not this time,' he said. Utter disappointment. Despair. Miss Kaye had to stop herself from trying to convince him to muster up some support. She knew what it was like to be young and alone. Although it was many years ago for her, the girls in The Institute were a constant reminder of how hard it can be to be young. Alone.

'Are you sure?' Miss Kaye asked. Flatline. One little double check never hurt anyone.

'She just keeps letting me down,' he said, his voice even more creaky than before. He told Miss Kaye that he had taken the girl in when she was three. Her mother hadn't been much of a mother and there had been no one else. He had loved the girl, tried hard to be everything he could for her. Her father, her mother, her friend. 'She was always troubled, always . . . like her mother,' he said in conclusion. Nature beats nurture.

'I'll let her know, sir. If you change your mind, give us a call back,' Miss Kaye said with empathy. It's hard to be a robot on the outside all the time.

She hung up the phone. The girl had quietened down, the staff had returned to the office and, when Miss Kaye looked out in the common area, all looked quiet. She busied herself with the mountain of paperwork required to keep The Institute ticking over. After a while, Miss Kaye took herself out to the rooms to check on the new girl. Too quiet. She knocked on her door.

'Piss off,' said the new girl. There wasn't much gusto in her tone. Miss Kaye opened the door just a little and poked her head through. 'I said piss off,' the girl said with even less gusto. She was balled up in the corner under the built-in desk. Everything was built in at The Institute. Miss Kaye wanted to say that you can't hide from yourself. You're always hiding there with yourself and you never go away.

Miss Kaye told Miss Broom that she had spoken to her grandfather. The girl's eyes lit up and she moved ever so slightly from her hidey hole.

'How is he?' she asked before explaining that she hadn't seen him for a whole two weeks. She went out one night, hit the streets and found herself stuck there. 'I wanted to go home, but I didn't.' The girl explained that she slept rough during this time. That she was bipolar and hadn't been taking her meds. So she found other meds.

That life just passed by while she was stuck. Miss Kaye nodded along with her tale. 'Can I talk to him?' the girl asked. She had become a child. Big hope-filled eyes.

'He's not ready to talk to you at this stage,' Miss Kaye said. No point lying. Delusions never end well. The girl fell to her side and wailed. In between her loud racking sobs, she spoke about how she was trying, how it's hard to be on meds, how they take who you are away and leave a shell of who you were walking around like a zombie. 'It's no way to live,' she said, wiping the snot away with the sleeve of her jumper. The wailing hit its inevitable decrescendo. Nothing lasts forever.

'Well, you can always write to him. Tell him your feelings. Tell him you're sorry,' said Miss Kaye. The hope provider. There's always another option. Mostly. The girl stopped sobbing and looked up. Beagle eyes.

'Do you think he'll answer me?'

'I don't know, but it's worth a go,' Miss Kaye said, adding that she would get her some paper.

'Will you read it, Miss? Will you read it?'

Miss Kaye wished validation came in a never-ending ink stamp. Stamp, stamp, stamp across the lives that passed through. Stamp, stamp, stamp across herself.

'Sure.'

Miss Kaye went back to the office to rip three sheets of paper from a pad. Three. The acceptable amount to give according to The Institute. No wonder they write on the walls. She popped back to the girl's room and slid them under the door.

'Thanks, Miss.' Miss Kaye didn't respond.

As she walked back through the common area, all the girls looked at her. Watched her back and forthing. Wary. An alien in their turf. Miss Kaye pointed out that the area needed a clean.

'State of your room is the state of your mind,' she said. Her father had taught her that one. Invaluable. True.

'Your mind can't be a room,' said a timid middle-aged waif. Her face sagged in the middle like an old sofa.

'State. State. Victoria is a state,' said a pudgy young girl with sprinkles in her eyes. Miss Kaye laughed.

'What does that even mean, Miss Kaye?' Miss D asked. It was nice to see her inside. On a couch, not a pole. She smiled her Mrs Shrek smile. Her time in intake would be over soon. Time to move to the cottages.

'If the space around you is clean and organised, it helps your mind be clean and organised.' Miss Kaye had never imagined that the expression could be misunderstood. Not understood.

'You can't clean your mind,' Pudgy Girl said.

'I see it, I see it,' said Saggy Face. She bounded up off the couch. Catapult. Headed for the cleaning cupboard and wheeled the vacuum cleaner over. The girls followed suit. Up they went, busying themselves. Puzzles and newspapers were removed from the coffee table and put back down in different spots. Over and over. How to tidy up when there's nowhere to put things. Move them. Re-place them. Stack them. Unstack them. Put them in the corner of the table. Put them in the middle. Moving, shuffling, moving while the vacuum scooted around the floor.

'Chux,' Pudgy Girl said. A contagious epiphany. They all headed to the kitchenette, they all headed back – led by Pudgy Girl with a Chux held high. Trophy. The group lifted the puzzles and papers, Pudgy Girl wiped and wiped while they stood there watching with forensic eyes. When she stood to examine her work, the others leaned in and peered at the table. One nodded, then the others nodded, and the puzzles and papers were put back down. Exactly as things were before they tried to clean their minds. They sat back down, the vacuum was put away and they looked at each other.

'Is your state of mind better?' Saggy Face asked Pudgy Girl, who furrowed her brow in concentration. In she looked.

'You know, I think it is.' A proclamation. They all looked around at each other, looking for dissent. None. Smiles all around.

'Thanks, Miss Kaye,' Miss D said. The group representative.

'You're welcome,' Miss Kaye said as she headed back to the office. Peace doesn't cost much.

ADC

Two giggling girls passed by Miss Kaye's office window. Hmm. There's giggling and there's giggling. This was conspiratorial. Not two girls who had seen someone trip; or heard a joke. Two girls who were up to something. Miss Kaye went for a wander down the accommodations. Alert. Nothing. It went into her filing cabinet for later.

And there would be a later.

She returned to her never-ending paperwork pile. She didn't mind. Each piece led to action. No paper, no action. Needs were met through paperwork.

A bloodcurdling scream came from the left. Before she had stood up to find its origin, a tall blonde girl-woman with creamy latte eyes emerged at the office window. The two giggling girls looked in from outside – giggling harder than before. Eighteen going on seven. One had tears on her cheeks. Miss Kaye waggled her crooked forefinger, signalling her to come hither. Latte Eyes was standing there in shock, rubbing her hands together maniacally.

'What happened?' Miss Kaye asked indifferently. The emotive train was at the station, beckoning her with a cake-filled dining car. One must not hop on the train.

'SOME CUNT'S BEEN IN MY ROOM AND MOVED MY SOAP,' Latte Eyes said. Staccato.

'Hmm,' Miss Kaye said, shaking her head. Empathy. She looked over to the girls who were no longer giggling. One had Newton's third law on her face. The other still had amusement in her eyes.

What to do.

'Let's go and see what's happened,' Miss Kaye said. Distraction. Latte Eyes stormed back down to her room. Miss Kaye followed. When Latte Eyes was just out of hearing range, Miss Kaye told the two girls to stay. Right. Where. They. Are. Laughing Face went to move off; Newton's Third Law held her arm, planted her feet and nodded at Miss Kaye. Newton's Third Law knew Miss Kaye better than Laughing Face. It was always better to stick around. Regardless.

Miss Kaye walked into Latte Eyes' room and saw her standing ramrod straight, arm fully outstretched, pointing to the soap with outrage and hurt plastered across her face. Miss Kaye had seen her room many times before and had marvelled at its perfection. No 1940s nurse could compete with the hospital cornered sheets. Her few possessions were equally spaced on dust free shelves and the floor could be licked without fear. Miss Kaye had never joked about Latte Eyes's OCD. Most had.

It was a monument to how things should be. How things would be for Miss Kaye if she had the skillset. Sure it comes with consequences, but what doesn't. Miss Kaye took an extra step inside the compact space and looked at the soap on the lone tray in the shower. A bedroom and ensuite in one. Latte Eyes turned the soap over, revealing the remnants of a brand icon. No soap slime. Miss Kaye wondered whether she washed and dried her soap after use. It appeared so.

There was no point asking whether, perhaps, she had been forgetful when placing her soap back into the built-in tray.

This was clearly a case of soap interference.

'I'll kill the cunts,' Latte Eyes said, her body in attack mode, a lightning soul and two tightly clenched fists.

'That's not going to happen,' Miss Kaye said softly. 'What is going to happen, is you're going to be more careful about locking your door. Is anything missing?' she asked casually. Deflection.

It could have been worse. Genius.

Latte's eyes scanned the room. She hadn't thought of that. Each item was ticked off an internal list and Miss Kaye waited patiently for her to finish. Tick, tick, tick. Latte Eyes shook her head and sat on her bed.

'I want an apology,' she said, stiffening. Miss Kaye gave her best 'let's see what happens' face and sought assurances that revenge or comeuppance was on the backburner for now. Latte's eyes rolled but she didn't move. Miss Kaye waited a beat for just in case and then returned to the office. As she sat, she signalled Newton's Third Law and Laughing Face over to the window. She looked at them one after the other. The first person to speak loses.

'It was a joke, Miss, it was just meant to be funny,' Newton's Third Law said, trying not to whine. Miss Kaye knew she understood that it wasn't funny. That it was wrong. Sometimes saying nothing has its own impact. She turned her face to the other girl, who had clearly not seen the error of her ways. Out of the corner of her eye, Miss Kaye saw Latte Eyes lurking in the corridor. Inching her way towards her potential opponents.

'Jesus, Miss Kaye, it was just, like, a joke. You know, she has ADC and we just thought . . .' Laughing Face began to say as she sensed Latte Eyes' presence. 'Fuck, man, I'm really sorry,' Laughing Face said. Her face was no longer happy as she walked backwards until she hit a wall.

'I'm really sorry too,' Newton's Third Law said, her hands in front of her chest in defence of what might come. Whining was getting the better of her.

There were milliseconds before Latte Eyes lost her temper and Miss Kaye searched her mind at the speed of light for a distraction. Time. It's all there is. She stood and picked up every pen within reach and started placing them in colour and size order on the desk in front of her. Nimble hurried fingers banging each pen down as loudly as she could. Latte Eyes took two large menacing steps towards the girls then stopped dead. She looked down at Miss Kaye's desk; at the fan of ordered pens. Miss Kaye sat without notice, going about her business with ease. When she looked up, Latte's eyes blinked slowly. With the slightest of nods, she headed back to her room. Laughing Face peeled herself off the wall and wandered towards Miss Kaye. Newton's Third Law let out a sigh of relief and turned towards the exit to create some space between her and what nearly was.

'Hey, you think Miss Kaye has ADC too?' Laughing Face asked Newton's Third Law as they walked off.

PART THREE
LEFT UNSAID

CHAPTER 21

Sydney. From the moment she got off the overnight bus she felt liberated. She sat on a bench outside Central Station and watched the people going past. It felt different to Melbourne. More vibrant. She wondered if it was her or whether it was real. It had to be real. Her eyes hadn't failed. The tan suitcase was heavy, so she went inside the station to catch a train to Circular Quay. From there she had been told to catch a ferry. A ferry! Her bus arrival was too early for Geoffrey's parents to pick her up and besides, she was quite capable of taking care of herself thank you very much. Geoffrey said driving in Sydney was way worse than Melbourne and Susie asked where he got this conclusion from, given that they weren't quite sixteen yet and had never driven anything but remote-control cars. Susie only had a few weeks until the milestone. Geoffrey said you could get your Ls earlier up here and Susie nearly fainted. Imagine the law letting her drive. Although she felt mature, she couldn't ever imagine getting a driver's licence. Besides, she didn't have a car, so there was no point.

The trains were double-decker, which she didn't know. She sat on the small platform between the two levels and decided she would travel in the top part when she didn't have baggage. When she got to Circular Quay she had to sit for a while. It was just too beautiful looking out across the harbour. There was even a Luna Park over the water and under the bridge. It looked way better than Melbourne's, even from this far away. It had to be at least three times as big, which meant three times the rides. Susie put it on her mental to-do list.

She didn't want to be late to Geoffrey's. To make them worry. To have them notice her at all. It was all too good to be true and she didn't want to muck it all up before it even began. On the ferry she went. She was worried about missing something, so she darted her head left and right to take it all in.

The first thing she noticed was all the apartments. Row after row of skinny apartments along the hills and inlets. On her left there was an old stone building, right in the middle of the water with a lonely palm tree on it. It would have made a wonderful jail. There was a lighthouse section at the back and Susie decided that being a lighthouse keeper was a most desirable job. She could wave all the ferries and boats around like the Fat Controller with his trains. But she wouldn't be so grumpy.

There was a lady having a nap near her and she contemplated waking her up and showing her all the things she was taking for granted. There was a mini white lighthouse with fanned wooden slats around its base and random differently coloured poles sticking out all over the water. Susie had no idea how they drove them into the deep-water ground. There were inlets full of boats and even more apartments. In one inlet, there was a massive rock at the bottom of the hill that looked like a giant toucan sunning his face.

She could never tire of this ferry ride. It ploughed through the water and she didn't even feel like she was on a boat until, all of a sudden, the ferry went from side to side. One second she was looking at water then all of a sudden she was looking at sky. Over and over again. She wasn't sure if she was going to vomit or not.

A lady in a floral dress with a cross around her neck came over and told her not to close her eyes. That she would feel better if she watched the horizon. Susie felt doubtful, but she didn't really have any other ideas – other than feeling like she was going to die. Besides, ladies in floral dresses were usually nice and not liars. She diligently looked at the horizon while the lady said they were going through the heads and that the water would be calm soon. Susie wondered what the heads were, and what heads had to do with sickening seas; other than her own head feeling quite dizzy. The floral lady was right on all accounts and Susie thanked her for her kindness. The lady smiled and went back to her seat.

Susie looked around, feeling embarrassed. There was a blond surfie boy whose sunglasses were tied to his face with string, but he hadn't noticed Susie having her turn. His head was firmly focused on a bible. As they neared Manly even more apartment blocks sprouted from the hills. Tall ones, skinny ones, square ones, oblong ones, mini ones and even a fanned out semi-circle one.

Before she knew it, the ferry pulled in and Susie watched the man throwing ropes and winding them around twin poles. Then he pushed a button and the big metal gangplank squeaked its way down to the platform. There was only one way in or out, so Susie didn't worry about being able to find Geoffrey. She walked until a big under cover square revealed itself and there he was. She gave him a big hug and then held her arms out wide, threw her head back and told the world she had finally arrived.

'Look up, Geoffrey,' Susie said, pointing to the diagonal wooden slats on the ceiling of the shed. 'They're just like the ones in the Yarraville house.' He certainly did remember them. Before they went to Moomba one year, Susie's dad had asked them to help with the renovation – just for a few minutes. Susie and Geoffrey had held up the ceiling slats with the bristle end of brooms while her dad went across the room on his ladder nailing them in. It had taken way longer than a few minutes and their arms were so sore at the end they could barely hold on to the ride rails when they finally got to Moomba.

While Geoffrey was remembering his sore back from holding up the roof slats, Susie was remembering the time she helped her dad move the fridge across that house's kitchen floor. Her dad had been on one side with Susie on the other as they inched the fridge across the floor. THUNK went a jar on her dad's head. It had toppled from the top of the fridge. CLUNK went the jar as it hit the floor. Vrrr, vrrr it went as it rolled away.

'Fuuuuuuurk,' her dad had said as he hopped around holding his head between his forearms. Susie had run over to pick up the jar. One injury was enough. Tripping on it as well would be a double hit on her father's mood. Susie's heart fell into her feet as she looked at the black jar. It was full to the brim of ten cent piece sized dead black frogs. Tiny speckles of light highlighted the spaces between their entangled arms and legs. Susie's legs had given way as she remembered going tadpoling a year or so prior. She had poked holes in the jar lid and lovingly placed greenery around the tadpoles playing about in the water at the bottom of the jar. Only then did she realise she had put the jar on top of the fridge and forgotten about her new pets immediately. How much pain she had caused those innocent tadpoles as they grew and grew into frogs, ran out of food and water and turned to cannibalism to survive. Frog after frog must have eaten each other to survive until there was simply no more room to even move their mouths.

'What was it?' her dad had asked, looking to blame something for his sore head.

'Just an old jam jar,' Susie had said, throwing the jar of dead frogs into the bin. She brought his attention back to the job at hand. They both took their sides of the fridge to finish shuffling it across the way. Tears had streamed down her face as she silently punished herself over and over and over again. She had wanted to show him the jar and talk and cry about the dead frogs with him. But his head was as sore as hers already.

It had taken a long time to come to terms with the notion that she was a frog mass murderer, and the guilt was still strong as she stood there with Geoffrey. They both shrugged away their memories. Geoffrey told Susie that Sydney was very hilly and that they had to turn left and walk for ages uphill until they got to Fairlight. She idly wondered how many steps that would take, but she dismissed counting them. She was trying to put a halt to her counting addiction. It had just turned up one day. She had been sitting near a brick wall and just started counting. Then she had to do it again to check her calculations. And so it had begun. Bricks, lino squares, pavers, parked cars, pens, steps, cutlery, everything.

Geoffrey added that the streets were separated by stairs and two massive sets awaited them. Oh, and there was a nudist beach just down from their place. Susie told him that was gross and when he said that the nudists played volleyball there, she said that was doubly gross and they laughed. Although she didn't want any help with her suitcase, she accepted taking turns after about seventeen steps. It was going to be a hard walk and they had to stop all the time for rests. Every time they stopped, Susie looked out over the water in amazement. They walked along a beach that had a massive net square in the middle (Susie concluded this was to keep the fish and the humans separate), around a round building and up the first big steep stairs. They must have been built back when people had smaller feet because they were small and hard to balance on with a suitcase. The view from the top spread to the heads.

'We have to stop and smell the roses, Geoffrey, the blue rose of the harbour!' Her arms were out, her head back and the wind whooshed over her face. Geoffrey followed suit. On the way up the hill, Geoffrey reiterated that all of Sydney was hilly (it obviously bothered him more than it should) and that they only had today before they had to start school. Only one day, and it was disappearing before her eyes. Susie suggested that after she dropped her stuff off, they go for a big walk around Manly – to get to know their turf. The lie of the land. Have a swim. Geoffrey nodded in agreement. He said that they had to be home by six.

'Six?' Susie asked. 'That's a bit early.' Geoffrey explained that they have dinner at six and that evenings were for study. Susie rolled her eyes on the inside. There was a whole city to explore and how could they do homework when they didn't even know what homework there was? Geoffrey's mum was very diligent and had rung their schools to find out their English texts. She had also sourced the books from the library, under her name, so it was important to look after them. Susie promised Geoffrey she'd do what was expected of her. He looked doubtful, even when she pinky promised. On their last rest, Susie told Geoffrey all about the ferry ride.

'So far, I've learned that Sydney has double-decker trains, loads of apartments and heaps of Christians,' she said in conclusion as she stood for the last leg of their walk.

When she walked into the apartment, she was shocked by the view. She stopped still and looked out over the harbour, the boats, the cliffs. She couldn't imagine a better view in the whole world. She was shown her small room at the front of the apartment, which was like the back because she thought the view should be the front. It was cosy, and she was thrilled. She lay on her bed for a minute and then unpacked her suitcase. As she folded her clothes, she reminded herself of all the things she was going to do to stay invisible, so her new home wasn't taken from her. She would speak only when spoken to. She would be there when expected. She would go to school every day and never be late and she would hide in her room as much as possible.

After she unpacked, she poked her head out into the common area. The floorboards were lightly stained and stretched along to the large windows. There were two couches facing each other near the window and a small dining table along the left side of the room, down near Geoffrey's parents' bedroom. Susie gave the room a nine point five because of the view and the rich floorboards. Geoffrey's room was next to hers and she whispered his name as loudly as a whisper could be.

'My parents aren't home, they're at work,' Geoffrey said. Susie still felt she had to whisper.

'Shall we go for a walk to Manly?' Susie said softly. 'We can look at the beach,' she added as an extra incentive. Geoffrey was already sold and off they went. The winding paths down to Manly were full of bushes and glimpses of big apartment blocks. Susie noted that if the water and the trees were removed, it would all look drab. Aged. The older buildings were oblongs and made of grey or brown brick. Every now and then, though, there were rich creamy brown curved art deco apartment blocks that Susie could see herself in one day. Only two years of school and she would be thrust out there into the world to fend for herself. With a job and an apartment. Other than being an architect, she had never been driven in a direction. There had been a moment where she wanted to be a lawyer, but buildings were her passion. Even then, she couldn't see herself actually being an architect. It was a hobby, an interest, a part of her. Not her job. Maybe she could be a rope man on the ferry. Not the one who caught the rope on the ground, the one who took the trips and threw the rope overboard.

Before too long they were back where they started but without her suitcase. The Quay sprawled out over the water and Susie and Geoffrey headed left onto The Corso. It was a wide carless road with palm trees up the middle and a bunch of fat trees with multiple branches reaching up to the sky like hands. There were shops either side and there were people going about their business like they had on the streets of Melbourne when she sold papers. She could see herself with a store. Be her own boss and serve the people. It could sell lollies, or ice-creams. Definitely food, because people ate wherever they went. One day in the library, their friend Lotte had said that when she moved to Australia, the biggest difference in her new country was that people ate food while they walked down the street. She had said it like it was an unusual thing to do. Susie looked around and saw a little girl with a potato cake, and her mum eating chips as they walked along. Susie thought it was more unusual not to see people eating as they walked down the street. Yes, a food store would be very successful.

Susie and Geoffrey hardly spoke during their walk. That was often the case when they were somewhere they hadn't been before. The first time they went to the Botanical Gardens in Melbourne, Susie remembered them not talking for nearly the whole day. Except when Susie had an insightful observation to make. She often spoke like David Attenborough when they went somewhere new.

As they neared the end of The Corso, there was a massive beach with actual waves. Not like in Williamstown where the bay barely lapped. Even when she had eaten fish and chips with her dad on the back beach, the waves were pitiful compared to this. They crossed the road and headed onto the sand that was speckled with people lying on their towels reading, napping, soaking it up. Susie immediately took her shoes off and swivelled her feet through the sand, burying them. She urged Geoffrey to do the same. He looked at the sand like it was a spider and said no thank you. Susie had seen Geoffrey's feet with his knobbly bent in all direction toes and wondered if that was why he was keeping his shoes on. She had never said anything about his toes before in case she took away his ability to go barefoot. That would be a horrible thing to take from someone.

Susie looked along to the left and along to the right, and chose left. She threw her shoes at Geoffrey and ran. She ran as fast as she could through the soft sand, knowing it wouldn't look very glamorous. It was all about speed, not image. Her arms and legs flailed along at different rhythms, but she was free as a bird. She felt like she was flying. She ran and ran until she fell face first into the sand, laughing as she lay there rolling around in it. Geoffrey took a while to catch up to her, and she rolled and rolled until he reached her.

'We're free, Geoffrey. We're free!' she said at the top of her voice. Geoffrey looked around in the hope that no one was watching. They were. One man walking past smiled at Susie and then winked at Geoffrey, whose face reddened.

'We should all be a bit more like that, mate,' the man said as he passed. Geoffrey didn't think so at all. Susie hadn't heard a thing. She stood up and shook the sand off her.

'And the dog shakes the sand from his fur,' she said in her best and loudest David Attenborough voice as she shook from side to side, sand flicking everywhere. Even Geoffrey couldn't contain a little laugh, but he was careful it wasn't so big that she would find it encouraging. He didn't need an even bigger Susie performance. He needed her support. Unlike her, he was far from embracing change at all. He craved stability, sameness, routine. His mother was always talking about routine, to the point where he had become one. And then she had the audacity to rip his life out from under him. Here was Susie, acting like life was wonderful. She didn't understand.

Susie plonked herself down on the sand and wiggled her bum until she had created a bum crater. She patted the sand next to her and waited. She had learned that she had to be patient with Geoffrey. That if she waited and didn't speak, he would comply with whatever it was she wanted to do; within reason. She watched the waves and listened to their boom and crash sound. It was in her new top ten of sounds. Geoffrey planted himself next to her but wasn't half as comfortable. He looked at her sand covered face and smiled. She beamed back.

'Listen, Geoffrey. Listen,' she said in a whisper. They sat there listening together. His body relaxed a little. Boom; crash; boom; crash. Susie said they should go on a sound mission. 'We have never paid any attention to *sound*, Geoffrey.' She recalled some of their adventures and pointed out that not once – not even *once* – had they ever paid any attention to the sounds around them. She began listing all the things they could seek out. They could find a forest and listen to the trees swaying, they could stand on the edge of the freeway and listen to the different vehicles as they rumbled past, shaking their bodies with their noise as they stood close. They could stand outside a kindergarten and listen to little kids laughing and crying. 'We haven't experienced life to its fullest, Geoffrey!'

By the time she had concluded her monologue, Geoffrey was a believer. Perhaps they should go sound exploring. But then life came back and slapped his face. He said she had to stop being so silly. So fanciful. That life wasn't some magic land to frolic around in. 'But it is, Geoffrey, it is,' she said quietly but loudly at the same time. Geoffrey let his shoulders fall. He didn't know whether she was right or wrong, but he knew he didn't have the same enthusiasm for it all. But he also knew he was grateful to have her as a friend. Even if he didn't have all this spirit himself, and he was glad he didn't because it must be exhausting, he sure did love being around it. Watching it. He recalled her rolling in the sand shouting, 'We're free,' and instead of being embarrassed, he laughed. It was a proper case of the giggles. Susie had no idea what he was laughing at, but she joined in wholeheartedly. They sat there laughing at each other laughing without a care in the world.

CHAPTER 22

Susie and Geoffrey caught the same bus to their next-door schools. Susie said she didn't know whether to vomit or cry she was so nervous. Geoffrey was nearly as bad, but he reminded her that they had each other and it was only six and a half hours and that they would make it.

Susie got off the bus first and stood there having a good look at the school. It was on a hill, and there were loads of trees. Unlike her Melbourne school, it only had two levels. She watched the kids, took a few deep breaths and headed in to present herself at the office. By the time she had her orientation chat and was taken to her classroom, all the kids were already seated. The reception lady took her in and introduced her to the class. There was a brief moment of curiosity as the group looked up, but it died quickly. The sporty kids had no interest, nor did the girlie girls. They could tell she wasn't the same. The only person that looked at her for more than a glance was a girl with silky long dark hair, oh wait it was a boy, at the back. Susie headed in that direction and sat two seats away so she didn't show too much interest. Her face burned for a few minutes as the rejection peaked, and then she glanced around the room. The pretty boy had the most beautiful face she had ever seen. His smile revealed perfectly sized brilliant white teeth, he had enough cheekbones and not too much jaw. His eyes were dark, dark brown. And gentle.

Susie tried to listen to whatever was being said in the classes – the blonde bespectacled English teacher had been passionate about Mrs Macbeth, even though she seemed like a real meanie. Lunchtime rolled around eventually, and Susie wandered around aimlessly, looking mostly at the ground, until she saw a big student holding the pretty boy up against a tree with the back of his forearm. Susie raged. She walked over and pushed him. He was like an immovable tree trunk. A boy man. Her push only resulted in her nearly falling over as she bounced off him.

'Leave him alone,' Susie said with years of anger. The boy man dropped his forearm and smiled at Susie without smiling. It was a filing cabinet smile – the boy man was saving her for later as the pretty boy caught his breath.

'Thank you,' he said with years of relief. Susie knew what it was like to be a misfit too. He turned his head a little to the side and examined her hair. He reached over and pulled bits and folded bits and declared that she should shave the sides of her head.

'There aren't many people with a natural mohawk,' he said, smiling his beautiful smile.

'I like your face,' Susie said before she could stop herself. 'What's your name?'

'Louis.'

'As in Huey and Dewey?' He nodded and asked her name.

'Susie.'

'Floozy Susie,' he said, smiling that smile again. Susie returned serve and in an instant they were friends, comrades, companions, allies.

When they walked back to class, they were conjoined at the arms. They sat with each other, passing knowing glances as the day progressed. Two differents make a same; two outcasts makes no outcasts.

In the space between classes he asked her if she wanted to come to his house after school. He would sort out that mess on her head in no time as he flicked and placed her short locks like a florist. She reached over and twirled part of his long luscious hair into a ringlet and told him that he would look better with a fringe. As he shook his head, she said that it wasn't a one-way street. He shrugged, she shrugged, and a deal was made.

At the bus stop after school, Susie told Geoffrey that she would be home by six and introduced her new friend. Geoffrey wasn't as impressed as Susie. Scepticism scrunched his forehead. Susie didn't have time to assuage his fears, nor the desire. The rule was six and six it would be. Other than that, it wasn't his business. It didn't cross her mind that Geoffrey needed to debrief with her. His day had not resulted in a friend. It was simply hours of aloneness with the throngs being a salient reminder that he was nothing. Susie waved as she headed up the road with Louis, who was filling her in on who was who and what was what amongst the school rabble.

'Pooftas!' someone from a passing car called out. Susie looked at Louis' face to gauge his feelings. He shrugged. It must have been common.

'Looks like we're pooftas,' Susie said, making up a tale of two young boys who went to school and fell in love the moment they met. By twenty, one was a famous painter (Louis had pastel and charcoal embedded in his nails and carried a small black portfolio) and the other became his manager. When they turned twenty-five they adopted a baby and lived happily ever after. Louis loved Susie's make-believe land and added details, like the soft furnishings that adorned their apartment overlooking a tree filled park. It was so high that they could look out the window and the treetops looked like green clouds. By the time their imaginary life was mapped out, they had arrived at Louis' place. It was a square orange apartment block with cast iron balcony railings. She followed him up the stairs.

The apartment was tiny. Louis' bedroom was on the right immediately after the front door and Louis explained that his mum and sister shared the bedroom to the left. A small bathroom abutted Louis' room and there was a boxy living area with a small balcony off it. The right side of the lounge had a small galley kitchen containing a tubby teenage girl in a blue uniform. Louis and Susie's uniform was mission brown.

'That's my sister Donna,' Louis said, waving his hand dismissively in her general direction. Susie wondered how two children in the same family were called Louis and Donna. Louis was exotic, and Donna should have a brother called Wayne.

Susie nodded at his sister and was led into Louis' bedroom. It was big enough for a single bed and a miniature desk that was no wider than her shoulders. There was a set of drawers and a small glass oblong fish tank on top of it, but it didn't contain fish. It was full of twigs fashioned into a tree and there were small balls of fluff in the twig nooks and crannies.

'They're my silkworms,' Louis said as they both peered inside. Susie told him that was very glamorous. She'd never met anyone who had silkworms before. Louis seemed pleased with himself. He grabbed a pair of scissors and suggested they cut hair on the balcony. The last thing his mum would want to see when she came home was hair everywhere. Off they went.

There were two chairs on the balcony and they sat to plan their haircuts. Susie pulled her hands through his soft, straight black hair, pulling enough over his face to make a thick fringe. He said it was most important that it wasn't too short. That it must partially cover his eyebrows, but not fully. Susie said he had been specific enough for her to begin. She stood over him with butterflies in her stomach. It needed to be straight, otherwise she would have to keep going and going until his fringe was up at his hairline. That would be most unacceptable.

'And so the female analyses the male,' Susie began in her David Attenborough voice. Louis laughed and told her off. It was important not to be funny while cutting hair. One laugh, one slip and all of a sudden, he wouldn't be able to leave the house for three weeks while it grew out. That sounded logical, so she timidly cut piece after piece in silence.

Pleased with her work, she stood back and ruffled her fingers through the new fringe, looking for wayward strands that had evaded the scissors. There were a few and she carefully nipped at them. He was even more beautiful than he had been before the fringe, and she said so. He ran inside to the bathroom, Susie hot on his heels. He looked in the mirror, to the left, to the right, face down and face up.

'Perfect!' he said, giving her a big enveloping cuddle. 'My turn,' he said as she followed him back to the bathroom. He looked at her closely then reached into the bottom cupboard under the basin. He pulled out a bottle of mercurochrome. Susie had seen enough grazes and cuts to know what it was.

As he held it aloft, it dawned on her that he planned to put the orange solution through her hair.

'I don't think so,' she said defiantly.

'I do,' he said, ushering her back towards the balcony. 'We'll start with cutting your sides,' he said as he plonked her onto the chair by her shoulder tops. He used a comb to make lines on the side of her head and clipped the top of her hair together. The sides were hacked off and then he went for the clippers. Susie didn't know what clippers were. It turned out they were like her dad's electric shaver that he hardly used because it just didn't do the job. She used to love watching her dad shave in the bathroom. He would always put a dollop of shaving cream on her nose before he lathered up. Susie listened to the buzz of the clippers as Louis worked away. He was taking it very seriously, so she didn't want to start chattering and interrupt his flow. She might end up with only one ear.

After ages, he stood back and looked at the left side, looked at the right side and decided that the job was done. He followed her to the bathroom and they stood there together examining his handiwork. Susie quite liked it. Her hair had always stuck up in random spots, which worked very well with her barely there sides.

'See!' Louis said, throwing his arms around. 'A natural mohawk. You're blessed.' He pulled out the bits in between the bits that already stuck up.

'I look like a boy,' she said. Analytical, not critical.

'I look like a girl,' he said similarly. They giggled. 'But I haven't finished yet,' he said, pushing her gently back out to the balcony. Susie decided that he had done a great job so far and there was no point protesting his vision. He swathed mercurochrome through her remaining hair, carefully pushing up the rivulets of orange that kept trying to run down her head. In the end he had to contain the liquid with a towel dam. He said it was important not to let any on her bald bits because it stained like a bastard. Susie knew this. She had orange knees for weeks at a time as a kid. He stood there holding the towel dam until it was dry enough for her to go and have a shower. He handed her a clean towel and she hopped straight into the shower, washing her hair vigorously.

Once she was under the water, he came into the bathroom and sat on the toilet. They yacked away about their families, relationships, likes and dislikes. Now that they were friends, they needed to get to know each other. They spoke quickly, with urgency, there was so much to know. After a while she kicked him out, but he only left after she promised not to look in the mirror without him. Dry and dressed, she called him in. The door opened instantly. He said he was listening for sounds that may indicate she was going to cheat and have a sneak peek. Susie wondered what cheating sounded like and insisted that she never cheated. Louis said everyone cheats. He grasped her by the shoulders and together they turned to the mirror. Susie had never seen such a beautiful orange.

Blood orange. Her hair stuck up all over the place with slightly different shades of reddy-orange all over her head.

'Thank you, Louis,' she said. She meant it. She'd never looked so good. So . . . *her*.

'You're welcome,' he said with that smile. They went out on the balcony and looked out over the other apartment blocks flowing down the hill towards Manly until Susie said she had to be home by six. She asked for directions before she left, because she had no real idea of where she was in relation to where she needed to be. She looked at the sun and placed a compass on the roads she could see.

'I'm so glad you moved from Melbourne,' Louis said sheepishly as she was leaving.

'Thanks for being my friend,' Susie said as she gave him a hug.

As she walked home, she smiled at everyone and everything. This was her place now, and it seemed to like her as much as she did it.

CHAPTER 23

*L*ouis and Susie spent most afternoons together, often heading down to Manly to walk along the beach or The Corso. Louis loved Boy George, and Susie would follow him into the biggest newsagency she had ever seen and head to the pop magazines to pore over pictures with him. The newsagency was called Humphries, and Susie decided that if she ever had a child or a dog, she would call it Humphrey. Susie much preferred Boy George's friend Marilyn because she liked his long blond dreadlocks and he was understated. The new romantic era was fading, and the gender benders were emerging. Louis looked like he would fit right in the magazines alongside the makeup wearing effeminate singers and bands like Pete Burns, Annie Lennox and Grace Jones – Susie wondered what Grace Jones actually did as her pictures flicked past her eyes. Susie was slender and gender neutral herself, but it was more her genetic makeup than an intent.

The derogatory comments people shouted out of cars at the pair had increased. Sometimes they were called pooftas, sometimes dykes. It wasn't the words themselves they found offensive, it was the way they were said. Even the air felt homophobic. Talk of AIDS was ramping up and fuelling the hatred. Susie and Louis felt right at home on the odd occasion they wandered up and down Oxford Street on a Saturday, and one day they had the idea to go at night. To be with colourful people and to dance their shoes and bums off. Susie said she didn't know how to dance; Louis said all she had to do was move around and be herself. That she could do. They talked of their cover stories and logistics all the way to Manly.

When they got to the newsagency, their feet took them to the music section and they pored over the new releases. Out of the corner of her eye, Susie saw Louis run his fingers all the way around a picture and before she knew it, he had placed the picture itself right into the magazine she was holding. Her face burned, and she put the magazine down like it was an infectious disease. She walked off to the puzzle section, full of memories of the sunglasses incident. She had no idea how he was doing it, but she watched him follow the border of Boy George pictures with his finger, magically pull the picture out and put it into the same magazine Susie had been holding before. The ravaged magazines were then put back on the shelf. Susie was mesmerised as she pretended to show real interest in crosswords. After a while, Louis picked up the magazine that had all the pictures in it and headed to the register. The lady behind the counter was wearing a navy pinny and it reminded Susie of her old boss's overalls. It was the only colour that didn't show the ink, she supposed. A newsagent's colour.

Louis passed the magazine over and Susie watched the lady locate the price in the top corner before keying the amount into the register. Susie closed in. As the lady passed the magazine back to Louis, the magically removed pictures fell out and fluttered to the floor. Louis mumbled something about stupid advertisements as Susie froze in place. He picked them up and shoved them back in the magazine like that was where they belonged and then simply walked out the door. Susie was amazed by his composure as she jogged up to him and joined him by his side.

'Hoooow?' Susie asked as they sat on a bench seat. Louis looked at the seven Boy George pictures he was going to put in his collection and revealed a razor blade in his hand. There was also a Marilyn picture, which he gave to Susie. His present to her. She thanked him and put it in her canvas shoulder bag. Louis placed his pictures and blade into the algebra section of his maths book as the conversation returned to their Saturday night out.

As was the case most evenings these days, Susie headed back to Louis' for dinner. Geoffrey's and Louis' mums had conversed over the phone to rubber stamp her presence in the beginning, but they didn't seem to worry about it anymore.

Susie would just ring from the phone box and say she was going to Louis'. Louis and Susie were cognisant that Louis' mum was a single mum and doing it tough so they both ate small portions and pretended they were full. Even though the unit was tiny, Susie loved sitting around the lounge room with their dinner plates on their laps. The old velour couches sunk so low that one edge of the plate sat on the tops of her knees and the other smacked into her boobs (such as they were). Louis' little sister, Donna, wasn't as annoying as when they had first met. She was quite a nice girl, despite being a bit beige. Susie didn't like that she had no sense of adventure, or any dreams. Although Susie couldn't pinpoint her own dreams, she was certainly full of them. And Louis' mum was just terrific. She had a job in a bank, but she wasn't weighed down by life like most parents. She was young and not too serious. Once she told Susie that she was her age when she had Louis and that blew Susie's mind. She didn't think she was capable of driving, or full-time work, and most certainly not having a baby. Although she didn't fit the profile of the perfect mothers Susie had imagined during Merry Christmas' mental fluctuations, she was perhaps even better. She was patient and kind and her eyes sparkled with enjoyment at her kids; even when they'd been stupid. Her name was Sondra, which Susie thought was exotic, but she started calling her 'Nearly My Mum' after the sixth dinner at the unit.

When she first met Sondra, she'd been frightened. She wanted Louis' mum to like her so desperately that she lost self-control. Susie began over performing and flouncing around like she was on stage spilling verbal diarrhoea; but Sondra had just laughed, ruffled her hair and told her to sit her backside down for apricot chicken. Susie did. She'd never had apricot chicken and she wasn't terribly excited about it. It sounded gross, but she didn't show it on her face. In fact, she lied and said apricot chicken was her favourite except for sweet and sour pork. Sondra had been pleased with this comment, and Susie was pleased with herself for thinking of another dish with fruit in it.

The apricot chicken had been amazing, and Sondra even drove her home. Susie would have preferred to walk, but it wasn't time for an opinion. It was time to be grateful that Louis' mum liked her. And so, within a few dinners, Susie had become a part of the household. Luckily there weren't any more dinners with fruit in it. It was mainly plain stuff, like sausages and mash, which Susie liked. When the sixth dinner came, Susie found herself eating fish and chips on the floor of the little unit. She couldn't have been happier. They spoke of their weeks and Susie's impersonations were lauded. She did the kids at school, and even though Sondra hadn't met them, Louis did terrific introductions of their characters before Susie did their actions and voices. Even Donna laughed along with them. The impersonation highlight was Bob Hawke. Susie could hold the guttural 'eeeeer' for ages. In the middle of eating half a piece of flake (no thanks, Louis and I will share one, it's plenty) she called Sondra Nearly My Mum for the first time. Everyone seemed delighted and clapped as Susie became part of the family.

Being able to tell Geoffrey's and Louis' parents that she was at the other house freed her and Louis up. After a while, they just said they were at the other one's house so they could wander. Louis had continually given Susie different haircuts, and he even stole some gel for her. Susie accompanied Louis on his picture gathering expeditions but did not participate in razoring magazines herself. What she did participate in was clotheslining. They lived in a wealthy area and they hopped over fences and walked through backyards as dusk became night so they could peruse the clotheslines in the backyards. There were rules to justify their clothes gathering, like only one item to be removed off each clothesline at one time. That way the residents wouldn't miss anything. There was one house where Louis nearly wet his pants at the range and style of clothing of the obviously trendy man who lived inside. Susie whispered demonically when Louis removed four whole items off his line. Louis whispered it was designer stuff and the man had plenty of money to replace them. Susie said in her loudest softest whisper that it broke their rules and she would go and knock on the man's door this instant if he didn't put them back. Louis rolled his eyes and said she needed to be more flexible as a person. Susie did a cartwheel and said she was flexible enough before pegging two items back on the line. Louis won because he got two items (a pair of white pants covered in zips and buckles and a red top with diagonal soldier buttons down the chest). Susie won because he hadn't taken four things and they snuck over the next fence.

The extra clothes were justified to Geoffrey by saying that op-shopping was their latest craze – 'You should come, Geoffrey, we can get you something other than button up chequered shirts,' Susie said playfully. Geoffrey was finding her less amusing these days.

Final arrangements were made as they sat on their regular bench on The Corso. The hardest job was finding fake ID. They listed the older sisters and brothers of people they knew, with the idea of borrowing licences. Louis was always talking about a girl called Sissy, who was living in a share house and going to art school – just like Louis was going to do – so Susie suggested Sissy for her ID. Louis thought that was tremendous. He said she was great at thinking outside the box and that Sissy would know a boy for Louis' ID.

Cover story: the movies in George Street. If asked, *Poltergeist*.

Actual destination: The Exchange Hotel, Oxford Street, Paddington.

Time: Arrive at 7:30 pm, last ferry home at 11:45 from Circular Quay.

Safety: Walking home together – perhaps a sleepover at Louis'.

What could go wrong?

Once plans were in place, Susie tried to cajole Geoffrey into coming. It could be the best night of their lives. Geoffrey explained numerous times that he had no interest whatsoever in going out, but that if she actually wanted to go to a movie, he would be very interested. But not if it was *Poltergeist*. He didn't know her new friends. Susie said she didn't know them either, except for Louis, and that the pair they were going with were from Geoffrey's school. Surely he must know them better than she did. Geoffrey was a little bit jealous, but Susie didn't notice. At the very least he wished she would talk about them less. He missed the way it was.

Susie got Sissy's ID the day before their outing. She had memorised the name, the middle name, the star sign, the address and she had practised the signature. Born in '65, currently nineteen. It was now ingrained, like her timestables, and she practised looking casual in the mirror as she answered questions about her imaginary life. As she stared into her reflection, she almost saw her face change. She became Sissy Pervis, who finished second in Year 12, had plenty of friends and was currently studying medicine at Sydney Uni. It sounded more serious than fine arts. She had a part-time job in a bar. A fancy bar. And she wore glamourous dresses, had long flowing locks and didn't look like a drag queen in a dress. Susie looked ridiculous in a dress. Sissy had small elegant fingers with painted nails. When Susie was being

Sissy but not Sissy in the mirror, her hands were smaller and had purple polish.

'What are you doing in there?' Geoffrey called through the bathroom door. Sissy but not Sissy returned to being Susie and she hopped out of the bathroom. Susie had told Geoffrey every detail of the plan and he made her promise not to miss the ferry. Although Geoffrey's mum wondered why he wasn't going to the movies too, she wasn't displeased because she considered Louis a bad influence.

•

The big day arrived, and Susie was exhausted by the time she needed to leave. All the anticipation and overexcitement had drained her. When she got down to the wharf, she smiled and waved at Louis. He was with Aaron, who had the tightest imaginable curls atop his head, and Jess, a tomboy with swaggering hips, a constant smirk and a high dose of indifference. Susie wanted them to like her. Although she had met them casually, Louis had been rabbiting on about how amazing they were for ages. She pepped up as she approached the group.

When they hopped on the ferry, Susie kept reminding herself not to get too carried away. There's no way they would like her then. She just let the conversation happen, with music and image being the main topics. Susie was a little bored. There was an older lady sitting nearby with a cane and knowing eyes. When their eyes met, Susie beamed at her. The old lady winked. It was the slowest wink she had ever seen. Susie winked back as slowly as she could. It ended up being more of a blink and the old lady laughed like crepe paper. Susie giggled. Louis shot her a 'what are you doing' look and Susie stuck her tongue out at him.

There was a brief debate about who would buy the cask wine. Susie said that she had practised being Sissy but not Sissy and that she was up for the challenge. There was a moment's silence before Louis said that she was definitely the person for the job. Susie revelled in his confidence in her and ignored the doubt on Jess' face. When they reached the Quay, they walked and skipped their way up the city to Oxford Street. Susie's Sissy but not Sissy performance when she purchased the wine went smoothly and they sat around the corner from The Exchange on a set of three concrete steps that went nowhere. They drank as quickly and as much as they could without being sick. At one point Aaron said they'd feel more drunk if they went for a little run. Jess said that was crap and drinking out of a straw definitely made you more drunk. Susie didn't much care. Her head was woozy and she wanted to stay just the way she felt. It was pleasant, and the group became more interesting the more she drank. They practised getting past the bouncer and then walked over as a group brimming with confidence and belonging.

Mission accomplished. After walking past the bouncer's line of vision, they all hugged each other and revelled in their success. They headed to the dance floor, and Susie moved and swayed along to the music that was so loud she could feel the beat in her bones. She sidled up to a tall woman with a fairy floss wig and complimented her on her accessorising. The woman kissed her on the cheek and Susie kept moving. She wiggled and smiled at a couple of serious leather clad men, shook her shoulders at a human doll and danced with a trio of shaved headed ladies that looked less angry when she left than when she had arrived. Susie moved around the whole floor, song after song.

At some point her group left to retrieve their cask from a bin near the going nowhere stairs. Susie let the wine and the wind rush over her and smiled at the sky with her arms up. Aaron sang the Rocky theme song and Susie extended her arms up even further, as far as possible then more, and moved her feet like the best boxer in the world. Louis joined in and they laughed like hyenas. Except for Jess. They returned to the dance floor and Susie went off on her own again, unaware that Aaron was parodying her. Jess laughed, and Louis pretended to. He felt bad for not telling Aaron he was being an arsehole. Susie always stuck up for him when people picked on him, but he didn't know how.

The night went by in an instant and the group found themselves running to catch the last ferry. They made it and Susie did her best Rocky as she stood at the front of the ferry with the wind in her face while the others sheltered inside. As they went through the heads, Louis came out and stood with her.

'We should go to the movies again next week,' Susie said. They smiled and snuggled together against the cold as the ferry rocked and rolled.

CHAPTER 24

The golden period came crashing to an end. Susie had drunk way too much wine on one of their 'movie' nights. She lost her friends and stumbled towards Circular Quay, determined to make that last ferry. When she got to Central Park, she decided to cut through it to be quicker, but her foot caught on a rock and over she went. Despite the pain in her face, she soldiered on. She staggered her way down to the Quay and ran higgledy-piggledy all the way through the ferry bays. She made it. As she sat, she wiped the sweat from her brow with her shirt sleeve and sat there trying hard not to vomit as the ferry went through the heads. It was the longest trip of her life. When she got to Manly, she headed up the hill to the apartment, snuck in and fell into bed.

The following morning, she got up at nine o'clock, even though she could have slept another eon. Geoffrey's family had breakfast together by hook or by crook every Sunday morning at nine. It was a time to catch up, to reflect on the week, to plan the following week and to just sit together. Susie liked it more than she had at the start. And there was always a proper big breakfast with eggs and bacon and thick tasty bread. She headed out in her dressing gown and sat at the table. Geoffrey's head dropped to his lap. Susie wondered what was wrong. She looked at Geoffrey's parents, who were also looking down.

'How was the movie?' Geoffrey's mum asked. Her voice was cold.

'Good thanks,' Susie said in a small voice. She knew something was wrong but didn't know what.

'Go and look in the mirror,' Geoffrey said to her in a whisper. The family all sat in silence while she went to the bathroom. Susie turned on the light and looked in the mirror. There was dried blood smeared all over her face. She thought back through the night before and remembered wiping the sweat off her forehead. It must have been blood from when she fell on the rock in the park. Susie washed her face, brushed her teeth and went to the table to face the music. She slunk into her seat and told the truth. She said that they had gone to a pub, that she had a fake ID when Geoffrey's mum asked what sort of establishment served children alcohol, that she had drunk too much wine, fallen over in the park and caught the last ferry home.

'What sort of friends let you walk home with a cut head and blood all over you?' Geoffrey's mum asked. Susie admitted that she had lost her friends at some point and came home by herself.

The table was quiet. Even Susie was looking down now.

'While we're at it,' Geoffrey's mum said, 'I got a call from the school yesterday.' Susie's heart sank even further. It was sitting in her stomach like an anchor. She could not work out what she had done wrong. She'd been going every day and handing in most of what was required of her. Geoffrey's mum said that the school was concerned because another student was bringing in lunch for her and the school had accused her of not providing food for a child in her care.

Susie's eyes filled with tears. It had all gone so wrong, and it was all an accident. She had no idea how to explain what had happened. A couple of weeks prior, Susie had been sitting under a tree at lunchtime. The smart group had been sitting nearby and a Greek girl called Mary asked if she wanted to sit with them. Susie most certainly did. The Greek girl was eating a big fat sandwich full of colours Susie hadn't seen before. She had asked her what was in her sandwich and the Greek girl spoke of eggplant and charred capsicum and some sort of cheese Susie had never heard of. She offered Susie half her sandwich, which Susie accepted with great anticipation. It was the nicest sandwich Susie had ever eaten. She hated dry food, and sandwiches topped the list of driest foods in history. Except for chicken, which was like eating a ball of string. She had the option of making a sandwich in the morning before school, but she couldn't do it. No matter how much butter or how many toppings she slathered on, sandwiches would never be nice. Except now. Susie was most complimentary, and Mary said she would bring her a sandwich the following day. Which she did. Susie had eaten it and when Mary had quizzed her over a few days regarding her lack of lunch, Susie had indicated that making lunch at home wasn't an option. It wasn't quite a lie, she just didn't finish her sentence by adding that she didn't like dry flavourless sandwiches. She hadn't meant to cause any harm, and Mary had seemed so nice.

Susie's face burned as she sat there at the table. There was only one option – to get out in front and save face. She explained that Mary's mum made the nicest sandwiches in the history of sandwiches and that she hadn't meant to cause any harm to Geoffrey's family's reputation. Her voice got softer as she explained, and she realised how pathetic she sounded. Between the school practically calling child services and her getting drunk and coming home with blood all over her face and the lies, she knew her run was coming to an end.

'I think it's best if I find somewhere else to live,' Susie said. She waited for protestations, but there was only silence. She apologised for all the trouble she had caused and asked for some time to find an alternative place to go. She also asked if she could talk to her father herself. To explain. Geoffrey's mum was reluctant as she was worried that Susie would misrepresent what had happened. But she relented and agreed to the terms and conditions of Susie's departure. She suggested a two to four week timeframe for Susie to find new accommodation. Even at this stage Susie was under the misguided belief that they would change their mind. Give her a chance. They didn't. She waited until she got to what was no longer her room, threw herself under the covers, put a pillow over her head and cried her eyes out. Even Geoffrey hadn't stuck up for her. Geoffrey sat at the table knowing he should leave her alone for a while – even though he wanted to rush to her, to hug her.

Eventually Susie fell asleep. When she woke up a couple of hours later, there were a blissful few seconds where she hadn't yet remembered what had happened. But only a few seconds. It all flooded back, as did a shipload of dread. She couldn't raise her head. It was whirring and spinning with stress and worry and guilt. She listened to the house and decided to wait until no one was around before emerging. The family often took a Sunday evening stroll down to the Corso.

When she poked her head out of her room as dusk fell, the family had gone out. She was alone. She sat looking out over the harbour, ruing her life. She knew she had to ring her dad but a variety of tasks became more important than the phone call. Like washing up the breakfast dishes and sweeping the expanse of floorboards from top to bottom.

When she returned to the kitchen to put the dishes away, she took two saucepans from the cupboard and put her feet into them. She stomped and stomped across the floorboards and began to sing at the top of her lungs. She sang 'I am Sailing' by Rod Stewart and had no idea why. She hated Rod Stewart, but there she was singing his song at the top of her lungs. In between 'I am Sailing's, there was a tap on her shoulder and she got the fright of her life.

'Jesus, Geoffrey, you know I hate frights,' she said, holding her chest with both hands. He looked worried as he explained that he really had no choice but to frighten her. How else was he going to tell her he was home in amongst her cacophony? Susie said she liked the word cacophony and began shouting it over and over as she stomped in her saucepans. Geoffrey eventually smiled. She stopped momentarily and asked where his parents were. He said they had gone to see a movie, so he and Susie could have some time together. To talk.

'I don't want to talk, Geoffrey,' Susie said, 'I want to sing!' She resumed stomping and singing. Geoffrey disappeared into the kitchen and came out with saucepans on his feet too. Together they marched and clomped and stomped and sang 'I am Sailing' at the top of both their lungs. All their arms were up, punching the air in time with the song. They smiled and laughed their way through two choruses and then Geoffrey seemed to vanish in thin air. Just as Susie got to the can you hear me part, she saw Geoffrey and a man in the front back doorway. Susie stopped dead in her tracks, her face getting redder and redder by the second.

'This is Glen, the man who lives downstairs,' Geoffrey said sheepishly. Susie muttered apologies and removed the saucepans from her feet. The man's face seemed to soften a little as she explained that she didn't mean to cause such a ruckus, she was just expressing her anger at herself.

'It's not easy being angry with yourself,' the man said, his face full of reminiscence. Susie was pleased that she wasn't the only person in the world who had hated herself. He left, and Susie and Geoffrey were left in silence. They put the saucepans away and sat looking out over the harbour.

'I'm sorry,' Geoffrey said. Susie said he had nothing to be sorry for. That she was the only one who should have had regret pie for dinner. Presently she burst into tears. Geoffrey sat across from her, helpless. After she had wailed herself dry, she told Geoffrey, with a bravado that didn't match her insides, that everything was going to be fine. That it would be quite the adventure heading out into the world. He took her literally and told her that he'd never met anyone so brave. So enamoured by life.

Encouraged by his compliments (she almost believed him) she asked whether he had any strategies to use when she eventually rang her dad. He reminded her that her dad had said he would pay her board as long as she went to school and she felt a bit better. Her dad could be distant, withdrawn, even a little cold. But he wasn't a liar.

CHAPTER 25

Susie went to school the next day with a peanut butter
sandwich. She had to go to school to keep her dad's
support, but she was petrified about seeing Mary. Mary who
must know that she had been cheated out of sandwiches.
Susie could explain. Tell her that her sandwiches had been
so delicious that Susie was caught up in their magic; so
much so that her mouth didn't tell the truth. The Smashing
Mary Sandwich spell. She could tell Mary the whole story
about the mesmerisation of her spirit and soul that led to
her misguided actions in order to have just one more. The
whole planet could be spellbound by the Mary sandwich.
They could go into business together and sell Magic Mary
Sandwiches from a cart on The Corso. Susie was a friendly
person – she would work the counter while Mary would
stand at the back of the cart in a crisp white uniform with
those old-fashioned embroidered cotton hook and eye clasps

making Magic Mary's Sandwiches. Yes. Susie would talk to Mary and clear up this nonsense in no time.

When she got to school, she didn't see Mary. Admittedly she was a little relieved. Louis was there though, with his big smile and a hug. Susie fell into his arms and held on a little longer than normal. She needed recharging. He started spouting that the actual Sissy who went to actual art school needed to take pictures set way back in time when women wore gowns even just to go to the lounge room. He said that Susie, yes Susie, would be perfect to feature in the photos that Sissy needed to take as part of her art project. They could go straight after school and he told Susie not to worry because her eyebrows would grow back.

'What does that even mean?' Susie asked, wide eyed and caught up in the olden days of velvet gowns and downcast faces. Susie thought they must have thought sad was beautiful back then, because women in those days never seemed to smile. Louis explained that women shaved off their eyebrows back then and that Susie would need to shave hers off today to make the pictures more authentic. Susie shrugged. She saw herself as authentic and if that meant having no eyebrows, then having no eyebrows it was. She asked him if this added to olden day ladies' sadness and explained her sad theory to him. Louis said that this was before toothbrushes were invented and they probably didn't smile because they had no teeth. They laughed their way to class.

At lunchtime, Louis told her they could walk to Sissy's flat in Harbord to do the photos straight from school and opined about how wonderful it must be to live on your own. With your friends. With no parents. Susie thought this was most misguided. It wasn't fun at all. She told him that she had thrown herself out of Geoffrey's place and that she needed to find somewhere else to stay. Soon, because living there was simply untenable for much longer. She told him she had two weeks to find somewhere. Louis flapped his arms around and said how exciting it was. How adventurous. Susie did not feel adventurous. She felt alone.

'We'll get the local paper on the way to Sissy's place,' he said, standing up and brushing the crumbs off his pants. He had eaten his own and Susie's sandwich. She told him she wasn't hungry because of the stress ball in her stomach. When he asked her what a stress ball felt like, she said like one of those metal pot scourer things, rolling around and around, cutting all her insides up as it spun. He said she was prone to being dramatic and should consider acting as a career. They could both go to the same fine arts college and he could do painting and she could do drama. Susie said she was a terrible pretender. He said pretending is about truth. She said if it was about truth she would win an Oscar.

They sat through the afternoon classes and Susie kept checking for Mary without success. When the bell rang, she followed Louis out past the bus stop. As the bus went past, she waved at Geoffrey who was looking out the window for

her. He raised his shoulders in question and Susie pointed
to where her watch would be if she had one and held up six
fingers. The rules would still be respected. She didn't want any
unwanted attention at the moment. She didn't want any at all.

As Susie and Louis walked and walked, they talked of
what their classmates were doing. They tested their own
moral compass against the actions of those around them and
concluded that they were much better all-round humans than
the others. It didn't cross their minds to hold the mirror up
to themselves as they meandered through the hilly terrain.
Finally, they came to a wooden gate. Louis pressed a small
bell that Susie would never have found, and they followed
a windy path to the front door of a dark honey apartment
block. It was surrounded by plants, bushes and small trees,
and Susie had to hold her forearm up in front of her eyes so
the branches didn't flick off Louis and into her face. They
waited at the glass entry doors until a woman with purple
hair and a really short fringe came to open the door. She was
wearing an old-fashioned dress that stuck out from the hips
with a bunch of netting holding it in place. Her lipstick and
headband matched her hair. When she spoke Susie thought
even her voice sounded purple. Susie was feeling shy, so she
stayed back as they all went up the three flights of stairs.
Louis and the purple lady were blabbering about images, and
how they spoke to them. Susie sort of listened, but mostly
she just felt embarrassed and shy and she wondered what on
earth to do or say as she was ushered into the apartment.

The first thing she noticed when they got to the living area was a mural painted on the wall opposite the balcony window. There was a lake and grass and trees and sky, but it was not quite real. It was a washed-out watercolour version. Susie thought it was just terrific. And the light from the balcony gave it a glow. Like the light was inside the mural.

'I'm Sissy. Pleased to meet you, Susie,' the purple lady said, shaking her hand daintily. There was a wooden stool next to Susie that hadn't been there before, and Sissy was patting it, indicating that Susie needed to sit down now. Sissy turned Susie on the stool so she was facing the balcony and she just stared at Susie with her head tilted left and her head tilted right and her head tilted down and then back to the start. 'Perfect,' Sissy said to Louis, who nodded vigorously in the background. He even clapped his hands. Sissy rubbed some gooey stuff on Susie's eyebrows and Susie flew off the stool.

'We spoke about this at lunchtime, Snooze, remember? We're going to dress you up like the olden-day ladies, shave off your eyebrows and take some pics for Sissy's project.' Louis always called her Snooze or Snoozie when he wanted something. He was almost whining. Susie sat back down and apologised to Sissy. She explained that sometimes she got the real world and story lands mixed up. Sissy laughed and tousled her hair. She told Susie not to be scared and that she had a perfect face. Susie reddened as Sissy put the gel on her eyebrows and sat there not moving as her eyebrows were removed.

Susie didn't feel any different without her eyebrows, not that she had much time to analyse it. Within minutes, she had been stripped down to her knickers and Sissy and Louis were draping pieces of velvet over her. There was a large blue oblong that had been fashioned into a gown from the front. It was clipped together at the back with bulldog clips, paperclips and sticky tape. It was pinched at her waist and had a boat neckline.

'That's a lovely long slender neck you have there, Susie,' Sissy said, running her finger down it. She looked at it like she was looking through a microscope. Louis held a red velvet piece over her head and a veil emerged. It reminded Susie of Sister Sylvester's habit with her little red curl that would never stay inside. Bouncing around like a puppy. Susie laughed at the memory. There was so much she had already forgotten. Sissy asked her to please not laugh. It shook the fragile construction and she was worried that the velvet pieces would simply fall to the floor. What goes up must come down, Susie thought to herself. But she didn't say anything.

When Louis and Sissy finally stood back and concluded that things were as perfect as they were going to be, Susie looked down at the floor. The intensity of their examination made her feel more naked than when she was standing there in her knickers.

'Perfect, don't move,' Sissy said so loudly that Susie froze. Louis was saying something about a perfect blend of sadness and contemplation. Susie thought she must be looking scared, but they said her vulnerability was spot on. Sissy clicked away with her camera as she fired off a bunch of mini instructions. Chin up, no down, no left, no a little to the right. Eyes towards me, eyes looking just past me, eyes looking at Louis, now look at Louis' shoes. Louis' smile was getting bigger by the minute and Susie couldn't help but smile on the inside. She didn't let it reach her face and then they congratulated her on being able to smile with just her eyes. An accidental success. Before Susie knew it, it was all over, and she was undraped down to her knickers. She put her clothes on and Sissy shook her hand vigorously in gratitude. She said she would send some photos to her once they were developed.

'What's your address?' Sissy asked, reaching inside her bra for a pen. Susie explained she was in between addresses and Louis said to send them to him. He would pass them on. Besides, he wanted to see them first.

'Isn't your roommate going overseas?' Louis asked.

'I'm too young to be a Mum,' Sissy said, 'besides, this one's too shy for my household.' And that was that. If Susie had known it was an audition, she would have been herself. She would have been chosen. Tears pricked the back of her eyes, but she stopped them dead in their tracks. She wasn't going to let Sissy think she was a baby.

Susie and Louis headed in different directions when they left Sissy's, but they stopped at a bus bench to have a debrief. Louis was glowing about Susie's performance and said she was just terrific. He explained that he had really wanted to impress Sissy. For when he went to art school too. Susie just listened. She was much more focused on her impending homelessness. Louis hopped up from the bench and retrieved a local paper from a nearby letterbox.

'Here, Susie, I nearly forgot that we need to find you somewhere to live,' he said sitting beside her and squeezing her knee. 'Don't worry, it's going to be fun finding you a new home.' He suggested she look through the accommodation section in the paper.

'How did you know there was even a section there?' Susie asked, incredulous at his knowledge. Louis explained that he looked through them every week and imagined what household he would choose if he was looking.

'Imagining all these places is so exciting, and now I'm doing it for real. With you,' he said, standing up and looking at his watch. He said he had to go home now, as did Susie, and they agreed she would circle the ads she liked. They would go through them together at lunchtime the next day. Susie didn't think it was exciting at all, but she was glad to have Louis by her side. That she wasn't completely alone.

CHAPTER 26

There was only one ad in the paper that appealed to Susie. It was for a place called Housemates, which matched people to suitable accommodation. She had called the number and arranged to go over after school the following day. Louis had been terribly excited about it and said it was like a smorgasbord. Susie asked what that meant, and he said a buffet. Susie remembered going to Myer with her dad and hoped it really was a buffet of houses to navigate. Even she was getting excited now. They sat under a tree at lunchtime and imagined all the places she could go. He wanted to go with Susie; to help. She said she would be just fine on her own and she headed there straight after school.

The address didn't seem to be an office. It was an apartment in a pale orange brick square block. Susie hadn't seen a home office before. The only office she had ever seen was the tax office, and this was nothing like it. The address said unit one, which was on the ground floor to the left. She rang the bell and an older European man answered the door and invited her in to what would have been the front bedroom. He said his name was Con.

'That's a short name,' Susie said. He told her it was short for Constantine. Susie said the name a few times before suggesting he use his full name. 'It sounds so . . . important,' Susie said, twirling her wrists and repeating his name over and over. She knew she should stop – this was a serious business and she wasn't behaving like it was an audition. She stopped and looked at the room as she sat on the visitor chair. There was a desk, a phone, filing cabinets and a bunch of stationery that made it all seem official enough. Her mind eased, and she looked at him expectantly.

'Tell me a bit about yourself,' Constantine said as he leaned back in his high-backed chair. It looked comfortable.

'Well,' she began, searching for what he was searching for. She explained that she was living up in Sydney and that her dad was down in Melbourne and that she was still at school and delivered pamphlets for pocket money, even though her dad gave her twenty dollars a week as well. This reminded her that money was going to be important, so she told him that her dad would be paying her board – as long as she stayed at school and didn't wag. Oh – and she needed a fully furnished room please. His head leaned to one side and he said it was an unusual arrangement. She gave him her dad's phone number and said he could speak to him regarding payment.

Susie had called her dad two days prior to say that things had been great at Geoffrey's for the previous months, but that she had to move on. He didn't even ask her what had happened or why or anything. The call had been so much easier than she expected. She didn't know that Geoffrey's mum had called him and explained that Susie would need to move because they had a relative coming from Melbourne that would need her room. Geoffrey's mum wasn't used to lying and her face had been red as she told her lie, but she was fond of the effect Susie had had on Geoffrey – even though she wasn't terribly fond of the girl herself. Geoffrey's mum didn't know why she lied, except that she wanted everything to go smoothly. If it went smoothly for Susie, it would go smoothly for them too.

Constantine dialled the number and handed the phone to Susie, who explained to her dad that she was in the Housemates man's office and that he would like to speak to him. She was a little embarrassed when he asked what a Housemates man was, and she explained that he ran a smorgasbord of houses out of an apartment office and handed over the phone.

Constantine and her dad had a conversation that involved Constantine making 'hmm hmm' agreement noises and nodding his head. Her father did most of the talking. Every now and then Constantine would begin sentences with words like 'the payment method' and 'she's only seventeen'. Susie liked that her father had answers for everything – in this instance anyway. The phone call concluded, and Constantine told Susie that he would need to closely examine the available options on his books due to her age and the unusual payment setup. He gently told her not to worry when he saw her stricken face and requested that she return the following day after school. He said it would give him time to contact suitable people and explain her situation to them. Susie said it shouldn't be unusual just because she was young. Constantine said that's just how it was as he flipped open a big fat diary and wrote 'Susie' in it for four o'clock the following day. Susie shrugged and took her leave.

The atmosphere back at Geoffrey's was only awkward because of Susie's regret and trepidation at walking in the door. She explained where she had been to Geoffrey's mum and then asked Geoffrey if he wanted to go for a walk. They were doing a lot of walking recently, mainly because Susie needed to get out of the house and Geoffrey needed time with Susie. Although she was spending the majority of her time with Louis, she still craved her old friend. The only one who had known her through her ups and downs and sideways and glorious embarrassments without judgement. She loved him dearly and was sad now that they were at different schools. It was fine while they were in the same house. She was going to miss sitting on his floor in the night as they folded their pamphlets up in groups before their

Friday after school delivery. They would chat about their futures and what they would buy from the pamphlets to insert into their imaginary lives. They were going to live in the same street and Susie was going to get silkworms. She had told Geoffrey all about the caterpillar-style worms that looked as soft as their silk balls, and how much fun it was to watch them crawling around their mini trees. It was even better than a fish tank, she reckoned. Geoffrey didn't think so. He had no affinity with any type of creepy-crawly at all.

When Susie and Geoffrey hit the paths, she told him about Housemates man and how he had a gross hairy chest and he wore his shirt with his top buttons down and black hair tufts stuck up all over the place like spiders. But she also said he seemed really nice, and that he took time to explain things to her instead of fobbing her off.

There was a rounded rock not far from the apartment that overlooked the water. It was one of their spots and their feet took them there without discussion. There was room for them both to sit on it and enjoy the view.

'I'm sure going to miss this view, Geoffrey,' she said with sadness.

'I'm sure going to miss you,' he said, looking the other way so she didn't see his eyes. She reached over and took his hand.

'We've done a lot of sitting since we met,' she said to change the subject. She had decided she was going to be stronger. To cry less. Geoffrey laughed, and they recollected their favourite spots. Leaning back on the swivel chairs and looking at the State Library dome, the Flinders Street steps, the tram floors, the milk crates on top of Geoffrey's boat and under at least a squillion trees.

'Trees are my favourite,' Susie said, waving her arms like they were branches in the wind, 'I'm going to live in a tree house one day.' Geoffrey said she was not going to have enough lives to live in all the places she imagined.

'You want to live wherever you are,' he said matter-of-factly. Susie said he didn't make any sense because she didn't want to live on the rock they were currently perched on. 'It's all about the stooooorrry,' Geoffrey said in his best Susie voice. He stood up and flounced about, telling her about the time they caught the train and she said she wanted to live in a train, and how she wanted to live in an old tram in her backyard, and how she wanted to live on a boat when she was on his old houseboat, and now she wanted to live in a tree, impersonating Susie all the while. They both laughed until they had good tears and Susie pushed him in the arm. They went back to the apartment and had dinner. Susie ate as quickly as she could without being rude and kept quiet before going to her room for the evening.

The next morning, Louis ran up to her as her bus arrived.

'What happened, what happened?' he asked, skipping along next to her. She caught his anticipation and gave him a rundown on Constantine's hair before explaining that she was going back after school to see what options were available. 'At this rate you'll be thirty before you find a place,' he said, putting the back of his hand to his forehead and sighing dramatically. Susie laughed, and they set off to class.

The day was interminable, although Susie found the English class interesting. She loved *1984* and was glad the real 1984, which was nearing an end, was nothing like the one in the book. Other than that, it was a slog to the last bell and she raced out of school at full speed. She made the bus and got off earlier than usual, pointing out the Housemates place to Geoffrey as she alighted. They waved to each other. Susie hadn't noticed that he didn't sit with anyone other than her on the bus until then. Maybe they could get a bus one day and drive all over the country.

When Constantine answered the door, Susie swanned in and plonked herself on the visitor chair. She told him that the visitors deserved a throne chair, just like his. Constantine said it would be impractical given the size of the room. Susie hadn't thought of that. Nor had she noticed the bonsai tree on the filing cabinet until then. It was intricate and looked as old as a real life old tree. Constantine saw her looking at it and pulled a leather case out of the top drawer full of bonsai tools. Like a fingernail kit for trees. Susie smelled the leather case and pulled out each tool one by one while Constantine spoke about how much care was involved in having a genuine bonsai. He said you couldn't just put it somewhere and forget about it. Susie said it would be a lovely addition to any home, especially if you lived in a train carriage, or a tram. Constantine smiled and agreed wholeheartedly. She liked that he liked her.

Constantine got out a large two ring binder and began flipping through it. Sorry to say, there weren't as many options as he had hoped, but he had found a viable one for her.

'It's important not to be too judgemental about the look of a house,' he said, settling on a page in his folder. 'They are an older couple,' he began to say when Susie interrupted and asked whether he meant old or old-old. 'Just older,' he said, 'like me.' They lived not too far from where they were now which would be perfect for Susie's school. She could walk there in ten minutes, he said, like it was a plus. It was not a plus to Susie, because she liked catching the bus with Geoffrey. Constantine said their names were Jan and Dave and that he had spoken to them about her situation and that they were happy to meet with her. Another audition. Susie wondered whether being grown up involved a series of auditions, to add to the big fat pile of regret and little chats. She thought 'having a little chat' was a lie anyway, because in her growing experience it usually meant a long and difficult mostly one-way conversation.

Susie was inwardly disappointed that she didn't get a smorgasbord, but at least there was a light at the end of her homelessness tunnel. He asked whether she would be happy to go there now and added that he could give her a lift. Susie asked for directions and said she could use the walk.

If she was going to move, she needed to know the area and walking it was the best way to do so.

'Feel free to come back to talk about it,' Constantine said as he handed her a piece of paper with directions on it.

Susie headed off. The streets were not as hilly and windy as they were in Fairlight. Nor did the name run off her tongue so smoothly. Harbord. Haaar-booard. Harb'd. She kept rolling the name around inside her head as she walked along briskly. There weren't people everywhere, like in Manly; in fact she only saw seven in her whole trip. Three of those had been in their own gardens and only one was walking their dog.

Before too long she found herself outside a ramshackle weatherboard with a yard full of weeds and four shopping trolleys. The house would have had a veranda originally, but it had been turned into a room. The front door had a sign on it saying the doorbell doesn't work and to please knock loudly. At least it said please, she thought to herself as she waited for someone to answer the door. A short frumpy woman in a grubby chequered dress opened the door and smiled, but it didn't reach her eyes.

'You must be Susie,' she said, opening the door and ushering her in to a dark stumpy hallway. Susie introduced herself as she followed the lady to the kitchen out the back. There was a man reading a newspaper on the formica table. He was wearing an under singlet on the outside and said his name was Dave. At least his eyes smiled when he said hello. The pair weren't dirty, but they seemed grubby. Same with the overcrowded kitchen. There was kitty litter near the back door, so Susie thought she'd break the ice and ask about the cat. Dave told her his name was Holden, after the book character not the car. Susie asked if he was called his full name when he was in trouble. Dave said he called him Mr Caulfield when he sicked up his food in the house. Susie liked Dave.

Jan said she'd better show her the room and they headed back to the front of the house. The veranda room was the one available, and as she could see, it was fully furnished. There was a single bed in the corner under the windows, a set of drawers at the opposite skinny end of the small oblong and a small round side table with a crooked lamp on it. There was no desk, nor room for a desk.

'You can sit at the kitchen table if you need to study,' Jan explained. Susie wondered if she was a mind reader. A crystal ball did not seem out of place. They watched telly in the lounge of a night, so she could have the kitchen all to herself. 'Dinner's at six,' Jan said, like she was reading from a list. Susie wondered if she would ever escape from the six o'clock dinner. Back at her dad's, life had been more fluid. Susie explained that she was often at her friends' places at that time, and Jan told her not to worry, she'd keep a plate for her to heat up when she got home. Susie was instantly sold. She had no curfew, no expectations. The shape of the place didn't matter anyway. She had a bed, and she had her freedom. She was suddenly full of joy and asked Jan when she could move in. The following weekend was decided on as she was shown around the rest of the meagre house. The lounge was as dark as the hallway and only had two recliner chairs in it. The bathroom was as long and skinny as her lean-to room, but it had those old-fashioned four-pronged taps with balls at their ends and an enamel H and C at their centre. Susie loved those taps. Yes, this would be fine. She took her leave and headed back to Housemates to tell Constantine that she was moving the following weekend.

When she got back to Housemates, Constantine invited her into the house part of the unit. He was finishing up for the day and said he needed a coffee. Susie didn't like coffee. There was a big open space at the end of the hallway with an ornate wooden dining table, a kitchen and a lounge room all in one. The walls were covered in bookcases, like the walls back at her dad's. She felt at home immediately.

'Well this is very different from Jan and Dave's,' Susie said, smiling broadly. Constantine laughed and said that it was very different indeed. She sat herself down at the dining table and declined the offer of a soft drink. Susie said that the Harbord place was dilapidated, but that Dave seemed nice. She added that Jan probably hadn't smiled in ten years, but that it would do.

'There's a bed to sleep in,' Susie said, shrugging her shoulders. Her eyes were bright with the future and Constantine said that if it didn't work out they would find another place. It was cheap and furnished and she would give it a good go.

Susie looked at the clock on his wall. It was made of a shiny metal and trapezoid shaped. It was also dangerously close to six o'clock. Constantine placed a small plate with some olives and cheese on it in front of her. Susie picked away as she told him how she liked to score houses out of ten – Jan and Dave's was barely a one. He pulled out a book on Victorian architecture, and Susie flipped through the pages longingly. Most of the houses in the book were a ten and it made her sentimental about her bike rides. She hadn't had a bike in Sydney – it was probably too hilly for one anyway. After forcing six olives in to be polite (she didn't much like olives, even on pizza) she said she'd better get back to Geoffrey's. She told Constantine that she was excited about not having to walk through a door at six o'clock anymore and he held up his coffee and toasted her new-found freedom before she left.

CHAPTER 27

*A*s the months went on, Susie drifted from house to house. She joked with Constantine that he was the only constant in her life. She had lasted six weeks at Jan and Dave's place. It wasn't the condition of the house that was the problem, it was the condition of the occupants. They smoked joints all the time, and inside the house at that. Susie had a few puffs of a joint while she was out with Louis, but she didn't like the smell of it in her face every day. Besides, they were always home. Always. Susie told Constantine that she didn't know how they went to the shops when they never seemed to leave the house. Perhaps they had a Tardis.

The next house was just as dilapidated, but it had more charm. There were three art students living in it and there were murals on every wall. They had been told that the house was going to be demolished in six months, so they decorated to their heart's content. Susie was quite happy there, she told

Constantine, even though she had nicknamed it The Crack Den. The students kept dreadful hours though and it was impossible to get to school every day when she lived with a bunch of noisy night owls.

Back to Constantine's folder she went. She had taken to having dinner there regularly as she reported in on her new house or reported that she simply couldn't continue there for another moment. He enjoyed finding her houses, and their dinners, and used them as an opportunity to give her good books to read and to attempt to discuss philosophy and her future. She shadow-boxed discussions about her life adeptly and in the end he had taken to showing her slide shows of pictures from Greece. She told him she could well imagine living in a white stone house overlooking the water and drinking wine. He asked her about drinking and she said she drank wine with her friends and to keep his judgements to himself.

Following The Crack Den, she moved into a house with a mother and a sullen daughter with an eating disorder. From the moment the girl saw Susie, she demonstrated complete contempt. For the whole twelve weeks Susie stayed there, the daughter said not one single word to her. It didn't bother her, but the mother's complete lack of humour put the final nail in that coffin.

Constantine suggested she try a bungalow in the backyard of an old-old couple. The bungalow even had a toilet and shower, so she hardly had to go into the house at all. Dinners were pleasant there, but she found more and more of her evenings were being swallowed up by their tales of the past, which were riddled with deep sadness. Their children had no interest in them whatsoever, their friends were passing away by the month, they got lonelier by the minute and their eyes filled with almost running tears at every turn. No matter how many times Susie tried to change the subject, they were human brick walls. She spent more and more time at Louis' and less and less in her bungalow. She would try and sneak around the back when she got home, but they had ninja reflexes, microscopic hearing and Superman x-ray eyes when it came to spotting her.

'Hello dear,' one of them would say as she snuck under the kitchen window, and into their vortex she would go. Each entrapment got longer and longer. Even when she went out late on a Saturday night to Oxford Street, they would see and hear her no matter the hour. The jubilation of being tipsy and dancing without a care in the world dissipated the minute she was called into the house for a cuppa. The good thing was that Susie discovered she quite liked a cup of tea. Milkier than average, and not too many teabag dunks, but she found them comforting. It was a shame the company sucked.

'I can't stay there any longer, Constantine,' Susie said when she plonked herself down on the visitor chair. When he had no other appointments, they headed straight out to the dining table and he heard a list of her issues again. This time, the place itself was perfect. She had plenty of space, but the sadness of the old-old people was contagious. She didn't want to spend her life living in a cycle of death and loneliness. Constantine put some brie cheese in front of her and she put thick slabs on some crackers and wolfed them down. She had grown to love olives and many cheeses, except blue because it tasted like sweaty socks, and she was at home when she sat at that table. Louis said it was weird that she hung out with a middle-aged hairy man and that he probably wanted to get in her pants. She said no way, he was a good person who didn't look at her like she was a toffee apple.

One day she had taken Louis there for olives and cheese, so they could meet. Much to her horror, he straight out asked Constantine what his intentions with Susie were. Constantine said nothing untoward was going on and that he should chew with his mouth shut. Susie had laughed and coughed up an olive that flew over the table and landed in the kitchen after two bounces. They all laughed at that and Louis didn't mind so much when she went there after that.

Susie saw Geoffrey less and less. It was no one's fault. Susie was flitting around a carefree life with no boundaries or curfews, while Geoffrey was stuck in a routine that didn't suit her. They didn't have the same interests. Geoffrey repeatedly refused to go into the city with them to drink and Susie repeatedly refused dinner invitations to the apartment. Susie had tried to lure Geoffrey into going out – she told him she had befriended Tony, the man who worked in the Freshwater Ferry kiosk, and she got a free snack each time she caught his ferry. She even did the announcements for him: 'Welcome aboard the Freshwater Ferry; there's a kiosk on the upper deck offering a wide variety of hot and cold refreshments.' She told Geoffrey that the announcements were meant to stop there, but she provided a comprehensive list of the available items from Cherry Ripes to hot pies.

'You need to come just to hear me do the announcements, Geoffrey, I could do it professionally,' she said as she flounced around the bus. Sometimes she caught the bus just to be with him, but Geoffrey was never tempted to join her and Louis on their nights out. Even though he would love to watch Susie do a theatrical ferry announcement, it wasn't enough to sway him into tagging along.

Susie caught the bus with Geoffrey the day she went to Manly to view her next abode. She was excited by the location and asked Geoffrey if he wanted to come along. They could walk along the beach afterwards. Geoffrey had exams and reminded Susie that she did too. Susie sighed and got off the bus. She was happy to walk the rest of the way.

Susie told herself her luck had turned when she arrived at an apartment block only one building back from the beach. It was ugly, the building had no lift and the apartment was on the fifth floor. Susie swore she wouldn't smoke again when she got to the top, except for when she went out with Louis, and knocked on the door. There was a lady with thick glasses that made her eyes look gigantic standing in the doorway.

She took Susie through the small flat and Susie fell in love when she saw the glass sliding door that led to a tiny deck. The rest of the roof was bare, and she asked why the deck was so tiny when it could take up the whole of the roof. The lady called Alison said they weren't allowed on the other part of the roof, that it was dangerous. Susie leapt over the deck railing and ran across the roof screaming 'Hello Manly' at the top of her voice as she looked out over the water. She failed the audition and didn't get an opportunity to live with Alison and the mini deck.

Susie told Constantine that she was prone to getting over-excited sometimes, and people needed to relax a bit. Alison had apparently been very unimpressed with the teenager with purple hair. Susie told him that her hair colour should be irrelevant, he said that people are judgemental, she said that was wrong and he said that was judgemental in itself. She rolled her eyes and promised she would behave herself after he explained that his reputation was also at stake. Susie said she would love another bungalow, any bungalow – it gave her more independence, except when it was in the yard of non-sleeping super-powered old-old people.

The next house he sent her to was on the main street in Harbord. It had that fake brick cladding, which Susie thought was a shame. She was sure there were beautiful well-preserved weatherboards under the baby poo brown cladding. She rang the bell and waited. A tall girl answered the door and she looked familiar. It didn't take Susie long to place her.

'You're one of those Christians in my year group at school,' Susie said.

'I recognise you too,' the girl said with happy eyes. Susie wasn't sure about this at all. The girl said her name was Rosemary and Susie said that was a good name for a Christian. She burst into the Simon and Garfunkel song about parsley, rosemary and thyme. Rosemary joined in.

The house was labyrinthine. The front door opened straight into a lounge room that Rosemary said no one used. No wonder, there was thick plastic all over the yellow and brown velvet couch. They turned into a mini hallway and Rosemary's room was down the dogleg back to the front of the house. There was a bathroom straight ahead, Susie's room was behind her and a formal dining room completed the four exits off the mini hallway. Susie's room was large and had a double bed in it. There was a set of big drawers at the foot of the bed with a telly on it.

'There's a TV,' Susie said, wondering why a bedroom would have a TV in it.

'Yes,' Rosemary nodded. 'I know I'm a Christian, but I'd rather you move in than some random stranger,' Rosemary added, looking right into Susie's eyes.

'Well as long as you don't try to brainwash me into being a Christian,' Susie said, making her mind up on the spot that this house would do just fine. They passed through the old lady style formal dining room. The curtains were floral and heavy, the table and chairs were dark and chunky and the carpet was brown with different sorts of flowers to the curtains. Susie wondered if these people were colour blind. A big, tall, olive-skinned man walked into the room and Rosemary said his name was Piggy. Piggy nodded and smiled and welcomed Susie in a heavy Russian accent.

'That's my mum's boyfriend,' Rosemary said, rolling her eyes at Susie. He seemed quite young to be her mum's boyfriend, but Susie didn't say anything. She didn't want to fail her audition. They walked into the kitchen and a frumpy lady in a floral dress, who couldn't be more different from Jan even though she had been a frumpy lady who wore floral dresses too, smiled at her while she stirred something on the stove. Rosemary explained that this was Susie and she went to the same school and that she was definitely moving in. Susie shrugged and smiled.

As they went out the back from the kitchen, Susie saw the house was on a hill. Rosemary pointed underneath and said her mum was greedy and was currently turning under the house into more rooms for rent. Susie said she didn't look greedy; Rosemary said looks can be deceiving. In the space of the tour, Susie decided she liked Rosemary, even though she was a Christian, and they arranged for her to move in the following weekend.

When Susie returned to Constantine's, she told him that he had outdone himself and that he had finally got it right. They rang her dad and Susie told him all about the Christian, the Russian and the greedy lady who was turning the space under the house into more rooms. She was feeling so positive about her next move that she elaborated and said she was actually going to do some study and try to get better marks in her upcoming exams. Her dad sounded like he almost believed her.

CHAPTER 28

Susie moved in with Rosemary over the weekend. Moving wasn't difficult. She had a bus pass and a suitcase, and she didn't mind taking two trips. It gave her time to merge her imaginary new life and her actual new life. Each new house meant a whole new beginning, even though she was still going to the same school and seeing the same people. There was an added zest. New eyes.

Rosemary's mum thought it was terrific that she delivered pamphlets and Susie was told she could use the front lounge to fold them all up, so she wasn't too cramped in her room. She felt instantly at home in this place. She even attached herself to the variety and denseness of the thick curtains and the shag pile carpets. In her old scoring system, the interior wouldn't rate a one, but the way she felt inside raised the score to a seven. Liveability points would become part of her future scores.

Susie didn't like calling Piggy 'Piggy' but she hadn't been there long enough to ask him how he felt about it. Besides, he wasn't as approachable as most people. He was an amazing backgammon player, and Susie and Rosemary took turns in trying to beat him. Mostly they played round robin, and Susie lost thirty-nine games in a row before she managed a win. It was hard to lose that many in a row, even with the worst of luck, so she focused on learning the obvious set moves, how to stack the board to stop the other player from getting their pieces out and when to take chances and when not to. It took thirty-nine games for her to put it all together, which she suspected was way too many, but once she figured it out their competitions really heated up. Now that she could win she could banter along with the others. Rosemary's mum, who kept saying 'please call me Agnes', would walk through the dining room and stop and smile at the three of them. It seemed to make her happy, even though they spat dreadful insults at each other as they flew their pieces around the board. Susie told Rosemary that she was a big fat meanie for a Christian. Rosemary said Susie was too sensitive.

Louis came over once but told Susie that he didn't like it there. It was oppressive, he said, pretending to cower under an imaginary leaden cloud. Susie felt like she was spread too thin. She was still catching up with Geoffrey, having dinner at Louis', going out and playing backgammon at home. There wasn't enough time for it all. When watching Rosemary and Piggy play off for the Cheddar Cheese Trophy (a three-way first to fifty), her mind wandered over her life. She concluded that even though she spent time with her friends, she was really alone. At The Exchange she danced alone, despite being surrounded by her friends, she played backgammon alone, with the others being background noise, and even though she walked and sat with Geoffrey, she was really bouncing her alone thoughts out loud.

'Are you alone right now, Piggy?' she asked. He was the most experienced alone person she knew.

'My self is always alone, but I am not alone now,' he said as he rolled a six–one. Susie liked his accent and wanted to ask about his background. She said she was feeling unwell and went to lay down. It wasn't entirely untrue, it just wasn't her body that felt ill.

When she woke up, it was early evening and Rosemary was getting ready for church. Susie liked that Rosemary never harped on about God or tried to convert her. She invited herself along. They arrived at an oblong building with no crosses or anything that made it look like a church. There were swarms of young people all milling around chatting gaily. It could have been Susie and her friends as they hung by the staircase that went nowhere. Except they dressed like middle-aged people. The boys had button up shirts and actual trousers, the girls wore skirts below the knees. Susie was the only one in jeans and she felt a little self-conscious. Rosemary introduced her to a few people before realising that Susie was there as an observer only. She had seen the faraway look in Susie's eyes before and left her to her own devices. Every now and then she would look for Susie and they would make eye contact and pass a little smile. Susie appreciated that she was keeping an eye on her and didn't find it at all intrusive.

The group started making their way into the building and there was an electric atmosphere inside. Susie was surprised to see a full band kit up on stage. She was expecting a dowdy man with a pulpit, a microphone and a scratchy voice telling tales of redemption and the benefits and positive results of hard work. Some of the young people hopped up on stage and the crowd went mental. They played rock music. Susie couldn't believe it. The crowd was up and dancing and singing along with the words that were only a little bit God-ish. Susie smiled along and headed outside to sit on a rock and smoke after a couple of songs.

She was pleased that Rosemary had a sense of belonging and she realised she did too with her eclectic mix of people she went dancing with. Over the time they had been going to The Exchange, Susie had met people that always seemed pleased to see her. Collette was the smallest person Susie had ever seen, and she always wore a pointed hat that made her look like a garden gnome. She wrote poems and Susie had spent hours reading them on the stairs that went nowhere. Cranky Jess had turned out to be funny, on the odd occasion that she spoke. It was like she saved all the good bits and said them at once, so she didn't waste time filling in gaps like everyone else did. As Susie sat there smoking she thought Jess had been good for her. Susie herself was much less of a chatterbox these days. Well at least she tried. Stanley danced with her all the time. He was from the western suburbs and said that he had to have two personalities. His parents were Salvation Army people that hadn't had a real conversation with him since birth. He said he developed a home persona and realised his new persona was the real him and that he had been a persona his whole life – until he met the motley crew that sat on the stairs that went nowhere. Everyone hugged him as he revelled in his freedom discovery. Even mostly Cranky Jess.

It had been a while since Susie had gone out. Backgammon had taken a front seat. As she sat there waiting for Rosemary, she decided to reconnect with her friends. She wasn't alone after all. She stood and stretched out her melancholy and let it fly off into the wind before she grinned broadly at the trees; which was how Rosemary found her.

'You look as happy as I feel,' Rosemary said as she linked arms with Susie. The unlikely pair made their way home for melted cheese on Cruskits and a bedtime game of backgammon.

CHAPTER 29

Susie had wound up at some apartment near Oxford Street somewhere. It wasn't too far off the main drag and she was always able to find her way around. Training herself in knowing north, south, east and west had held her in good stead. Sydney wasn't based on a grid like Melbourne, so she had learned to do it from the time of day and the placement of the sun. Sometimes she imagined being on a boat on the high seas hundreds of years ago.

'Help us, Susie,' the captain would cry. 'We're going around in circles,' he would say over the sounds of the waves, which were so high they splashed everyone on the deck. Susie would navigate them out of trouble every time without fail and they would go on to discover many new lands. At the last dock, the captain would paint over the name 'Sea Angel' with 'Susie Shoes'.

But Susie wasn't a hero tonight. She was trying to stay afloat in a different way. She had smoked a joint after drinking over half a cask of wine and she felt so ill that she went to the bathroom to chuck up. She hadn't made it to the toilet, but she had made it to the basin. Which was now blocked and three quarters full of vomit. She sat on the edge of the bath to gather herself and find a solution. She couldn't leave the basin blocked with her vomit. When she was sure she had stopped spewing – for now – she looked under the sink and in every hidey place she could find in the bathroom. No plunger. She pulled up her shirt sleeves and went in. Using the palm of her hand and sparing bursts of water, she had managed to plunge half of it down. It was sickening work and she stopped to have a cry. Her head was spinning and she could barely stand, but her progress thus far encouraged her to keep going. She used toilet paper to line her hands and fed the toilet handfuls of vomit in between the slow work of hand plunging. Her head clock told her she'd been there for at least half an hour, and that was allowing for time being slower than normal. She took small sips of water from the bath tap to keep her going and she washed her hands and forearms regularly.

Eventually the job was done and the bathroom looked as though no one had even blocked the basin with vomit. She made her way back to the living area. The people she had come with had gone. There were two men sitting on the couch under a window. They were in their own world and

Susie was not in a state to be able to walk yet. Her brain was clag, her mouth was sandpaper, she had double vision and she was very close to chucking again. She slid down the wall and sat on the floor half listening to the two men. Her head throbbed.

'*I really need a Coke.*'

'*Well, you can't go and get one now.*'

'*Yeah, I know. I'll have to wait until the market closes.*'

'*Unless you want to walk through it.*'

'*No, I don't want to disturb those fish sellers. They seem pretty aggressive. They'll make me buy a fish and I only have enough money for a Coke.*'

'*Well don't buy fish unless you want fish more than a Coke.*'

'*I won't. But I'm thirsty now.*'

'*Well, you'll just have to wait until the market closes then. Unless we borrow the money off someone.*'

Susie made herself look small. She didn't have any money to lend them. She was actually beginning to see the imaginary fish market in the lounge room.

'*Like who?*'

'*Roger.*'

'*Funny you should say that, there he is! In the fuckin' market.*'

'*He is too. ROGER.*'

'*No, don't bring attention to us. Those fishmongers'll make me buy a fish.*'

'*Well, we could take a chance on Roger lending us the money for a fish so you can use the money you've got for a Coke. I want a sip.*'

'*But if Roger can't lend us the money then we're fucked. We'll just have to have fish then.*'

'*This is absurd. There's always a way around problems.*'

Susie wanted to leave but still didn't have the required skills to get herself to the door. Aside from the fact she couldn't quite get up, she didn't want to walk through the imaginary market to the front door across the lounge room. She didn't need any attention right then.

'*Feeling rather optimistic, aren't you?*'

'*Yeah, well it beats being a constant misery guts like you.*'

'*I'm not a misery guts. I'm realistic. I want a Coke. There's a fuckin' market in front of my front door. I can't get to the shop. Fact. What's the solution, oh wise one?*'

'*Sarcasm's the lowest form of wit.*'

'*Even if it is, it's not as unstylish as using clichés.*'

'*You're really grumpy when you need caffeine.*'

'*Yeah, well I'm trying to address that by getting a fucking Coke, aren't I?*'

'*Mmm. The only way is to get Roger's attention and ask him for help.*'

'*Shit, did you hear that? It was the doorbell. Why don't we get whoever that is to buy a Coke and come back and then they can walk through the market. See if THEY can*' *manage to get through without buying a fish, and if THEY can, WE can.'*

'We'll already have the Coke then, dickhead, and there's no need to whisper.'

'True. But we don't know if the market's ever going to close. We could be locked in here for days. Then we won't be able to get the paper tomorrow, but we will if whoever's at the door can get through, because then we'll know if it's possible. The mafia own the markets you know, we don't want to fuck with the mafia.'

'All right then, WHO IS IT?'

'DAVE.'

'WHICH DAVE? THE ONE WITH THE RIGHT LEG OR THE ONE WITH THE LEFT LEG?'

'THE ONE WITH BOTH LEGS, BUT TWO CRUTCHES.'

Susie couldn't believe what was happening in front of her. If she didn't feel so ill, she was pretty sure she would have laughed by now. Another wave of nausea hit and she put her head in her hands, willing herself not to throw up on the market.

'HANG ON. What are we going to do?'

'If we ask him to get a Coke he'll be gone all night. Imagine how long it took him to get up to our door on his crutches, let alone to the shop. Then again, we have no choice. PRICE OF ENTRY IS A CAN OF COKE.'

'I ALREADY THOUGHT OF THAT, OPEN THE FUCKIN' DOOR.'

'WE CAN'T.'

'WHY NOT?'

'THERE'S A FUCKIN' MARKET IN THE WAY.'

'JESUS FUCKIN' CHRIST. ARE YOU SERIOUS? EVEN IF THERE IS A MARKET, WALK THROUGH IT AND OPEN THE FUCKIN' DOOR.'

'CAN'T DO THAT EITHER. WE DON'T WANT TO BUY A FISH.'

Susie knew she was going to spew again. She took the hat off her head. It was a Greek fisherman's hat that she had saved up for, and she vomited in it. It filled right to the top but didn't spill over. She picked it up, reached around the doorway and put it on the floor out of sight.

'LOOK, I DON'T HAVE TIME FOR THIS CRAP. I'LL PUT FIVE BUCKS UNDER THE DOOR SO YOU CAN BUY ME A FISH. I NEED A FISH ... SO WALK THROUGH THE MARKET AND BUY ME A FISH, SEEING AS I REALLY WANT ONE, THEN I'LL SWAP YOU THE COKE FOR THE FISH.'

'BUT THEN YOU'LL BE SWAPPING YOUR OWN COKE FOR YOUR OWN FISH. I DON'T NEED ANY FAVOURS FROM YOU.'

'HAVE YOU GUYS GOT ANYTHING AT THE MOMENT?'

'MAYBE.'

'LOOK, I'LL LEAVE SIXTY BUCKS UNDER THE DOOR AND YOU WAIT TIL I GET DOWNSTAIRS AND THROW ME THE STUFF DOWN.'

'That's not a bad idea you know.'

'ALL RIGHT. GIVE US A YELL WHEN YOU'RE DOWN THERE.'

'Shit. Now he's put the money under the door and some passer-by's going to trouser it. Great fuckin' idea that was.'

Susie tried to stand up. She desperately needed to drink some water. Her legs were too wobbly and even getting halfway up brought a fresh wave of nausea.

'If someone takes the cash, we won't throw the speed down.'

'What if someone takes it after we've thrown it down?'

'Well, we won't throw it down at all. Just in case.'

'OKAY, I'M READY.'

'SORRY, DAVE, WE CAN'T THROW IT DOWN IN CASE SOMEONE PICKS UP THE MONEY.'

'FOR FUCK'S SAKE.'

'IF YOU FOUND SIXTY BUCKS ON THE GROUND, WOULD YOU KEEP IT?'

'THERE'S NO ONE FUCKIN' THERE. YOU'RE HALLUCINATING.'

'UP YOUR BUM.'

'I'M COMING BACK UP AND THE DOOR BETTER BE OPEN, BITCH.'

'*IT MIGHT HAVE BEEN IF YOU HADN'T CALLED ME BITCH. Can you believe that?*'

'*No one has the right to call you a bitch. You're the nicest person I've ever met.*'

'*That's right. Call me a fuckin' bitch. Now he won't get the drugs or the money. Now let's sit here real quiet and when he gets back, we'll pretend we're not here.*'

'*Yeah, what's he gunna do, call the cops?*'

'*Hah.*'

As they sat there quietly pretending not to be home, Susie dry retched. There was nothing left in her system to throw up. The men on the couch looked over at the noise.

'*Well, heeeellooooo,*' one of the men said. Susie knew instantly that she was in trouble. There was hunger on his face.

'*OPEN THE FUCKIN' DOOR.*'

'*S'ALL RIGHT, DAVE, I'M DOING THE WINDOW DROP NOW.*'

'*YOU BETTER NOT BE LYING.*'

One of the men threw something out the window, the other started towards her. She was equidistant from the men and the door. There was no more fish market. She looked at the door, pushed herself up with all her might and willed her legs to run.

All the times where she wanted to run from things she couldn't run from came back to her. She launched herself up and ran from Mack, from Wexley, from her dead mum in the hospital, from being removed from school, from Mary's Magic Sandwiches, from the shame, from the lies, from the regret, from the unsaid things – and from the men. She ran like the wind.

She didn't make it.

THE MOON IS BIG TONIGHT

She loped towards Miss Kaye in a body too big for her, sporting a crop of large loose curls that formed a natural Lego hair helmet on top of her head. Before taking a sharp turn towards her room, she poked a note through the staff window.

'I swallowed a razor,' it said. Miss Kaye watched her walk to the left side of the unit as she picked up the phone.

'Yeah, I'm going to bring someone down, swallowed a razor blade,' Miss Kaye said, noting that they shut down in half an hour.

'Are you sure?' Nothing depleted empathy more than a looming home time.

'Yep. I'll be there in five.' She hung up before any protestations then walked out onto the wing.

'Come on, grab a jacket. It's cold, I'll walk you to medical.' Matter of fact.

'Oooh, are you all right, love?' said a nearby resident, placing her hand on Lego Hair's arm, feigning concern.

'Yeeeaah,' she said. She always elongated her words, especially when she'd self-harmed.

'She's fine, I'm taking her to medical.' Staccato. No time for contributions. Out the door.

Once they had left the building, their pace slowed. It was chilly, but dusk seduced them, slowed them down.

Walking.

Miss Kaye counted steps. Ten so far. Medical was between eighty-six and ninety-one steps depending on how relaxed she was.

'Anything else you need to tell me about?' Miss Kaye asked. Casual. She idly wondered how much more troubled she'd be if she didn't have a hair helmet keeping her brain in.

'Yeeeaah,' Lego Hair said, taking three steps before lumbering to a stop. Step eighteen, just before the kangaroo paw.

Miss Kaye waited. She had time.

Lego Hair pulled up the arm of her windcheater to reveal perfect criss-cross cuts that would make a Christmas ham proud.

The wounds were examined.

'Okay, well don't forget to show that to medical.'

In the failing light Miss Kaye could see little blue fluff balls from her windcheater flicking across the cuts and blood puddles in the breeze. Tumbleweeds. Lego Hair pulled her sleeve down.

'Does it hurt?' Miss Kaye asked. She didn't usually feel the need to fill silences.

'Yeeaah,' said Lego Hair, walking again.

'So where'd you get the razor?' Miss Kaye asked. Nonchalant. Threw in a bit of lackadaisical for good measure. This was the one that mattered. How the heck did she get a razor?

'Sharpener,' she said. Just like that.

You give someone pencils to assist in raising happiness and this is what you get. Not two hours before, Lego Hair had walked up to the window, big dopey grin, holding up a coloured-in picture of a mermaid. Miss Kaye had been complimentary. And she'd even meant it; mostly.

'It's a shame you don't show that sort of initiative in other areas, Miss Poulson.' A lopsided grin spread up her face. Step thirty-seven, where gravel turns to concrete. 'So what are you going do when you leave here?' Miss Kaye asked. It was hard to imagine all these people scattered around suburban Melbourne. Like diseased trees. Hard to spot from a distance.

'They found me a supervised living house in Albert Park,' she said, standing a little taller. 'It's really nice.' Can't see her running the Tan. Can't see her running at all. Miss Kaye thinks that's where the Tan is. She doesn't run.

'Are they keeping it for you?'

'I hoooope so,' she said, doubt dragging her shoulders down. Oops.

'I imagine they would,' Miss Kaye said. Calm, non-committal. 'Are you allowed to have pets?' Animals. Genius.

'Nuuuuh, I n'used to have a puppy. His name was Book.'

Miss Kaye smiled on the inside. Step sixty-four. Corner near the chapel. On target.

'Why today?' Genuine.

'It distracks my mind. Mind pain is worse.' Shrugs. It's a fact. One and one make two. 'It's starting to reeaally hurt now.'

Miss Kaye had no words.

'The moon is very big tonight, Miss Kaye.' Lego Hair tilted her oversized head without falling over.

'Yes it is . . . Yes it is,' Miss Kaye said, glancing up. It had golf ball dimples.

Home stretch. Around the roses towards the fluoro light.

'Have you got anything on you?' Miss Kaye asked. There's always more.

'Nuuuhh.'

'You have seven steps to tell me,' she added in a last chance tone. Silence.

Miss Kaye opened the medical door and ushered her inside.

'Turn your pockets out.' Business is business. Nothing.

'I'm going to pat you down. Do you have anything on you?' Miss Kaye asked again. Last chance saloon.

'Nuuhh.'

Miss Kaye found nothing, handed her over and returned.

The big moon lit her way and she wondered whether she'd ever had mind pain. Not for many years anyway. Once the path became gravel, she revelled in the asymmetrical crunching. Boots, gravel. Her favourite sound in the whole world. The sea has nothing on gravel.

'Off we go, ladies!' one of her colleagues called out. Miss Kaye's turn to lock up.

A young girl with lank hair and spots in Room 16 was sitting on her bed, her face blue like her windcheater. Not sure what the ligature was made of. Could be leggings.

'Take it off,' Miss Kaye said. Calm like a pond. Firm like a brick.

She loosened it. Slightly.

'I want to die,' she said. Husky. Barely audible.

'I'll call medical,' Miss Kaye said to her colleague as home time ran away. It was between seventeen and twenty steps to the phone from this room, depending on the pep in her steps.

AN ACCIDENTAL SYLLOGISM

Night shift. Peace or havoc. Nothing in between. The women in this building are a danger to others; or themselves.

'Bzzzz.' Room 15.

'State your emergency,' Miss Kaye said. Disinterested. Emotion gets grasped within an inch of its life.

'What's the time?'

'That's not an emergency.'

'When you have no idea what time it is, it's an emergency.' Calm; polite. Seems reasonable. Miss Kaye has an intimate relationship with time herself.

'Eight-thirty pm.'

'Thanks Miss.'

'No worries.' Manners get you everywhere. All nooks and crannies.

'Bzzzz.' Room 12.

'State your emergency.'

'Is that you, Miss Kaye?'

'Correct.'

'Sweet.' That's it. Nothing else. She wondered briefly what they think of her. The thought passed. She hit her mundane night duties. Clean up, prepare the breakfast packs. Select random cereal packs, label the tops. Random pack for Room 17 is Cornflakes. She hates Cornflakes. Can't play favourites. Write 17 on the top with thick black marker. The 'Alexander Beetle' song slides into her ears. Cornflakes is her fate. Miss Kaye doesn't believe in fate. And yet she'll have Cornflakes. Miss Kaye made a syllogism by accident. She's in a night shift state of mind. Did a little unabashed two-step.

Buzzer hasn't gone off for seven minutes and change. It's too quiet. Miss Kaye put her hand over her keys, snuck down to the top of the corridor. Waited. Listened. She has time.

'Pffffffft,' the tightly rolled paper package said as it was expertly skimmed from under door 12 to almost under door 14. It's tied to a bunch of tampon strings knotted together. They're called snakes. The string allows for instant recall if it misses the target. It's recalled. Miss Kaye is too slow. Slippery snake.

'I saw that,' she said. Methodical.

'Saw what, Miss?' said Room 12. Innocence personified.

'Oh my god, did you see a mouse Miss? I haaaate mice,' said Room 14.

'Oh my god, did you see a spider, Miss? I haaaaate spiders,' said Room 10.

'Oh my god, did you see a ghost, Miss? I haaaaaate ghosts,' said Room 17. Raucous laughter by all. A wry smile by Miss Kaye. Admitting defeat is like being able to laugh at yourself. A must.

She returned to the breakfast packs.

'Bzzzz.' Room 12.

'State your emergency.'

'I can't guarantee my safety.' Terminology, not emotion. Miss Kaye's not worried. She lets her talk. And talk. And talk. Miss Kaye muttered 'hmmm' spasmodically. Threw in occasional 'I sees'. Between two very interested 'hmmms', Miss Kaye raced to the top of the corridor.

'Pffffft,' from 12 to 14 again. The chat on the buzzer was a ruse. She thought so. Had to be stealthy. Full stealth. She went back to the buzzer, a few 'hmmms' and 'I sees'. Room 12's telling tales about her family. Miss Kaye whacked out a 'beg your pardon?' after a long bit and bolted.

She scooted to the top of the corridor. Can't pass any doors, they'll see the shadow and alert Room 12. She's on the blocks; going for gold. Saw a slight movement in the light under her door. She's off. Seven gazelle steps. She's there. Miss Kaye stamped a boot down on the string, the other boot on the rolled-up paper. Picked it up. Retreated to the office with her spoils.

'You weren't listening to me,' said Room 12. Sadly.

'You were distracting me, so you could pass your package. I'll give you an opportunity to tell me what's in it,' Miss Kaye said. Restraint.

'Coffee.'

'Really? You've been known to pass your meds. This is an opportunity to tell the truth.'

'I said it was coffee, so it's fuckin' coffee!'

'No need to use language like that. Do you ever hear me use language like that?'

Silence.

Miss Kaye unrolled the magazine paper. Diagonal roll. Tight. Must be an aerodynamic thing. Delicate job. Unroll, unroll, unroll. Getting close now.

It's coffee.

Oh. She's a little disappointed; she thought it was contraband. Her job was playing chasey. She was 'it'.

'Bzzzz.' Room 12.

'State your emergency.'

'I told you it was coffee.' Hurt.

'I wasn't to know. You can't pass coffee either.'

'Are you going to report me?'

'I'm consistent.'

'Yeah, well I reckon you'd throw a good snake if you were stuck in 'ere.' Resigned. Maybe; but she's not.

What she is: two zip down and less than half an hour in.

Secret weapon: only twelve shifts left. Ever.

PART FOUR
SAID THINGS

CHAPTER 30

When Miss Kaye left after her night shift, she turned left instead of right. She drove to the Hepburn side of Daylesford down to the last street abutting a gully. There was a small cottage waiting for her. Her main indulgence had been buying an old red rattler train carriage – it had been thrilling to watch the crane lift it into place. It was a small house, but the backyard seemed endless. The cottage itself had a small living area, an adequate kitchen and a bedroom up the back. It only took twelve steps from the front door to her bed. The little veranda had decorative wood fretwork which raised the overall score from a seven to an eight. She had spent many of her days off trekking up to the falling down cottage until it had been lovingly restored.

The whole place was now painted mustard with heritage green trims. It even had a flower box under the front window. The Silver Moon wasn't there yet. But it would be. The original dream for the carriage was to remove the bench seats and turn it into a bedroom for when she wanted a change. Previously she had always had a refuge within her refuge for self-emergencies – but she decided that the train carriage was a train carriage, so she left it as it was. Still, she owned a swag, a kerosene heater and strong portable lights. If need be, she could always run an extension cord across the yard and camp out in the train aisle.

The only thing left to bring inside was the small suitcase of belongings she had needed in her last days in her Melbourne apartment. She had dropped the now deflated lilo at an op shop on the way. Everything else was ready for her. She unpacked her toothbrush and threw her dirty clothes in a basket. It was wicker, like the small setting on her miniature front porch. With one chair only. On the off chance she ever had a visitor, she wanted it made perfectly clear that there was no room for them. She stripped off her work clothes for the last time and took them straight out to the bin. She held off on throwing away the work boots.

'You are now gardening boots,' she said to them, waving her magic hands all around them. Their new role in her life needed to be clear. She hadn't wanted to keep anything connected to her past at all, but they were comfortable and had a practical new existence. A new life. She went and sat out the front for a cup of tea. The silence pounded inside her ears. She expected she would adjust at some point, so she just let them pound away without concern. At the end of her cup, she took the twelve steps and fell into her bed, pulling the covers up tight around her ears. She wanted to fool them into thinking that the silence was because of insulation. It worked. They slowly stopped throbbing and she fell into a fitful sleep. She was aware that she was too warm, but it didn't quite wake her up. Normally after a night shift she would be lucky to get an hour or two, but she managed a solid six. When she woke, it was three in the afternoon. It was autumn. Her favourite season. A perfect time to retire. She walked outside and headed over to her shed with purpose.

Not quite three weeks earlier, she had been driving to work in the early hours, listening but not listening to a radio show where people rang up to buy, swap or sell things. An old man had rung in to sell his collection of three hundred garden gnomes. Miss Kaye nearly drove off the road in excitement. She pulled into the emergency lane (this was as big an emergency as she could ever imagine) and got her phone ready to dial the upcoming number. She had been the first and luckiest caller to get through and she secured the gnomes on the spot. For extra security, she made him promise to keep them for her three times. This allowed her to go about her day with a light step.

After work she made herself drive sensibly to the old man's house and just stood in his yard with delight in her chest as she looked over the gnomes in various states of disrepair. She had secretly hoped there would be some restoration involved. Perhaps not as much as was facing her, but that didn't matter. Her favourite was already a gnome with his head slightly cocked. He was pushing a wheelbarrow and she could have sworn there were taut muscles pulled across the back of his concrete shoulders. As she leaned over to lift the sinking wheelbarrow, the old man came outside and introduced himself. He had pale watery blue eyes that shone in the dusk light. When she held out her hand to shake his, he stepped forward and gave her a hug. He pulled away quickly as his sense of propriety kicked in. He muttered an apology and she said that there was nothing he needed to be sorry for. At all.

'I'm Kaye,' she said, completing the introductions. He said she didn't look like a Kaye.

'Well, my mother always called me Susie Shoes,' she said, surprising herself.

'Susie Shoes it is,' he said. They both laughed, and he invited her in for a cuppa to discuss the gnome logistics.

'Well, young lady,' he said as he placed a cup in front of her, 'I am so pleased to see that you like the gnomes.' He sat across from her grinning. His teeth were slightly yellowed, and she saw he would have been a handsome man in his day. Heck, he was still handsome. She complimented the wonderful collection and told him that when she was a child, her mother brought a dilapidated gnome home. They had lovingly repainted it, giving him a new, rich dark blue hat in which to hold his head high. She told him they used glossy black paint for his boots, gave him fire engine red trousers and a bright green vest. He revelled in her memory and asked what had happened to the gnome. Susie said she didn't know. Perhaps it was still under the daisy bush that had more flowers than most because she pulled the dead ones off with great vigilance.

The old man insisted on taking no payment for the gnomes despite her protestations, and he put the outside light on so they could load them into her car in the now dark. It was agreed that she would need to make a few trips, so the gnomes didn't have to rub against each other in the car too much. They both knew that it could probably be done in two, but they arranged three trips because they liked each other.

On the second trip he brought out a biscuit jar from times gone by. It was round, lemon coloured and made of Bakelite. The top section was a translucent green with glittery bits through it, so you could almost see what biscuits were inside. It had a saucer sized lid with a diamond shaped handle. She admired it and told him that biscuits were life's great icebreaker. He agreed that this was the case in the past, but that people didn't do biscuits the way they used to. She kept touching the container with envy. He looked like he wanted to give it to her, but his ties to it were too strong. As a compromise, he asked her to pick something from the room to take to her new cottage; something to remember him by. She said the gnomes were plenty, but her eyes wandered the room anyway.

There was a round bird head with fluffy hair atop a long stem and a bulbous base. It rocked back and forth like it was drinking out of a glittery liquid-filled bowl next to it on its stand. There were three ducks in three sizes on the wall with deep, rich green necks. It was like a 1950s museum. There was a round black ball with hundreds of fine hairs sprouting from its top, all glowing in different moving colours. But her favourite were two little porcelain dogs. They stared into the distance with sad eyes and she tried to muster her manners and refuse his offer. He could see that she had settled upon the pair of terriers. And that she was wrestling with herself. While she wrestled, he stood up, took some pages from the newspaper on the bench and began wrapping each pup with care. She tried to stop him, but she didn't try very hard. She thanked him profusely and he told her in no uncertain terms that she needed to stop wasting her time with effusiveness. It makes others feel awkward and he said that he hoped she could quell this terrible characteristic. He said it seemed entrenched and she had probably been annoying people with it for years. She belly-laughed and agreed with him. Then they packed the second carload and off she went to the cottage to drop them off. She secured them in a shed with a freshly bought padlock because she was worried they might be stolen. Who wouldn't want a hundred and ninety-six gnomes and counting?

Before she collected the final gnome load, she went to a hobby shop and selected a wide variety of small paint pots, some brushes and some turps. 'The best quality oil-based paints only, please,' and she headed off to see the old man. She took the bag of paints inside to show him what she had amassed. He laid out some newspaper on the table and suggested that they paint one together; to start the slow process of bringing the clan back to life. They wandered outside to select the first cab off the rank. They chose a plain juvenile gnome with a spritely stance and hope in his eyes. After settling on his character and the life he'd lived thus far, they turned to the decision of what colours to use. Given that they'd agreed he was only seventeen years old, and not a mature seventeen at that, they decided on pale blue trousers. Bernie went to the shed and returned with some sandpaper suitable for a gnome. He sanded the gnome's front, Susie sanded his back, and within no time the gnome was ready for his new life.

Bernie had said that the young ones liked bright shoes, so he was painting them a glossy white while Susie rejuvenated his pants. It was a powdery light blue and although she didn't like any blue much, they suited him. Susie had brought along four shades of white and they discussed his shirt. As he was in his final years of high school, they gave him an ivory shirt. Bernie spoke of his days back at boarding school that weren't that bad. Or perhaps those years had become more palatable with time. He said he had been a middle of the road student to avoid attention. He added that was the best way to be. No getting strapped or highlighted in the classroom.

Like a fly on the wall, he said, but with a desk and a chair. They smiled at each other across the gnome. Susie asked him whether he'd had to wear a hat and Bernie said a straw one, curling up his lips in distaste. He said the squeaking of a straw hat as it moulds to a head was intolerable to him, just as fingers on a blackboard irritated others. He shuddered.

They found a pale yellow for the gnome's hat. Although his hat wasn't shaped like a standard straw one, it now had the vibe of one. It didn't make that dreadful squeaking straw noise either, Bernie noted. A couple of cuppas and a few biscuits later, they were done. They stood back from the table to admire their work. Susie had gone out of the lines a little above the pant line, but given that juveniles are generally scruffy, it was considered part of him rather than a blemish. They named him Godfrey because he was from a bygone era. His face was now flesh coloured and his eyes were blue. Like Bernie's. Bernie bemoaned never taking the time to fix the old fellas up when the one thing he had was time. Susie said she had time now and asked him what it was like.

'Overrated most of the time. But when it's not, it's just wonderful,' he said, flouncing his arms about theatrically as he ended his sentence. There was never a good time for goodbyes. They were both old enough to know that so they didn't make a fuss. They didn't bother with false promises of catching up because the likelihood is always miniscule. Together they loaded the last of the gnomes and Susie noted that there were three hundred and two. But she kept this anomaly to herself. There had been a small debate about leaving Godfrey right where he was, but Bernie said he belonged with his friends. Susie said that she would email him pictures as the clan came to life and Bernie said that he would like that. They waved at each other as she drove off and she bipped the horn spasmodically until long after he was able to hear her.

So there she stood, rested in her new backyard. There was a small back porch with a utilitarian bench attached to the house. Susie designated this the gnome zone. It was under-cover, so she laid out her paints and brushes and retrieved a jam jar from inside. She plonked its contents onto a saucer and rinsed it out. She waved her magic hands around it and informed it of its new existence. A turps jar. Out came the permanent marker. TURPS. If she got Alzheimer's, she didn't want to accidentally drink it. After all, it did look like water and it was important to be prepared for emergencies. Susie went to the shed, removed Godfrey and walked around the yard. She asked him where he thought he would like to spend the rest of his days. Godfrey was nonplussed.

In the end she decided that the only place you really belong is the place you're in, so she carefully placed him in the middle of what wasn't a mini rockery yet. But it would be. To anyone else, Godfrey looked like he was plonked in the middle of nowhere on some brown patchy lawn. But Susie could see the rockery around him, so to her he was in his

Garden of Eden. She went inside and wrote a to-do list for the next day. For a moment she worried that she was already busy when she had only just stopped, but she talked some sense into herself. She had to be busy to create the space in which she could do nothing. Tomorrow's date was written at the top of the page and underlined. Underneath she wrote 'rocks' and 'Silver Moon' and then headed to the shed to get her next gnome.

CHAPTER 31

Susie only had one neighbour and the fence was well over the other side of the property from the cottage. When she placed the train carriage, it was as far from the neighbouring fence as possible. Susie had completed her rockery, twelve gnomes and seventeen sleeps before she ventured over to the fence. It was only five foot and she contemplated replacing it with a higher one. Most of her face sat above the fence and she examined the yard beyond. She hadn't heard much from the other side yet, but the people at the café, who seemed to know who she was and where she was living without any input from her at all, said that a man from the city lived there some weekends. When he needed a break. Also, that he had friends come over, but that they shouldn't bother her much at all. Susie didn't think so.

She walked to the café every morning and it was a one-point seven kilometre distance each way. When she got there, she had a coffee and a piece of cake. She hadn't meant to form routines so early, because the whole idea of being free was to have none. Still, she told herself she was choosing to go each morning. On the fourth morning she left at 07:03 so she wasn't leaving at the same time as the other days. When she got there, her coffee was brought over with no one even asking if she wanted anything different. The girl, who had too many rings in her face, apologised and asked what she wanted. Susie explained that it was exactly what she wanted, but that she did not like being thought of as predictable. The girl said she wouldn't do it again and looked at her with kind eyes. Susie nearly told her to wipe that look off her face, but she let it slide. This time. The girl said she would get her a menu and Susie said not to worry because she would have orange and poppy seed cake. The girl said nothing about her having had the same cake each time.

Susie stood there looking over the fence for a while. There was a random concrete slab in the middle of the yard under a carport-style structure. There was a billiards table on it. Susie had only ever seen an outside billiards table on a trip to China. It made sense there, given how short they were on space, but to do it in Daylesford seemed a little eccentric. Besides, the weather here would not be good for the felt – even though it had a plastic cover on it.

She had been so focused on the pool table that she had not seen the man standing on the back porch holding a cup of coffee. The coffee smell wafted over, and she turned her head. When she saw him, she waved. There didn't seem to be anything else for her to do. She had been sprung peeking over the fence. It would look foolish to try and sneak away. Susie always put her hand up when she behaved badly, and it had been advantageous in almost all cases. He waved back. Susie had a brief memory of her first high school and the teacher that used to stand over the way with a coffee. She couldn't remember his name. Or what he looked like. Or indeed why she had remembered him at all.

The man was slowly making his way over to her. She thought it was best to pass some pleasantries with a new neighbour, so she stayed put.

'I like your saucepan,' he said. Susie liked that he stayed the right distance away. She stared at him blankly. It was an odd way to start a conversation, she thought, until she suddenly remembered that she was, indeed, wearing a saucepan on her head.

'Thank you,' she said. She had to own it, but it didn't stop her cheeks from going a little pink. 'I like your billiard table.' The man said thanks and told her he had the slab built especially. And the carport. He told her that if he had his time over, he would have built it with a wall or two, so he could have some shelves or perhaps even a bar. Susie said it was never too late to add a wall, but that it was hard to take them down once the structure was dependent on them. This meant he had built it in precisely the right order. He nodded in agreement and said his name was Morgan. She said Morgan wasn't a first name. Her surname was a first name, but she didn't tell him that. She introduced herself as Kaye and then said she was busy and had to run.

'What are you busying yourself with, Special K?' he asked casually. She thought this was rude and intrusive, but she liked her new nickname. Besides, two rudes don't make a right.

'I'm restoring two gnomes today,' she said. Then she pointed to her head and said 'Hence the saucepan on my head.' She felt she had to explain the saucepan – so she didn't appear odd. Morgan's Not a First Name was tall, so his head was quite a bit higher than the fence. He looked over and complimented the gnomes he could see. She explained that she had to sit with them awhile and find their identity before she painted them and added that the saucepan focused her thoughts while she investigated their souls. He said that made perfect sense. As she turned to leave, he said that he came up every three weekends and had a few people over for a game. Firstly, if she thought they were too loud or boisterous to please come over and say so, and, secondly, that if she felt like a game, to come over and join them.

'No need to call first,' he said.

'Well, you mustn't mind surprises then,' Susie said before she nodded and walked away. She appreciated him laying out his itinerary. It rested her mind.

Even though she had retired, she still hadn't fully relaxed. The girls and their troubles kept bobbing up in her mind.

How they were and what they'd been up to. She tried not to think about them, but their vulnerabilities and sad traumatic lives stuck fast to her soul. Now that she knew how cathartic painting gnomes was, she had to stop herself from ringing The Institute and suggesting that they start a gnome restoration program. She knew how ridiculous it would sound and the staff would think she had lost her mind, so she didn't. Besides, she wasn't sure how readily available gnomes in need of restoration were. She imagined they were generally quite difficult to find.

When she got to the shed, she looked over the haphazard pile of gnomes. There was a bespectacled fellow with an impressive beard practically putting his hand up. No toing and froing required. He was the one. She scooped him up and meandered over to the back porch. There was a not quite comfortable fold-out chair that she had found at a local garage sale and she sat on it and set herself up. She adjusted her saucepan and stared and stared at the bespectacled chap until she decided he was an ex-priest with a kind soul who had read so many books that he realised there just couldn't be a god. The priests at her mother's funeral jumped into her mind. But this ex-priest had never met them, and if he had, they would have had nothing in common nor engaged in any meaningful conversation. This priest, if he had known a young girl whose mother had suicided, would have stayed in contact with her. Would have been concerned for her welfare. Wouldn't have abandoned her and just wandered through life as if she had never existed. This priest would have been what a priest was supposed to be.

She called him Father Ted. After he left the priesthood, he became a teacher in a country primary school and he took special care of the children's minds. And the minds of their families. The townsfolk still called him Father Ted, even though he wasn't a priest anymore. He wore bland, yet warm, beiges and browns, but his bowtie was the brightest and glossiest of reds. Father Ted would be the elder of the gnome community. The guide, the mentor, the town father. The father that the younger people in the gnome community could go to with their problems. He would envelope them in his arms and tell them funny stories when they were sad. Instead of fostering independence and leaving the juveniles to their own devices and choices, he would intervene and protect them. But not in an intrusive way. In a way that would invite the young ones in. And so, his place in Susie Shoes' gnome village emerged.

There was an old brick barbeque that Susie had planned to pull down. But it would never be pulled down now. It was Father Ted's hearth. His pulpit. When he was complete, she took him over and placed him atop it, so he could look out over the whole yard and his people. Susie decided that one gnome was enough for the day and pulled a few weeds before taking herself inside for a nap.

CHAPTER 32

*A*nd so the months went by. Susie learned to light the perfect fire and discovered that she could stare at flames for hours. It reset her. After many trips to the café at the same time every morning, rain, hail or shine, she finally figured out what made it a necessary part of her routine. It was the time of day she got sentimental. Where she looked back on her life. Became circumspect. By allowing herself this indulgence while she drank a coffee and munched down an orange poppy seed cake, it freed the rest of her days up. To move forward. To not worry about the past. To not overanalyse her life or be consumed by legacy and what it meant. To not waste time on working out what she'd done; or hadn't. What her purpose had been. Whether she'd done anything at all that would be remembered by anyone.

Morgan's Not a First Name joined her from time to time. He had his own routines, his own demons, his own tri-weekly ritual of a game of pool. Susie often sat hidden behind the fence listening to him and his friends talk into the early hours of the morning. He didn't know this, so when he bumped into her at the café, and they both knew it wasn't an accidental meeting, she was able to espouse general wise observations that were remarkably on the money. So relevant to his life that he viewed her as an oracle – and he told her so. She told him about her new-found revelations regarding her routine and said that he was, in fact, robbing her of an hour of self-indulgence every time they met. Now that she was entering old age, she didn't have many hours left and he needed to show more regard before thieving her time. Perhaps he should only turn up every second or third week. He said he would steal as he pleased, and she had every right to stay home and self-indulge there.

The second time they had met, Susie again had a saucepan on her head. She had been looking over the fence and counting the empty bottles scattered around his pool table. Morgan's Not a First Name was again holding a coffee and standing a lovely distance from her. He was wearing a sarong and he asked if he could come around for a gnome tour. Susie accepted his invitation but said he was not to go into the house. Nor was she going to offer him any refreshments, but he was quite welcome to bring his own coffee. She said that the best beverages are ones you make yourself because you're the only one who knows what you like and how you like it. Susie introduced him to Father Ted and told him a bit about his background.

'I can see it,' Morgan's Not a First Name said with grand enthusiasm. His face transformed, and he was in Father Ted's world. They both told extensive tales of Father Ted's successes with the younger folk in the village. Morgan's Not a First Name wandered around the existing population and interviewed them about the effect Father Ted had on them. He became quite animated and Susie had a moment where she felt he was intruding too much on her world; trying to make it their world. He even asked if he could make a documentary about Special K's Village. It was at this time that Susie informed him that her mother used to call her Susie Shoes.

'Oh, that's much better,' he said as he got out his phone, turned it towards himself and began a soliloquy on where he was (Susie Shoes' Gnome Village), why he was there (to do a documentary on each of the resident's lives as told by the villagers themselves) and to do an exclusive, world first interview with the one and only reclusive Susie Shoes herself – the phone panned to Susie as he finished his introduction. She inexplicably grinned and waved to the viewers.

Morgan's Not a First Name put his phone away at that point to liaise with Susie about the impending filming. To make plans. Susie said she'd had quite enough attention for today and took him for a brief look at her new gnome station inside Old Red (which is what she had named her train carriage). When she took him to the shed, she placed herself between him and the combination padlock. You couldn't be too careful. She showed him the mound of gnomes in varying states of disrepair. The new selection process involved picking one at random and placing said gnome on her workbench. Then she just looked at them until their history transpired. She picked a gnome and they made their way back to Old Red. As they sat across from each other, she didn't notice that Morgan's Not a First Name's phone had re-emerged and that he was filming her as she sat there staring at a gnome, waiting for his story. One of his gnome arms was up in the air. He looked victorious and ready to tell his story.

Susie said he had a well-hidden, adventurous soul. That he had spent his younger years being the family rock. The one people leaned on. The one who boosted the gnome family members towards their dreams. And elevate they did. It was a most successful gnome family with all the younger family members skyrocketing into the world of self-made gnomes. Their parents had been classic blue-collar workers – Mum worked part-time at the pharmacy and raised their four boys. Dad took two to three jobs, from driving to factory work, to provide for them. The boys had thrived under their mum's love, their father's hard work and the sacrifices of their older brother.

After their father fell from a ladder at work and broke both his hips, the older brother had left school and worked to add to the family coffers. When they got into trouble, the older brother gnome would head out to the site of sin and tell the local policeman it was, in fact, him who had stolen the farmer's horse and left him draped in toilet paper in the wrong paddock. Or indeed he who had graffitied the local church; penning his brother's name to avert suspicion. He took the blame, he helped with homework, so the brothers' grades grew higher, and he looked after their mother after she got sick with cancer.

And so, Susie concluded, after many years of being the family bedrock, we now see the older brother do something for himself. He saved some of his pennies after pitching in to help the brothers pay rent while they each studied to be a surgeon, a banker and an archaeologist (the one our gnome was most proud of) and bought himself a plane ticket to Russia. This pose, with his arm raised in victory, was how he looked after traversing the country from east to west, from north to south. And now he had returned to his roots to see what he could do for his community.

Susie looked over at Morgan's Not a First Name at the end of her introduction, turned the gnome around and said that this was Peter. He was going to be Father Ted's right-hand man. To be there for the community when Father Ted was too sick or too frail to do it himself.

Morgan's Not a First Name gave Susie Shoes a standing ovation and reiterated his plans for a documentary. Susie told him he needed to grow more mind tracks. To be a little less fixated on things. He couldn't listen because he was so excited by the upcoming filming. Susie said there would be no such thing and asked him to leave. She said she had things to do on her to-do list and perhaps he should busy himself with his own list. Morgan's Not a First Name said he didn't have a list. Susie said that explained things and shooed him off. Peter was placed next to Father Ted, but down a brick. He wasn't the top of the heap yet and he had much to learn.

CHAPTER 33

Susie renovated less and less gnomes as time went by. She attended the café less and less too. Although she did pop in on Wednesdays when she was sure that they served freshly made orange and poppy seed cake. She listened to more and more music. Her ear buds transported her to other places, to other lives. During her Suzanne Vega stage, she was the Queen and all those who had walked through her life were the soldiers standing in her wake. She was always left strangling in the solitude she preferred. Except it didn't strangle her at all in real life. She simply preferred it. Boredom wasn't a factor. Her father had always said that only boring people get bored.

To entertain herself these days, she wrote about her life. She no longer wallowed in what might have been, or what she could have done. Or achieved. Life wasn't about that stuff at all. As it turned out she had lived a full life. It was a revelation to her. She'd travelled, observed, watched, lived, raised a child and made small differences to the lives not seen by society at large. Morgan's Not a First Name wouldn't even know that those girls existed. Their troubles and battles weren't seen by passers-by. They were just other people walking down the street in their own hell. She had devoted her life to looking after them because she could have been them and they could have been her.

She had avoided her neighbour successfully for some time now. He'd been another salient reminder that she was perfectly fine on her own.

On the odd occasion she would don her saucepan and head out the back to renovate a life. She still got great enjoyment out of the growing gnome village. She was their queen. The Fat Controller. In the summer months she did it on the back porch. The train carriage was stifling in the sun. But it provided shelter for her in the winter. She wrote her stories in the same spots, but she only wore her saucepan when she was fixing up a gnome. Which is what she was doing when she felt a presence nearby. She turned and there was her son. Just standing there. He used to do that when he was a child and she hated it as much then as she did now. She told her insides not to show her fright or her dismay. To be quiet.

'I don't know why you do that. WHAT DO I HATE MORE THAN ANTHING IN THE WORLD?' she asked at nearly the very top of her lungs. Apparently, she had been unable to contain herself.

'Surprises,' he said, amusement spreading through his eyes.

'You've just taken five years off my life. I hope you're proud of yourself,' she said, turning her attention back to her new gnome. Her ears were pounding.

'If that were true every time you said it, you would have died before you were born,' he said, still standing where he was. He knew her well enough to wait for an invitation. Sometimes they came, sometimes they didn't. She laughed and shrugged at the same time. He let out the breath he hadn't realised he was holding. Making her laugh at the start of anything augured well. She let him wait while she finished sanding the new gnome's hat.

'Where have you been?' she asked, knowing full well that he had been in Cambodia for the last three years building a school. She had the Facebook after all. She invited him inside for a cup of tea and a biscuit and told him he would need to bring the folding chair she was sitting on, so he had a seat. They went inside, and she sat in her armchair while he made himself a pot of tea. He pointed out that there was room for another chair in the lounge room. She hastily informed him that if she had another chair, people would feel welcome; which they weren't. She said her life was full enough and she had no room whatsoever for anyone else. At all. He smiled warmly as he plonked himself on the chair. In that case, he said, it was lucky she had more than one teacup. They laughed. She looked at the wrinkles around his eyes and told him he was old. He agreed.

It was time for Scrabble. It's what they did. They had played thousands of games over the years. Their meetings were sparse, but they both enjoyed them. Once he had said they should catch up more often. She had said that would ruin what they had. They both knew this to be true. She had taught him the importance of small words to get a big score and the value of big ones in the world. It was important to be economical when talking with people. It was crucial not to waste people's time with unnecessary words. It would amount to years over a lifetime. Susie got on her hands and knees and retrieved Scrabble from the bottom of the TV cabinet.

'I see you finally have a television,' he said cheekily. They hadn't had one when he grew up just as she hadn't when she did. She explained it was only there to remind her of what not to do. Although she liked some of those shows on the Netflix.

'Telly's not too bad, these days, as long as you have control,' she said, giving him a wink. He said he still couldn't wink. She thought it was simply outrageous that after all these years he hadn't managed it. They started a competition of what they could and couldn't do. She could trill with her tongue behind her front teeth, he could roll the outsides of his tongue in, so the sides touched. She blew the longest raspberry and on that winning note she put a halt to proceedings.

'Why are you here?' she asked. He muttered something about it being perfectly normal for a son to visit his mother. She said phooey and they played on in silence. She was heading for a three hundred plus score and he was close at her heels.

'I want to know who my father is,' he said for the gazillionth time in his life. She couldn't comprehend why this had been so important to him for so long. She said that it was time to let it go. He said he couldn't.

They played away. Susie got 'circus' on a triple word score and gave herself a standing ovation in her mind. It wasn't always about the score. While the crowd roared in her head, the silence grew thicker in the cottage. Susie didn't notice. The silence never bothered her much, but it ate away at him; as it always had. After the crowd had taken their seats, she sighed audibly, sat back and just looked at him. Perhaps it was time to put him out of his misery. To deliver the kill shot. The stupid boy didn't seem to have the capacity to let it go.

'There's a bottle of wine under the sink. I'm going to need it,' she said, slumping slightly in her chair. He knew not to speak. The bottle of wine was delivered, along with two differently styled wine glasses. She selected the stumpy cut crystal one that had been her father's. She also pointed out that he could only have one glass because he was driving. There was nowhere for him to stay. Nowhere at all. He said he could sleep in the carriage if he got too pissed. Again, she sighed. She had sighed more in the last hour than she had in the last year. There was always an out and it came to her quickly. She could always walk to town and find some accommodation to get away from him. There was more accommodation in Daylesford per capita than there was anywhere in the world, she figured. Being a Tuesday, there'd be no shortage.

She poured her wine and took a sip. She realised he didn't know much about her, nor her about him for that matter. Not that there was anything wrong with that. But it was time to put him out of his misery. He'd had decades to work out that his father had nothing to do with his identity and yet here he was, still searching.

She began her tale back in her early teenage years, when she had too much freedom and not enough hugs. She spoke about her mother's mental illness and added that she was pleased to see that society now addressed such things, instead of sweeping them under the carpet like they did back then. The mentally ill were hidden back then. She spoke of the guilt she felt at not getting to her mother's earlier. Perhaps she would have been saved. But the guilt of being relieved at her dying was much more potent, acidic. Her son sat across from her, managing to keep all emotion off his face. Any sign of pity and she would shut down and put him out on the street. Crying had been taboo in his childhood. He was taught to stand tall, to move forward. She spoke of her paper stands and leaving home with Geoffrey to go to Sydney. How exciting it had been. How impregnable and ready for the world she was. How it had fallen apart and the various share houses she flitted through. How much she loved drinking and dancing and having fun wandering the streets of anywhere.

And how one night she had found herself in a flat where two wasted men spoke of an imaginary fish market in their lounge room. And how the evening had become the next worst night of her life.

'And so, I. Don't. Know. Who. Your. Father. Is.' She downed the last of her wine. 'There's another bottle under the gnome desk out the back,' she said, flicking her hand towards the rear of the house. Her son went to get the wine, giving them both some much needed space. When he got back, he poured two more glasses and drank his down in one go.

'So, are there any other pressing issues or questions while I'm feeling so generous spirited?' she asked with twinkles in her eyes.

Long pause.

'But you and Grandpa were so close?'

'Not always. You need to know that you were a product of the worst night of my life. But if you hadn't come along, I would never have climbed out of the sinkhole that was my life. You were my lifejacket. It was the best worst night of my life.'

'The worst night, best result sounds better,' he said casually. Susie appreciated him keeping the tone light. And right. She held up her glass and they clinked.

'I don't know what you do with this. I was never going to tell you. You have badgered me, pushed me, cajoled me and nagged me endlessly about your heritage. Well, now you know.' She went on to say that his identity had nothing to do with who his father was, and that it was time to stand up straight and move forward. She added that she was sorry she hadn't told him decades ago. To prevent him spending so much energy on wondering where he sat in the world. She was also sorry that he didn't have the common sense to move on regardless. She said that worrying about what you don't know is a waste of time. She said he lacked common sense and asked whether he was happy with himself now? She knew she was being cruel and he sat across from her trying not to look wounded. At least he was trying, so she reigned herself in.

'There's no magical loving father sitting there somewhere waiting for you, love.' She wondered whether he had seen her as a dragon withholding his father from him for all these years. Perhaps. But there was nothing she could do about that now. She finally stopped her tirade and sat back in the chair. Exhausted. So was he.

'I don't know how to feel,' he said presently.

'Oh, you and your feelings,' she said dismissively. 'It's not my fault you were born sensitive.'

'It's a quality, not an affliction,' he said. She smiled admiringly. She liked it when he answered back. When he stood up for himself. 'You don't care as much as I do.'

Susie blew a staccato raspberry before saying he was wasting her time.

'You always cared more about the girls at work than you did about me.'

'Well, you've been bottling that one up, haven't you?' she said, shaking her head. She explained that her job had provided their life, but that she couldn't leave it at the door the way you can if you're an accountant. Working with the damaged, the outliers, the mentally ill wasn't easy and he should be more considerate of the effect it had on her. It isolated her. Chipped away at her fabric. Left lasting scars. 'Now stop being petulant. Poor you, having a mother that had more to focus on than little old you. You're sulking. You've always been a sook.' She wondered if she'd gone too far.

'You don't understand me,' he said. Defeated.

'Wow. What are you, twelve?' She waited a while. 'Is that it?'

He nodded. Nothing he had meant to vent had come out correctly. He hadn't expected such a long-awaited opportunity and he had frozen. The words that had come out weren't the ones in his head, but he couldn't fix it now. It was too late. He wondered if any of it even mattered anyway.

He knew how she hated pity and so he kept the devastation at his mother's story deep down inside. He could worry about that later. She looked at him. As always, he was looking at her fondly. God knows why. She hadn't been much of a mother, but they had enjoyed life most of the time. They often went to the zoo and made up stories of how the animals lived when the people weren't around staring at them. Pretending they were animal whisperers. This tradition continued well into his teens. Going out for lunch was a weekly ritual, and each time they pretended they were other people with other lives. They had both enjoyed these times and in between he learnt how to behave and how to stay in life's lines. She wasn't as liberal as her father had been and she wondered if he would have reversed the pendulum had he had children himself.

Presently she suggested a tour of the garden and the gnome village she had created. He jumped at the opportunity. He loved his mother's other worlds and had envied her imagination for as long as he could remember. Susie Shoes gave him a detailed tour, the wine providing previously unknown intricate details of the gnomes' lives. At the end of the tour, they sat on the rocks next to the train carriage. He asked her what else she had been up to and she told him she was writing about her life. It was cathartic and quelled her fears about not having lived.

'I might just end the story with this visit,' she said, winking at him. He contorted his face as he tried to wink back. She said he needed to stop trying because it made him look like he'd had a stroke.

'Well, this might add some meat to your story then,' he said, champing at the bit to tell her something. 'I'm having a baby,' he said. Just like that. Susie sat there with a mouth like an 'o'. He laughed. She liked that he found her funny, even though she wasn't trying to be most of the time. It had saved their relationship many times over. He asked whether she would like to meet his soon to be wife. Susie declined.

She reiterated that there were way too many people in her life and she simply didn't have room for another. He said she feared being rejected. She said that was nonsense and that couples should be left alone, except perhaps for Christmas. Or something like that. He said she didn't do Christmas – unless, of course, she wanted to do Christmas with the new baby. Susie said she couldn't be less interested. Even though she was. He brought a piece of paper out of his pocket with his new address and phone number on it.

'Only because I don't want to appear rude,' she said, placing the piece of paper gently into her pocket.

The visit had come to its natural conclusion. All his early life she had trained him to notice the nuances. To not overstay your welcome. To not be so arrogant that you suck up people's time. They hugged. It was warm and natural. She had been determined to see that he had enough hugs as a child, because she knew what it was like to have had none. Especially when he was a teen and thought he didn't want them.

And then he was gone.

Susie went inside and wrote tomorrow's date on a piece of paper. Under it she wrote 'Purchase fridge magnet for phone number'. She was worried she might lose it. But only a little. She looked around for a good spot to put the phone number in the meantime. But not too good a spot. Her spots were often so clever that she couldn't remember where they were at all. She settled on a teacup in the cupboard and she placed a saucer over it in case a stray bit of wind wandered through and stole it.

She didn't know what time it was other than bedtime. The real time didn't much matter anymore. She put on her favourite pyjamas and lay down in bed. In no time at all she found herself in that position that comes along once, or sometimes, if you're lucky, twice a year. Where you're so comfortable that you daren't lift a finger in case you lose it. For the briefest of moments, she contemplated covering her ears with the doona – it always stopped her pounding ears. But she didn't want to put her position at risk. Besides, she noticed her ears weren't pounding after all. And so, in her once a year comfy position and with her ears out to the world, Susie fell asleep.

EPILOGUE

Susie began taking her unrenovated gnomes in her bicycle basket to the café on orange poppy seed cake days. She tried to break routine and branch out into other cakes on other days, but neither the pear and pistachio slice nor the flourless chocolate cake days felt right. At her age, she could damn well eat orange poppy seed cake every day for the rest of her life if she so chose.

Word of the growing gnome village spread around the town and the locals began turning up for a look-see. It became apparent to all that one shouldn't arrive before twelve and it was best to wait on the other side of the road for an invitation. When she was in good humour, usually on Mondays and Thursdays (give or take), she would banter about the varying gnome lives and postulate names to call her village. Gnometopia, Gnome Man's Land, The Gnomestead, Game of Gnomes and Gnome-tre Dame to name a few. But Gnome

Village stuck, and an artistic local made a sign on the back of a shell pool for her to place out the front – when she felt like visitors.

She became accustomed to the drop ins but she still hadn't placed an extra chair on the veranda. Drop ins were fine; sit ins were not. She even took to making the odd cup of tea for the more mature passers-through. Before too long, the weekend tourists started coming by too. A washed out paint tin was placed at the side of the inverted shell pool sign for gold coin donations. At first, she thought she would use the coins for the cost of paints (which she now ordered on the line on her computer all by herself), but she thought it should be given back to a good cause. So far $711 gnome dollars and counting had been donated to that nice man riding a unicycle around the country for cancer research.

Susie contemplates calling her son most days but is yet to actually do so. His number is safely tucked away inside the teacup, even though she bought a lovely gang-gang cockatoo fridge magnet, because it was just too risky leaving it out on the fridge in case a stray piece of wind took it away forever.

ACKNOWLEDGEMENTS

*T*hroughout the many years of me trying very hard to not be a writer, my brother, Sam, encouraged, cajoled, badgered, pestered, advised and proposed that I needed to face the inevitable. Thank you, Sam. This wouldn't have happened without you. But it's your friendship for which I'm most grateful.

To the readers of the early drafts: Lucy Freeman, for loving everything I write; Kylie Doyle, for thinking that Susie became a horrible old lady; Sullivan Krueger, for loving Susie as an old lady and dancing around the imaginary gnome village with me; Myfanwy Jones, for having no doubt it would happen and opening my eyes to kumquat gin; Jonno Hinton, for pointing out the little moments I wasn't sure would be noticed; Austen Krueger, for listening to me read random chapters on the back porch; and Em Rooke, for that day and pressing the send button with me.

I nervously emailed Vanessa Radnidge at Hachette with an outline of this story with a few chapters attached. She wrote back saying she wanted to publish it. And that if I wanted to write something else instead, she would want to publish that too. This belief gave me the boost, the leg up, the wherewithal. Bless your cotton pickin' socks.

Lastly, to my dead. Mum, I didn't hate you. Dad, it took too long but I got there. And Connie, when others said I didn't finish anything, you always said I was merely eliminating things I didn't actually want to do and that I was brave for trying all the things. Well, I tried another one, Con. And I finished it. Here it is.

Hilde Hinton has been a dedicated big sister to Connie and Samuel Johnson her whole life. She avoided being a writer for many years but has finally succumbed. *The Loudness of Unsaid Things* is her debut novel.

She lives in a boisterous house in Melbourne with a revolving door for the temporarily defeated and takes great pride in people leaving slightly better than when they arrived. Her children are mostly loved.

hachette
AUSTRALIA

If you would like to find out more about Hachette Australia,
our authors, upcoming events and new releases you can visit
our website or our social media channels:

hachette.com.au

 HachetteAustralia

 HachetteAus